Spike and Babe

Jane Jorgensen
Philip A. Jorgensen

pbj house

First edition

Cover art by Maxtrella

This book was professionally typeset on Reedsy.
Find out more at reedsy.com

This book is dedicated to all who have reached their majority and are dreading aging. It is possible to remedy wrinkles and get help for a hitch in your 'get along,' but you can't stop the years from piling up. Don't dread this stage in your life! Someone aptly dubbed this time as 'Golden Years.' There is rewarding life over the hill! This book should encourage empty nesters to surround themselves with like-minded friends and step out and live their lives with panache. You'd be surprised at all the fun waiting for you over here!

Contents

Chapter 1

The morning sun shone brightly on Shady Oaks Condominiums. A small squirrel hopped through the trimmed grass. Following some unseen scent, she stopped below a bird feeder that dangled from a metal shepherd's hook, then climbed a small tree near the birdseed. As Harold and Gwen Miller watched out their kitchen window, the squirrel got ready to pounce. From her perch in the tree, she leaped to the rod, grabbed it, and scrambled upward toward the prized seeds.

"Does that squirrel do this every morning?" Harold asked. Until three days ago he had worked at Cromwell Heating and Air Conditioning. His skin had the leathery quality of a man who had spent a career installing machinery outdoors. He was born in Shelby County, Iowa and had lived there his entire life. Only days ago he had retired. It was a great goal to reach to know he no longer worked by someone else's clock. He and his wife now claimed the freedom to come and go as they pleased.

Harold Miller's smooth, balding head was edged with a fringe of gray hair. His genuine smile had etched wrinkles into his face over the years. His clothes fit tighter now than they once did, mostly due to the good cooking of the woman sitting next to him.

Gwen was what Harold respectfully called "pleasingly plump." "Pleasingly," because of their years of sharing companionable meals around their kitchen table; and "plump," because she was a good cook who loved to sample. As the years trickled by, her brown hair had turned white, but to her the change was a natural progression.

"Every morning the squirrels get to the feeder, but they don't always make it on the first try." Gwen took a sip of her coffee.

Gwen married Harold Miller forty-three years prior, and she had never regretted it. They had a relationship where, when passing each other, one or the other would give a little pat on the arm or shoulder. It was as if they were silently announcing, "I'm glad you're you." They lived in a small town where there had never been a sit-in, a breakout, or a drive-by shooting; it was a great place to raise kids. They had raised four boys, which Gwen considered her first career. Those four had flown the coop and started their own families, thus making Gwen and Harold empty nesters.

Gwen nudged closer to the window and said, "You know, I believe that squirrel is Milly."

"Do you mean the squirrel you named at our old house?"

"That squirrel climbing in the bird feeder. See that dark spot on her back? I think she's the one that came to our old house last winter. Remember she got so she would come right up to the door if I gave her a peanut dipped in peanut butter? Do you suppose she's found us over at this new place already?"

The maybe Milly hung by her back feet from the eaves of the feeder and gobbled seeds. She sprinted down the tree, across the lawn, and went to work burying. Then back up the tree she went after another load.

Harold poured himself another cup of coffee in his favorite

cup that read, "God only made a few perfect heads, on the rest he put hair." It was the only mug he had salvaged from the moving boxes so far.

Harold halted in mid-step and stared out the window. Muttering more to himself than to Gwen, he said, "I'm going to fix that little rascal! She has her jump down pat and can get the birdseed too easily!" Not even glancing at Gwen, he marched to the garage.

A mountain of boxes faced Harold in the garage. Some were labeled "Living Room," others marked "Kitchen—Fragile," and "Guest Bathroom." Most boxes remained sealed with packing tape, but a few were open.

Inside a box labeled "Workshop," Harold rummaged through nails, a spool of wire, the broken pieces of a doorknob, and finally found a can of Armor All. He grabbed the can.

"What are you doing?" asked Gwen as he returned.

"I can't stop the little critter, but this should slow her down!" said Harold as he popped the plastic lid from the Armor All and headed for the back door. Hearing the door open, the furry diner flipped to the ground and bounded for the safety of the nearest tree. Harold bent down to get the spray nozzle close to the rod that held the feeder. "Remember, my little friend," he muttered as he sprayed the rod, "adversity builds character."

Harold reentered the kitchen and sat down. He glanced at Gwen and explained, "I'm just leveling the playing field for the birds." Gwen smiled and nodded, knowing her husband must feel a bit guilty about using his can of Armor All to sabotage the squirrel's climb.

From the safe vantage point in the tree, the birdseed raider watched Harold trudge back in the house. Only then did she bound down the tree and across the lawn. Back up her vaulting tree she went, and halfway up she leapt to the pole. She tried to scramble to the top in her usual style; but while all four tiny legs were working at a frantic pace, her body was getting nowhere. Realizing she had no traction, the little raider slid to the ground. She bounded back to her starting branch and again leapt to the pole with similar results. Accepting temporary defeat, she scampered off to find easier pickings.

"I never get tired of watching their antics," said Gwen.

"It is fun to watch the little critter," agreed Harold. He lifted his newspaper again, but his mind was drifting with the breeze. Contentment warmed him like the morning sun on this first day of retirement. So much adventure was ahead for him and Gwen. He peered over at her. She was craning her neck to watch a pair of cardinals bathe in their birdbath. He leaned over and lightly pulled on her earlobe. She turned her head and smiled. Yes, Harold was going to enjoy the adventure of retirement, but he planned to take it easy for a while.

"What are you going to wear to your retirement party tonight, Harold?"

"Oh, the retirement party." Harold frowned. "I tried telling Mr. Cromwell he didn't need to put on a shindig, but he only smiled and told me to dust off my shoes and he would see us there. You know I don't like being in the limelight, but I guess I can't get out of going to my own party. The fellows at work have been coming up to me all week to thank me. Imagine! To thank me! I did my job. No more, no less."

Gwen said, "You told me once that working with new guys was like herding a group of kids working on a school project. That means you had the responsibility of teaching them when they started their job."

4

"That's right, Gwen, but Mr. Cromwell did the same for me when I first started. I was just passing 'know-how' along." He paused. "I'll probably wear the blue plaid shirt I got for Christmas. It's casual. No matter what I wear I'm going to be uncomfortable at a party like this."

Gwen laughed, patting him on the shoulder. "You aren't going to be able to just ride off into the sunset, Harold. Enjoy the limelight. It only happens once or twice in a person's lifetime. You have been with the company longer than any of their other employees. You are well-liked, and you like the people you work with. Let them give you a special send-off. Your only job tonight is to relax and enjoy it."

Mr. Cromwell, the owner of the company, had announced the dinner was to start at seven o'clock. A little before seven Gwen and Harold headed to the town's only cafe with a meeting room. They parked beside the company truck. It read "Cromwell Heating and Air Conditioning—Your Comfort Is Our Business" in large printing along the side.

Gwen opened the car door and got out, but she paused when Harold remained motionless. He said, "You know, I'm going to miss these guys."

"Then you need to tell them that tonight."

Only a few customers sat in the actual cafe. The woman behind the cash register motioned toward the back room and said, "They are in the back waiting for you, Harold."

Gwen grabbed Harold's arm in silent encouragement as they entered the party room. There, all standing, were his boss and his fellow employees. They belted out, "For He's a Jolly Good Fellow" as the couple entered the room. Gwen had a lump in her throat and patted Harold's arm.

The dinner of lettuce salad, roast beef, mashed potatoes, and green beans with bacon was splendid. Harold and Gwen had been seated in the middle of the head table, with Mr. and Mrs. Cromwell flanking them on the right, and the co-owners of the company, Cromwell's son and daughter-in-law, flanking them on the left. The tables had been set in a giant U-shape. The other employees sat at long tables that extended on each side of the head table. Harold thought it felt weird to be with his fellow employees in such a formal setting. Weird, but nice. Anyone outside the meeting room could hear the dull roar of good conversation and the occasional guffaw, the sound of closeness.

They finished their apple pie dessert, and Mr. Cromwell got to his feet. The room grew quiet.

"I hired Harold Miller shortly after I opened the business, and the business has succeeded. Part of that success is thanks to Harold. He has gone above and beyond his assigned work. He trained many of you, and I know there are those of you who called him when you had a problem at work. We will miss Harold, but we wish him well." He turned to Harold and added, "You have worked hard and deserve your retirement." Looking around at his employees he said, "Would anyone else care to say something here?"

Several hands rose, and Mr. Cromwell nodded at Richard Petersen. A quiet man, not prone to talking unless he has something important to say, Richard stood and began, "I want to wish Harold good luck. He pulled my feet out of the fire at work more than once, and I thank him for that. I am a much better employee because of his guidance. But more important than that, he gave me some personal advice once that made me a better man and a better husband. Thanks Harold. I'm going to miss you."

Next, Glen Kloss stood to his feet. He grinned and said, "I wish you well too, Harold. I have been here almost as long as you and we've seen a lot together." He looked down at the table; and, looking up again, continued, "You newer people should be advised that this business can be difficult at times. You may run into a situation like this, so listen up because you can learn from it. I can tell you this now because the wonderful little lady is no longer with us."

He had everyone's full attention as he continued. "Mrs. Wiggs called the office one day, and the secretary couldn't make heads or tails of what she wanted. So Harold and I jumped in the truck and went to see her. We had no idea what to expect."

Harold chuckled at hearing Mrs. Wiggs's name. He rubbed his hand over his forehead and shook his head. Mrs. Wiggs had been a good customer, and her age never held her back. She was small, but as lively as a new puppy, and as personable as anyone you'd ever meet. Once, she called about trouble with her air conditioner and asked if Harold would pick up a quart of milk and a loaf of bread on his way to her house to fix it.

Kloss continued, "We got to her house and rang the bell. She was there in a flash. We asked her if she had called and she said no, she didn't need anything hauled. Then Harold asked her what was the matter, and she gave him a strange look and told him she didn't have a ladder. With the patience of Job, Harold kept asking. It became clear that our first problem was that Mrs. Wiggs couldn't understand what we were saying.

"Harold kept pressing her. He pointed to his own ears and asked if she had hearing aids. She told him yes, but she had lost them. Harold turned to me and told me in no uncertain terms that our first job was to find those hearing aids. We'd have to find them before tending to the problem she called the office about.

"We asked her where she had last seen her hearing aids. She thought it might have been when she went to bed the night before. We searched her bedroom, looking things over well; even taking the bedding off, piece by piece. Then we made a clean sweep of the kitchen—drawers and all. No luck. We were still looking an hour later, searching under furniture, in every nook and cranny and still nothing. Yes, this is part of the job when you work in a small town. We looked everywhere. Mrs. Wiggs stood in front of us shaking her head. Harold must have noticed something because he stooped down and peered in her ear. He reached over and pulled a hearing aid out of her right ear, then looked in the left ear. There was the other one.

"Mrs. Wiggs threw her arms in the air and said, 'Well, I declare!' and headed to a drawer to get some new batteries. The problem she had called the office about was that she thought her thermostat was broken. It took five minutes to show her how to reprogram it, now that she could hear the directions as clear as a whistle. I want you newer guys to know that the problem is sometimes more than heating or cooling. Always look for the obvious."

Others gave short comments and best wishes for retirement. A genuine admiration was evident from all who spoke.

Finally, Harold got to his feet, rubbing his chin with a nervous hand. He cleared his throat. "I want to thank the Cromwells for this party. It has been great. And I want to thank Mr. Cromwell for my job over the years. He is a top-notch boss. I could never have found a better one." Harold looked along the two flanking tables. "And there's no greater bunch of guys to work with than all of you. We've run into some tricky problems, but together we've solved them. I'm going to miss you guys."

Harold stopped for a moment and cleared his throat again. Gwen knew he was having a hard time saying goodbye. He continued in a husky voice, "Thanks to every single one of you for the years of laughter and standing side by side with me. Be sure to stop to see us anytime." He had to sit down then. They socialized with the group for another hour before the party broke up.

While driving home, Gwen commented, "It sure was a great party, wasn't it?"

"Yep, that is a great bunch and I'll miss them. But I won't miss going to work every weekday or being called out in the middle of a winter night to work on someone's furnace."

Harold chuckled and glanced over at Gwen. "And we are now officially starting our retirement, something we've worked toward for a long time. Great times are ahead, Gwen."

"Harold, when you say 'great times' it sounds like you have something in mind other than unpacking all the boxes in the garage. To me, 'great times' sounds more like planning a cruise or taking that train trip across southern Canada. To me, that's what puts the 'great' before the 'times' part!"

"I hope good things are in store for us. It doesn't have to be big things, just things we'll enjoy doing together. But for now, let's enjoy not having a schedule that calls all the shots. I want to sit around the house doing nothing but what I choose to do. I do some of my best thinking and planning from my recliner, and I need your input to make these coming years the best they can be."

Chapter 2

Dust motes floated slowly in the warm kitchen, illuminated by the light through the windows. Harold leaned back, sipping lukewarm coffee as he mentally checked off his chores. The paper read? Check. Bird feeders filled? Check. Birdbath filled? Check. The birdbath refilled after all the robins splashed the water out? Check. The patio swept? He went out the back door, grabbed the broom, and began sweeping.

Harold stood with his chin resting on the broom handle, surveying the open space that made up the communal condo backyard. The space was lush green and full of trees. He noticed the mowing trailer pull up on the street in front of the house.

Harold went back into the house and peeked into the guest bedroom where Gwen knelt on the floor unpacking a box of decorations. "Gwen, if anyone calls this morning, tell them I'm in my patio office."

Gwen paused, and the crinkle of newspaper stopped as she smiled. "Oh, back to work already I see. Today must be mowing day, and I imagine they will need a supervisor to make sure they don't miss any spots. You go enjoy your retirement . . . I mean, get to work!"

Harold sat down in his "office" as the men finished unloading their trailer. The four men worked like a well-oiled machine; two on riding lawn mowers, one with an edger, and one wielding a leaf blower. They made their way through the backyard of the condos, never missing a spot.

After twelve minutes of watching the mowers work, Harold returned inside to fetch the paper. He had already read it, so instead he sauntered back to the guest room. Gwen had finished with the box of decorations and was now putting guest linens in the small closet.

"Done so soon? I still hear mowers out there."

"Yeah, they are. I was thinking about planting something in our flower bed. Want to go to the gardening store with me?"

"Actually, I met the neighbor the other day; and she said that ever since she moved here, she has had terrible luck planting in beds like ours. Apparently, the deer make nightly forays and eat the plants as fast as she can replant them. She thinks it is a losing battle and has pretty much given up growing flowers or anything else back there. Maybe we should quit while we're ahead."

"What about that little slope off our patio? I could make it look better if I leveled it off."

"Well, Harold, is that our problem to deal with, or the condo association's?"

Harold sauntered back to the kitchen to see if there was still coffee in the pot. Gwen followed him, putting the last of the breakfast dishes in the dishwasher. He divided the remaining coffee into their cups, switched off the coffee maker, and sat down at the table. This was one reason they had decided on condo living. Not much for Harold to do. But there was no getting around it; Harold was bored.

"Gwen, honey," he mused, "you have been at this retirement

thing longer than I have. Do you ever feel that we're missing out on some excitement in life?"

"You may want some excitement, Harold, but I had about all the excitement I wanted when the boys were teenagers! There was always something going on, and some of it I'd put in the hair-raising category. You have to remember, you retired a few days ago, and it is natural to feel that you want to be doing something. Why don't you sit down and let your mind, as well as your body, relax for a change?"

"But don't you get tired of the same old thing every day?"

Putting the last of the dishes in the rack, Gwen closed the dishwasher and walked over to the table. She massaged her husband's shoulders. Actually, she thought life was good for them: a comfortable home, beautiful grandchildren, friends to share their leisure time, and a keen enough sense of humor to appreciate their own foibles. She smiled as she reflected on their life. They had each other and were compatible, healthy, and able to come and go as they pleased. Their sons were raised and had families of their own. There wasn't a lot of money in the bank, but there was enough to keep them in the quiet lifestyle they had chosen. In her book they were blessed. What could be troubling Harold?

"Don't you ever get tired of the same group of cardplayers? Our circle of friends is great, but nowadays when we get together we talk about the same things we talked about the last time. Don't you ever want to bust out and do something different? Don't you ever get tired of this humdrum life?"

"I've never thought of our lives as humdrum. How would you change things? Are you talking about taking a vacation to some exotic spot or renting an action movie tonight?" she asked smiling.

Harold leaned way back as he lifted the front legs of his chair off the floor. He put his thumbs under his suspenders and stared at the ceiling. Gwen waited for a response. But Harold kept staring at the ceiling while fiddling with his suspenders. Gwen thought back to last year when Harold announced the addition of suspenders to his retirement attire. At the time, she scoffed at them as a fashion risk, but now they were a part of his apparel and looked fine to her. If comfort meant suspenders for him, and low heels and elastic waistbands for her, fine! Comfort before style, right? Both had gained enough weight to stretch the integrity of their buttons, but that was part of being comfortable. Life was good. Thank you, God.

Gwen returned to the present when Harold burst out with, "I should have bought a motorcycle years ago! I always wanted one when I was young. I even started saving for it at one point. Yes, I should have gotten a motorcycle when I was young and fancy-free!"

Gwen could hardly believe what she was hearing. A motorcycle? Her Harold? Her conservative, conscientious, conventional, cautious Harold wishing he had a motorcycle! More to stir the pot than anything else, she said, "Well . . . go out and buy one. I'll probably never see you, but if a motorcycle will make you happy, you should get one. Plus, you don't have a job to go to now, and the condo association mows your lawn and scoops your snow for you. You're more fancy-free than you've been in years."

The chair legs hit the floor. Harold's thumbs came out of the suspenders, and he looked as if Gwen had thrown a glass of ice water on him.

"Now don't—just what—" and he laughed. "I'm only day-dreaming when I talk about it. I always dreamed of having a motorcycle when I was younger, but now it's insanity to even consider it. It's an expensive toy for just riding around." He hesitated and then added, "Even if I did go a little offtrack and buy it, we have a one-car garage. Where would we put something like that?"

"Well," Gwen responded, "that garage is full of stuff bordering on junk; all just sitting there taking up space. When we moved, you insisted we bring all sorts of stuff along. There are pots and planters you'll probably never use. There is the mower, the edger, and a couple of tree trimmers we don't need anymore." She hesitated, then laughed and added, "If you do decide to get a motorcycle, remember to wave as you ride by the house so I'll know you are still in one piece!"

Reaching over and pulling her earlobe, he said, "I've gotten used to having you around, old girl! I couldn't think of riding my hog without you!"

"I thought you said you wanted a motorcycle? What's this hog business?"

"That's just a fancy name for a motorcycle."

"Oh, well make sure to wave as you are out riding on your hog."

"No, Gwen, I would want you to come with me!" He raised his hands shoulder height and took hold of two imaginary handlebars. "Vroom! Vroom! Can you see it? Wind in our faces, heading out for a spur of the moment trip!"

Getting back on point, Harold said, "What about a motorcycle with a sidecar? Then you could ride right next to me."

Raising her eyes to the ceiling, Gwen replied, "Have you forgotten last year's New Year's Eve party when you turned into Ardie and Joe's driveway too fast and scraped their hedge with my side of the car? I'm lucky I was safe inside the car

14

and not in one of those open-air sidecars you're talking about. No matter how much I'll miss your company, I'll pass on that suggestion."

Harold would not give up easily. "Well, then ride on the back!"

"What? And just hold onto your waist?" She thought a moment and went on, "Well, you do have a waistline that would be handy to grab on to, honey," she joked. "I've fed you too well! Pardon me for taking the credit."

Harold said, "If you keep cooking like you have, there will be even more to hang on to. My waistline is your rider's insurance!"

"Yes, but then there is the issue of my waistline. I'm wondering about whether I am even built for a motorcycle seat! If a muffin top is what hangs over belts, what do you call what hangs over a motorcycle seat? A motorcycle muffin? I think I might be a bit overweight and past my prime to go gallivanting around on the back of a motorcycle!"

"Gwen, you're looking at this all wrong. Think of it as an adventure, a breaking away from the norm. I want you there with me. We have always done things together, and I want it to stay that way."

Harold's pleading eyes reminded Gwen of the time their sons tried to convince them to let them use their college money to buy a used Jeep. Was he being serious? And what if he was?

"OK, Harold. I would learn to ride behind you on one of those things if you promised not to take chances while driving. And, obviously, you would get your license and practice awhile before we bought one."

Harold sarcastically replied, "Practice? I've ridden a bicycle my whole life. How much different could it be? And where is the rebelliousness in that?" He raised his fist. "No license! No rules! No learning! Just us and the road!"

This was one step too far for Gwen. She gave him a no nonsense glare. "Harold, dear, let's get one thing straight before we talk any more about going anywhere on any motorcycle. I'll go along with this harebrained idea you have, but there is one thing I insist on. I insist you learn motorcycle rules of the road before either of us do any driving or riding. I don't know if a motorcycle is any different than a bicycle, but I don't want to find out by hanging onto your back for dear life! I feel strongly about this, probably stronger than you know. I love you, and maybe it's because I love you that I insist you learn and *then* get a license! I'm not going to change my mind on that!"

Gwen turned and walked out of the room. As a wife she had never in her memory taken that firm a stand before. She had never needed to. But horrors danced in her head—ditches, bridges, speeding cars, wet roads. Not knowing for sure all the regulations only added to those fears and made things worse in her mind. He had been strict with their boys when they started driving, so she hoped he would now sympathize.

Harold immediately followed her. When he reached her, he held her tight and whispered, "You are right, Gwen. I'll get it done as soon as possible. None of this putting my cart before the horse anymore."

Gwen turned and buried her face in his chest, putting her arms around his neck. Her voice was husky as she muttered, "You're special to me. If you have this hankering, we're going to look at motorcycles, crazy idea or not." Her tone became lighter as she said, "I made a 'for better, for worse' commitment years ago; and this motorcycle business might qualify under the worse category!" Laughing, she added, "I remember someone once told me that happy motorcyclists are easy to spot. They have bug stains on their teeth!"

"That's what toothbrushes are for, Gwen," he quipped.

Chapter 3

Every other Wednesday afternoon Gwen played a card game called Dirty Queens with a group of seven older ladies, making two tables. For years her mother had belonged to this group of mostly widows in their eighties and nineties. One time, when her mother went into the hospital, she asked Gwen to fill in for her. What started as an occasional game for Gwen turned into full-time membership when her mother passed away. Through the years Gwen had suggested other older women who might join and take her spot. But the ladies kept finding problems with each of Gwen's nominees. Over time, as Gwen continued to play with this group, she actually came to enjoy their company more than she ever thought she would.

Today's meeting was at Agnes Bolton's condo. It wasn't far from Gwen and Harold's condo, but nothing was far in this small town. You could get through town in a hurry but not as quickly as gossip traveled. This group professed to abhor gossip but always found a special way to pass along any they heard. They had learned to deliver any juicy tidbits by asking questions in a particular way. It was a good group, perhaps older than Gwen's usual crowd, but interesting anyway. After all, she was retired now, so maybe it was a good thing to rub elbows with this age group, if for no other reason than to see how "the other half lived."

Just as Gwen was parking her car, identical twins Tess and Bess Smith arrived together. As they were walking to the front door, Tess, who was always the spokesperson for the duo, greeted Gwen with "Lovely day, isn't it?"

"Yes, wonderful day!"

"How is Harold acclimating to life as a retiree?"

Gwen smiled as she answered. "Sometimes he seems a little bored, but I believe he enjoys not having a nine-to-five job to go to every day."

"Men are like that!" said Tess smiling. "I remember when my Larry, God rest his soul, first retired."

At the mention of Tess's late husband, Bess covered her heart with her hand, looked skyward, and murmured, "Yes, yes!"

"Larry just couldn't give up farming habits when he retired. He continued to get up at 4:00 a.m. each day as if he still had cows to milk!"

Agnes opened the door to their knock and welcomed them. Once inside, as they made their way to the kitchen, Bess added, "When my Rupert, may he rest in peace, finally retired, it took weeks before he would admit he was bored."

At the mention of her twin's husband's name, Tess covered her heart with her hand, looked upwards, and murmured, "Yes, yes!"

The ladies entered the kitchen where Frances Fullerton was sitting with Betty Alcott. The women exchanged greetings, and then Bess included the others in their earlier conversation. "Gwen was just telling us how poor Harold is trying to acclimate to his slower retirement lifestyle."

The other ladies went into full suggestion mode. The deep-voiced Frances offered, "Find him a hobby. It will keep him out of trouble."

Betty was quick to offer, "It will give him more time to do projects around the house." Betty was the oldest in the group but was probably the handiest with a hammer.

"My advice to everyone, no matter what the situation," added Agnes, "is to accept what is, let go of what was, and have faith in what will be. Those are rules to live by."

At that moment Mary Alice Wonder appeared in the kitchen doorway. Seeing her, Agnes suggested they draw for their seats. "You know Lettie will be here at the last minute, as always, so let's go ahead and draw. Gwen's seat was at a table with Frances, Tess, and the late-coming Lettie, while the other table held Bess, Betty, Agnes, and Mary Alice.

Just as expected, as the clock struck two, the sound of an engine signaled the approach of Lettie Tool. The sound was Lettie's husband Bert's prized 1957 Chevy that, in spite of its age, looked as if it had just been driven off the assembly line. There was never a speck of rust or even dust on its entire turquoise and white body. Bert had been babying that car for years and must have added or subtracted something because you could hear the car coming from a distance. The car was just loud enough to turn heads without making an unpleasant racket.

The ladies looked at each other in a knowing way. They knew Bert liked to bring Lettie at the last minute so everyone could see his car. He liked to be sure they all noticed the car in a way that couldn't be construed as bragging. Agnes headed for the door to welcome Lettie.

All the ladies were in their assigned places, and the cards were dealt to start the day's game. Many ladies in town liked to get together to play bridge, but not this group. They claimed bridge was a "snooty" game, and they thought of themselves as more down-to earth than bridge players.

As the last of the cards were dealt, timid Mary Alice spoke up. "What if, for a change of pace, once every few months we play dominoes instead of cards?"

Gwen immediately saw it was the wrong question to ask. The majority, at least the more outspoken in the group, furrowed their brows and frowned. There was a long pause until Frances spoke up. Her low voice was even deeper than usual as she said, "Dominoes are for children, and this group is beyond that age, wouldn't you say?"

Mary Alice didn't respond, but Gwen saw Agnes give her a consoling look, and Gwen wondered if those two would start up their own clandestine game of dominoes someday. If they did, Gwen thought they might want to wait until dusk to meet so as not to be seen by the others.

* * *

Gwen and Harold pulled up to Murry's Motorcycles, the only motorcycle shop for miles around. Operating lessons for new motorcycle drivers were given there twice a month. A neon sign lit the area as a few men sauntered about, lining small orange cones to cordon off one side of the parking lot. Harold parked the car and they got out. Shivering, Gwen hugged herself as Harold zipped his coat to his chin. The cold early morning temperatures seeped into the heavy layering of their coats.

"Are you sure you don't want to stay and learn how to drive a motorcycle with me? Maybe even get your license too? Someday you may wish you had it," Harold said as he rubbed his hands on Gwen's shoulders to keep her warm.

"Goodness, no! If I didn't freeze to death, I'd probably fall and break something!"

"Well we wouldn't want that, would we?" Harold smiled at Gwen. It was colder than he would have liked, and he had to admit he was nervous. But his excitement made him forget the weather and his nerves.

The roar of motorcycles filled the air as bikes were pulling into the parking lot, and a few were coming out of the store as loaners. Two people were setting up a small table next to a sign marked "Registration and Coffee."

"You be careful, you got that?" Gwen called after him. She wagged her finger at Harold as if scolding one of their sons, but she meant it. He hugged her tight and gave her a peck on the forehead; then Gwen climbed back into the car. Watching the others line up their motorcycles and get ready to earn their licenses made Harold quicken his pace in their direction. This would get him one step closer to having his own motorcycle.

As Gwen watched him meander, hands in his pockets, over to the instructors, she prayed. "Lord, please don't let him fall off and hurt himself . . . unless it will knock some sense into him!"

While Gwen was waiting on Harold, she ran errands and puttered around town. After the post office and the bank, she pulled into the local resale shop, Second Chances. Gwen loved coming to this store. It might need a fresh coat of paint and a deep scrubbing, but it was a fun place nonetheless. There were always new things to see.

The owner, May Jepsen, was a member of their Sunday school class at church. She started Second Chances as a ministry to the homeless in town and the surrounding area.

22

The donated clothes were available to the homeless first, and what they didn't need stocked the store. Incoming money from sales helped with building upkeep, plus purchasing other necessities for the homeless.

Gwen was on her own mission this morning. During her errands Gwen kept imagining Harold on some ghastly bike. She finally reached the conclusion she could eliminate at least one peril: the cold. Living in Iowa they had plenty of winter gear, but none of it allowed for as much movement as Gwen thought Harold might need on a motorcycle.

"Morning, Gwen," came a raspy voice.

"Good morning, May," Gwen replied to the woman behind the register.

Gwen was bound and determined as she headed for the men's department. On her way she might make a quick peek in the women's clothing department.

She figured she had hit the jackpot when she found one red blouse, two navy dresses, and a tan top. She draped her finds over one arm and continued looking. As Gwen flipped through the pants rack, she froze in mid-swipe. Hidden between two pairs of blue jeans, half dangling off a hanger, was a pair of jet-black leather pants. Her hand attempted to continue filing through the jeans, but the leather pants kept her frozen. She looked at them again. Why were these so interesting? As soon as she asked herself that question, the answer came to her. This was what motorcyclists wore.

She reached forward and took the pants off the hanger. The leather was softer than she expected. A large hot pink label inside said, "Threshold Threads." The letters were connected by a vine with roses on it. The knees of the pants showed a little wear, and the stitching around the ankle hems was coming loose, but Gwen didn't notice. In her mind a breeze blew through her hair as she thought how surprised Harold would be if she brought these home.

Gwen looked around the store to see if anyone was watching. She was nervous May would see her eyeing these pants. Oh, the embarrassment at church on Sunday. May was ringing up someone's sale, and no one else showed interest in what Gwen was doing. She laughed to herself about how silly she was being about a simple pair of pants. Even so, she stuffed the pants under the other clothes and hurried toward the dressing rooms.

The cramped dressing rooms at Second Chances gave very little privacy. Each of the three rooms was about the size of a water heater closet, and the doorways were covered only by skimpy curtains. Gwen took the room on the left and carefully tugged the curtain to make sure the entire opening was covered. She wanted to make sure no one would accidentally see her—Gwen Miller in leather pants.

As Gwen slipped off her tan elastic-waist pants, she checked the curtain one more time and stuck her toe into the right leg of the black leather pants. Immediately she saw they would be tight, if they fit at all. She tugged the pants to her waistline and realized just how tight they were. Three whole inches separated the button from the buttonhole. But it wasn't like she was going to buy them anyway, she reminded herself.

She turned toward the mirror and wanted to kick herself when she saw the broken mirror. The entire bottom half of the mirror was gone, and she couldn't see herself from the waist down. "Probably for the best. I'd look silly in them anyway," she muttered. But she couldn't leave it at that.

She moved to the far corner of the dressing closet. It didn't help. She moved closer. No luck. She thought about trying to stand on the chair. In her imagination she saw the headline, "Senior citizen breaks neck in dressing room." The article would have a picture of her sprawled on the ground, lying there in unbuttoned leather pants! How embarrassing.

The dressing room to the right of this one probably had a whole mirror. But should she risk it? She could put her own pants back on and then change rooms, but the leather pants with the brass beads decorating the side seam made her feel like a rebel.

Gwen peeked around the curtain. There didn't seem to be anyone close, and May was at the other end of the store reading a magazine. It was one thing for a total stranger to see her, but the last thing she wanted was to be seen by someone she knew. She decided to be adventurous. If she got caught, she would have something to laugh about later with Harold.

As soon as she slipped out from behind the safety of her curtain, she was inside the second room. She straightened up, and her reflection pleasantly surprised her.

"Not half bad, Gwen," she muttered to herself. She twisted a little to the right, then a little to the left, checking her behind. But there still was the matter of the three inches at the waistline.

"Three . . . two . . . one." She sucked in hard and tugged at the zipper. There was minimal movement. She tried again, with somewhat better results. A third and fourth try got the zipper all the way to the top. She still wasn't able to button the pants, and they were definitely tight. Gwen pulled her blouse all the way out and pirouetted again in front of the mirror. With her blouse on the outside, it wasn't even noticeable that the pants were unbuttoned. Plus, she knew there were extenders for button holes. "Ha! Listen to me! Acting like I am buying these pants!"

Gwen twisted a few more times, admiring the tight pants. Of course, there was zero room for growth or movement. But as she stared at herself in the mirror she felt a little breeze through her hair from deep inside. A *vroom vroom* whispered in her mind. She imagined she was holding onto Harold as they zipped down a Paris cobblestone avenue. In her mind she was in leather pants and a leather jacket. Her hair was tied with an imaginary red ribbon blowing in the breeze. They were laughing and having the best time together. Why Paris? She didn't know. And wouldn't riding over cobblestone streets be bumpy to one's derriere? Either way, she smiled as she returned to her daydream.

She might get these pants.

She looked around for her own pants. She had brought nothing into this dressing room when she dashed over. As she whipped the curtain aside to run back to the original room, a woman was standing directly in front of her.

"Gwen?!"

Gwen stared into the eyes of Mrs. Peabody, the pastor's wife.

Chapter 4

Mrs. Peabody, with a dress draped over her arm, stepped back from the dressing room, her mouth wide open. Her eyes moved from Gwen's mortified face to the tight, jet-black leather pants.

"What in the *world* are those things?"

"Oh! I . . . uh . . ." Gwen scrambled back into her first dressing room and tugged the small curtain shut. She inhaled deeply. Why did she have to try these pants? What was wrong with her? She stripped off the leather pants and pulled on her own respectable clothes. She inhaled again. She scooped up the other items she had planned to try on and exited the dressing room.

Mrs. Peabody was still standing with her mouth gaping wide open. The look on her face was as though she had caught Saint Paul himself, dressed in overalls, skinning a cat. Gwen nodded in her direction, not even able to make eye contact. She marched down the aisles of clothes towards the pant racks. Mrs. Peabody's gaze followed her, zeroing in on the wadded bunch of clothes under Gwen's arm.

Gwen began to toss the clothes back on the clothes rack but then hesitated. She wasn't doing anything wrong. What she *was* doing was loving her husband, which was actually quite wonderful.

"I'm going to buy these pants," she declared to herself, barely above a whisper. She thought about turning to Mrs. Peabody and saying something, but she feared what might come out. But, by golly, she was going to buy these pants.

Gwen put the clothes back she hadn't tried on, but kept a tight hold on the leather pants as she marched to the register. She got to the checkout and wondered if May would comment on her buying leather pants. She also wondered if either May or Mrs. Peabody were gossips; and if so, how fast this would get around town. This meant there were two people to light the gossip fire if they chose. Gwen shook her head and straightened her back. It was her business if she chose to wear leather pants trimmed with metal beads down the side seams. What other people thought shouldn't matter. She was doing this for Harold, for goodness' sake.

"Nice choice," May said with a wink as she scanned the leather pants. "These came in a few weeks ago. There is something so fun about them." She smiled at Gwen. "That will be $6.13," May said as she put the purchase in a plastic grocery sack.

Gwen thought $6.13 was a small down payment for a new life of adventure, or something to get a laugh out of Harold at the very least. Gwen was ready to begin her life as the wife of a motorcyclist.

She smiled as she approached Murry's, where Harold was taking his instruction. She saw Harold driving carefully through small orange cones. He was a little shaky on the bike while turning but controlled it well. She smiled as she pictured herself riding behind him on the motorcycle.

After the class was over, Harold walked over to the car, and

Gwen scooted into the passenger seat. "How was it?"

"Oh, it was great!" he said, with an enormous grin plastered over his face. "I'm getting the hang of it, too. It took a while getting used to the power, but it is so much fun."

"Good! I'm glad you had fun."

Harold told her about the class. After a few miles, he glanced over at Gwen and asked, "So, what's in the bag? Did you stop and get something for supper?"

Gwen clutched the bag in her hands. "No, I didn't stop at the grocery store this time. I stopped at Second Chances."

"Find any bargains?" he asked. Then he added, "You have a funny look on your face. What's going on?"

As they pulled into their driveway and got out, Gwen said, "Promise you won't laugh and I'll show you." She opened the bag, reached in to remove the leather pants, then stopped—pulling her hand back out of the bag and closing it tightly. She said, "You'll never guess what is in this sack. I'll give you three guesses, and if you guess what's in the bag, I will bake you any kind of pie you want! If you can't guess correctly in three tries, you will take me to see *Hairspray* at the Civic Center in Council Bluffs, which you refuse to see!"

By this time both were laughing. Harold squinted thoughtfully and said, "New pajamas."

"Wrong, try again! You have two more tries!"

Harold looked at her, grinned said, "You found a shirt for me, but you're not sure I'll like it!"

Gwen laughed. "That's two wrong. I'm getting closer to going to that musical that you don't want to see! One guess left." She rattled the sack with its hidden contents.

"This is getting serious," said Harold. He turned to see Gwen and the sack better. "Hold the bag up a little." He took a quick glimpse of the bag as she held it up. "I can see whatever it is, is dark colored. Give me a hint. Is this a normal purchase or is it something that we would hardly ever buy?"

Gwen countered with, "I have never worn anything like this before. I've never seen them before at Second Chances or anywhere else in town for that matter!"

Harold shook his head, saying, "I should never have made that bet because I don't want to see that musical. Musicals are weird! In musicals people sing songs running down the street hand in hand and hanging on lampposts. They sing whether they are happy or sad. They are just plain weird! I have to get this right! Come on, Gwen, you have to give me another hint!"

Grinning, she said, "OK. Another hint. These are for me, but you might like some too."

"Is it some kind of pants or jeans?"

"Close enough, and these are for me," said Gwen, as she pulled the leather pants out of the bag.

"Ah, Gwen!" said Harold as he held up the pants and looked them over. "You are going to ride with me. You must be planning to ride with me if you bought leather pants!" He reached over and patted her knee, and she looked up into his eyes.

In a soft voice Gwen said, "Yes, I'm going to ride with you, Harold, but I'm going to have to get used to it. It isn't my cup of tea by a long shot, but that's changing. You know how you feel about musicals, that they are weird? Well, that's how I am about this motorcycle business. Then she squeezed his hand.

"Gwen, honey, get us tickets for that musical! I'm just going to power myself through it, weird or not!"

Gwen and Harold sat in their van and stared at the neon sign reading Murry's Motorcycles. Their van's engine clinked and pinged as it cooled, but the couple still sat motionless under the store's neon sign. Out of the corner of her eye, Gwen watched Harold's face. His gaze followed a man wearing a leather vest and black boots entering through sliding glass doors.

"Well, are we going in?" Gwen's chipper voice broke the silence.

Harold turned towards her, while his eyes remained fixed on the store entrance. Several days ago at the kitchen table the idea had sent his blood racing and had reminded him he was alive. While getting his license, this very parking lot had made him feel adventurous and free. But he was miles from his kitchen, and this store looked different with all the lights turned on. The idea now felt as uncomfortable as a shirt a few sizes too small.

"Do you think we are getting too old for this?" Harold turned to meet her gaze.

Gwen bit her lip as she felt a small laugh bubbling forth. Deep inside, Gwen might have thought the idea of getting a motorcycle at this age was a silly idea. But she also knew there are times when seemingly silly things matter most. She loved Harold, and she wanted to encourage him if he wanted to go this route.

Gwen put her hand on his shoulder. "Now, I don't think they will sell a hog to someone who looks as mopey as you do right now. You go in that store and you look confident."

Harold grinned, nodded, and got out. He only needed a little encouragement. "Well, then, what are we waiting for? Let's go!"

They entered the store with a *whoosh* of the electronic door, and for a moment they both stopped in their tracks. Bold colored vehicles of all shapes and sizes cluttered every inch of free space. The aroma of leather and oil filled their nostrils. Several customers inspected a display of unknown tools. A muscular man wearing a leather vest and bandana glanced at them as he left the store. Gwen gripped Harold's arm a little tighter.

It was Harold's turn to exude confidence. He cleared his throat, tried remembering all the motorcycle lingo he had ever learned, and stepped toward the closest row of motorcycles.

He reached the first row; and as he walked, his fingers lightly touched a variety of bikes. He sensed their power and felt an imaginary wind whip around him.

A squeaky voice cracked, "Good morning, sir. How may I assist you?" ripping Harold from his thoughts.

Harold turned to look at the young man who had spoken. Harold wondered how this young boy was old enough to have a job, much less a motorcycle license. He was lanky and thin, and Harold noticed peach fuzz trying to pass for a mustache and a beard.

"Oh, we are only looking."

"For someone else or for yourselves?"

"For . . . uh . . . ourselves."

Gwen caught herself looking around. She halfway expected everyone to be staring at the old couple playing with toys. No one was looking.

"Oh, great!" The squeaky voice continued. "Are you looking for a cruiser, sports bike, naked bike, dirt bike, or scooter? And what do you want weight-wise? And height?"

"I . . . uh . . ." Harold figured they would soon see how little he knew about motorcycles.

Gwen sensed his hesitation and spoke up for him. "He wants to look at a *hog*," she said with a satisfied nod.

Harold blushed slightly and continued with, "You know, just something to ride around town on."

The young salesman furrowed his brow, as if deep in thought. He stroked his peach-fuzz-covered chin, looking back and forth between the two for a moment. Suddenly a smile burst on his face. "OK, I have the perfect bike for you!" The boy waved for them to follow. He led them through a maze of bikes to the center of the store.

A monstrosity towered above them. Four feet off the ground, the bike angled upward as if in mid-jump. It was made to look as though it had broken through a wall, with a few bricks suspended around the bike in midair. The bike itself was a dazzling jet black with long, bright orange stripes along the sides. The model name *Terminate X5000* glowed a soft orange.

"She is a beautiful bike, isn't she? Brand new. Only a $58,000 base price—a little more with some of the amazing extras. Imagine yourself roaring through town on this baby. All eyes, I mean, *all* eyes on you. What a thrill!"

Harold steadied himself on the railing around the display. The price thundered in his ears—$58,000! What was he thinking? This dream was unaffordable. Even the *thought* of spending that kind of money made him want to get his old job back. Harold held his stomach and looked over at Gwen. Wide-eyed, she stared at the bricks hanging in midair and fanned herself with a pamphlet about the bike. She kept imagining Harold crashing into a wall and all the explaining she would have to do at his funeral.

Harold thanked the salesman, Gwen placed the pamphlet

back on the stand, and the two looked for the door. They walked to the exit, half wanting to run. They were so dazed they almost ran into a short display of trail mix by the front door.

In another part of the store, a man had watched the entire ordeal. He had seen them enter, seen their reaction to the *Terminate X5000*, and saw their beeline for the door. He was a broad-shouldered man with large hands that were stained dark from working with machines. A thick, white ponytail dropped down from an American flag bandana. He wore jeans and a mustard yellow buttoned-down shirt.

"Excuse me!" His voice boomed through the store as he lumbered after Harold and Gwen. They half turned as they were nearing the sliding glass doors. They were ready to put this misadventure behind them but were curious as to whether the deep voice was intended for them. It was. This made Gwen want to pick up their pace, but Harold slowed. It was difficult to disobey such a commanding voice.

Chapter 5

"Can I help you folks find something?" the man asked.

Harold didn't quite know what to say. But he didn't want to wait too long and have Gwen answer by repeating they were looking for a hog.

"Oh, we were looking at motorcycles, but we may go home now and mull it over." He took a half step further outside.

"That's fine. I didn't want to let you nice folks leave before I met my newest customers!" the large man said with a genuine smile.

This caused Harold and Gwen to take a closer look at the man. On the expanse of this man's chest they saw a nametag that read *Murry*.

"So, you are the Murry of Murry's Motorcycles?" Harold asked. He took a step back from the door.

"I sure am! Chuck Murry. When I wanted to open my own motorcycle shop my wife kept calling it Chuck's Chuckwagons, but we decided on Murry's Motorcycles. It rolls off the tongue a bit smoother." Chuck laughed a deep belly laugh that was so infectious it drew Harold and Gwen toward him.

Chuck wiped tears of laughter from his eyes as he asked. "Anyway, what are your names?"

"I'm Harold Miller, and this is my wife Gwen. Nice to meet you." The two men shook hands.

"So . . . Gwen, Harold, what can I do for you today?"

Harold felt queasy again, remembering the $58,000 they didn't have. Gwen had flashbacks of Harold's funeral after he busted through the wall.

"We came to look at some motorcycles." He gestured towards the *Terminate* towering in the center of the store. "But we will be fine with just looking today. This dream seems a little out of our price range."

"I see you met Stephen." Chuck motioned toward the boy they had been speaking to earlier. He was standing again at the foreboding bike in the center of the store, talking to another wide-eyed couple. "Yes, Stephen loves that bike." Chuck continued. "It's all I can do to keep him from running all the new folks out. I keep telling him not everyone is as enthralled as he is about something that expensive, but he is a work in progress."

Harold smiled and looked down. Sometimes it is nice to know you aren't alone in being overwhelmed.

"So, is there anything in particular you would like, or are you just wanting to feel the wind in your hair?" Chuck beamed.

"Fringe of hair, you mean!" Harold joked, pointing to his head.

"Oh, and we can sell you some hair fit for bike riders!" Chuck laughed as he pointed to a row of helmets with mohawks protruding from the tops.

"Well, I've been in this business for a while, and I may have something that would fit you a bit better. Would you care to see it? If this is your first bike, it's smart to start off with something with less muscle, easier to ride. Then if the day comes you want something bigger, come see me again and I'll put you on something larger."

Chuck led them through the store away from the *Terminate X5000* until they reached a door marked *Mechanic—Employees Only.*

Harold and Gwen stepped through the door as if entering another world. The fluorescent lights were bright, and the aroma in the area was a mixture of oil and gasoline. Wood workbenches littered with tools lined the long walls. Chains and strange tubes hung from the ceiling. Large black, puddle-shaped stains marked the concrete floor. Several workstations had piles of what appeared to Harold and Gwen to be no more than twisted metal junk.

Chuck led them to a bench and a pile of metal parts on the far side of the room. As he stood above the shell of a motorcycle, he said, "Here she is, my current basket case. I call her *Hog Wild.*" Harold and Gwen tried to see a motorcycle in this pile of junk. The metal was a bright silver color with sleek oily black accents. They could recognize a seat and handlebars lying on the bench, but most pieces were foreign to them.

Gwen smiled at the name *Hog Wild.* She had asked Stephen to show them the hogs right from the beginning. She looked over at Harold to gauge his reaction. His eyes were riveted on the pile of metal on the ground, and she saw a glimmer in his eyes. It was the first glimmer she had seen since the young salesman had shocked them. Chuck pointed and spoke what sounded like absolute gibberish to Gwen. He spoke about blocks and cylinders, spoilers and kickstands—all of which whizzed right over Gwen's head. Had Harold ever heard these terms before? Either way he nodded wherever Chuck pointed. His lips pursed tight as he was deep in thought. She watched as a smile would begin to emerge but then recede as his brow furrowed. His grin grew more and more as he inspected each part of the proposed machine.

After a while, Chuck stopped pointing and Harold stopped nodding. Gwen mentally rejoined the conversation. "This has been my pet project for a few months on and off, but I have needed a reason to press on and finish it. When I saw you two, I thought maybe *Hog Wild* is right for you. It is an easy first bike, or it will be when I get all the pieces back together."

"How much?" Harold asked.

"Once she's all up and running again, I'd say around $3,500."

It might have been the price drop from the *Terminate* to the *Hog Wild*. But almost before Chuck finished his sentence, Harold jumped in with, "We'll take it."

Gwen was in a daze as she watched Harold fill out the paperwork. As she sat there, she kept staring at the large wooden desk in the small paneled office. She stared at it, but her mind was on Harold's split decision. She backed him, but he was so spontaneous these days.

Next they looked at helmets. Gwen chose a ruby-red helmet with misty swirls. Harold's choice was a black and blue helmet with tiny triangles down the center that looked like miniature spikes. Gwen reached over and tried her helmet on. How could anyone drive a vehicle with such a limited range of vision?

Gwen put the helmet down and looked at Harold again. She felt somewhat dizzy. Minutes before, she had been watching as people walked in and out of the store. Had those people bought motorcycles so quickly? What felt like only seconds ago she had been terrified thinking about Harold busting through walls. She supported him, but soon this death machine would be a part of their lives. She wondered if she should have been less supportive. She had heard the term "hog wild" before, and it had meant someone going off the deep end. Was that what was happening to Harold?

Chuck turned to look at Gwen. "I will finish putting your bike together by the end of the week, and we will get it to you as soon as possible."

Gwen stayed in a daze as the men talked financing and signed papers. She hardly noticed Stephen chatting with Harold on the walk to the front door. Gwen, thoughts dominated by *Hog Wild*, walked right into the small display of trail mix.

The next morning when Harold woke, he jumped out of bed and headed straight for the garage. He had been dreaming about the new purchase all night. He stood in the doorway, imagining his brand new motorcycle ready and waiting for him.

Harold showered and was ready for the day by the time Gwen even stirred. She found him, coffee mug in hand, sitting out on the porch.

"Well, aren't you up early and ready for another day!" Gwen said as she cracked opened the door to the porch. "Too excited to sleep?"

"Yeah, Chuck still has a while to go before he finishes with *Hog Wild*, and waiting that long is going to be hard for me."

"Even if we did get your new hog this instant, I don't know where you would put it! It definitely isn't going in the living room! How about clearing out some space in the garage," Gwen said with a smile. Before she could say another word, Harold was on his feet. He now had a mission to keep him busy until he got his bike.

* * *

Gwen heard the garage door opening. They had brought *Hog Wild* home the previous evening after Chuck had called to say it was ready. Harold drove the thing home while she followed in the van. As she was driving, Gwen shook her head and thought to herself that this was the craziest thing she had ever been a part of. Harold went at a safe pace, but she still put a death grip on the steering wheel every time he turned a corner. She found herself wishing again the thing would quit running on the way home and just fall apart as it stopped. She wondered how long it would it take for Harold to come to his senses! That might be $3,500 down the drain, but they could chalk it up to experience.

Between corners, when she wasn't in fear for Harold's life, Gwen remembered what her dad had told her long ago. It was the day before her wedding, and she had been heading to her room with some packages. Her dad was in the living room. No one else was around; and as she smiled at him, he put up his hand to stop her.

Gwen's dad looked up at her from his chair, smiled, and said, "It's exciting, isn't it?" She nodded, radiating joy. He hesitated a moment. "Gwen, you must always remember: married life isn't a 50/50 proposition. It is more like 60/60. There will be times when both of you will have to give 10 percent more than you think is fair. Remember that, and your marriage will run smoother in hard times."

Gwen remembered her dad's words now as she heard the commotion in the garage. Harold was moving garbage cans to clear a space for the new cycle. She shuddered a little thinking about climbing on that thing and hanging on to Harold for dear life when it moved! Over the past weeks life seemed to have gotten a lot more complicated. But maybe this was one of her extra 10 percent situations.

Harold appeared in the kitchen doorway, smiling as if he'd won the lottery. That's all it took to melt her, and she thought, "10 percent is nothing with Harold." She grinned back.

"Still happy with your purchase?" she asked.

"Oh, Gwen, it's the greatest feeling in the world to sit on *Hog Wild* and rev the engine! Let's go for a ride."

Gwen looked out the window and realized dusk had fallen. At least if they went around the block this late, no one would recognize them. Even as a long-married couple riding around on their own motorcycle, she could imagine the comments of some people. It was one thing for Harold to ride the thing. But she felt that reaction to her riding behind him would be right up there with an overweight retiree flaunting a skimpy dress with deep, deep cleavage. She smiled to herself as she imagined what Harold would say if, prior to any rides, she asked him to drive to some deserted spot to pick her up so she wouldn't be seen. It seemed silly, but it would be more comfortable for her.

Still hesitant, she stalled, saying she had to empty the dishwasher. She wanted to stall the first ride a day or two longer. When the dishwasher was emptied and refilled, and the kitchen was spotless, Gwen peeked around the corner. Harold's shoes were still on, and his motorcycle keys were still in his hand as he sat reading the newspaper. She had to think of another excuse.

"Harold, I need to go over and see Aunt Julia. You know how she gets when I don't stop in every now and then. You go for your ride, and I'll take the car over to Aunt Julia's."

Stopping to see Aunt Julia wasn't his favorite way to pass time. The old girl was OK, but she always seemed rather judgmental. He'd seen her clamp down on various family members at family gatherings, and he wasn't looking forward to his turn. Take, for instance, when Julia heard one of the young cousins had been seen buying a six-pack of beer. The next time Aunt Julia saw him, she told him if he planned to be a beer drinker, she wished he would change his last name. Then she added that they had never had a drinker in the family, and they were not ready for one now. Yes, Aunt Julia called them like she saw them, and it didn't matter who was around. But even that thought didn't stop Harold's excitement of taking his first ride with Gwen.

"Aw, come on Gwen, you have to come with me on this maiden voyage. We can stop and see her on our little jaunt."

Gwen just couldn't dampen his spirits and say no. Feeling nervous, she put her sweater on and headed for the garage. She drew in a big breath and looked at *Hog Wild* standing there so innocently, as if no one had ever gotten hurt (or worse) riding on one! She hoped Harold would never discover how scared she was about this motorcycle business.

The garage door was up, and Harold was sitting in the seat waiting for her. She approached, her head cocked to the side. "How do you get on one of these things?" she asked.

"Throw your leg over the seat, grab hold of my waist, and hold on!" Harold answered as if it was the most obvious thing in the world.

Away they went at what seemed like breakneck speed. Gwen held tight onto Harold's waist. She opened one eye and realized they weren't going as fast as she had thought. She turned her head this way and that, trying to see their neighborhood through her face shield. The breeze was blowing, and she had to admit it felt good. "This isn't half bad," she thought. "What is better on a quiet night than a ride in the open with your arms around your husband?"

Suddenly Harold turned a corner. He didn't slow; he simply leaned to the right and turned. She grabbed hold of his belt, pulling hard trying to slow them down.

Harold half turned around but Gwen couldn't hear what he was saying. He tried turning around again. He was saying something, but the noise around them drowned him out. She leaned closer with their helmets touching to hear him better.

"Quit screaming, Gwen. You'll break my eardrums and wake people up in this quiet neighborhood! And let go of my belt! You're cutting me in half! We're three blocks from Julia's house, but I will bet she can hear us coming!"

Had she been screaming? She closed her mouth and loosened her death grip on his belt one finger at a time. No wonder he was complaining. She would have to toughen up and get better about this. She let go of the belt, while taking a deep breath, and put her arms back around his waist.

As soon as she relaxed, she remembered something startling. They were going to Aunt Julia's on this machine. What was the old girl going to say? Why, she'd have a fit. Luckily it was dusk and perhaps Aunt Julia wouldn't notice how they got there.

Chapter 6

The front room light was on when Gwen and Harold arrived at Aunt Julia's house, so she was most likely reading or watching TV.

"Harold, leave the motorcycle on the street. Don't drive up in her driveway or she'll hear it."

"Quit stewing, Gwen. She'll find *something* not quite up to her standards, and it might as well be this." Gwen noticed, however, that he parked the bike in front of Julia's big elm tree so it wasn't as noticeable from the house. They also left their helmets on the bike so they wouldn't be a clue for their aunt.

They climbed off the bike and Gwen reached up to tidy her hair. She straightened the collar on her blouse and pulled down her sweater. She turned and straightened Harold's collar. They were climbing the front steps as the door opened.

"Well, look who's here," Julia said, holding the door open for them to enter. Julia was petite, thin, and had a ramrod-straight posture. It was difficult to tell the age of the woman. She rarely smiled and had all-knowing eyes that seemed to look straight through a person. "I've been wondering when you'd come by. I've been hearing things about you two that I'm having a hard time believing."

Aunt Julia, the older sister of Gwen's mother, had never

married. She had been engaged once, but shortly before the wedding her fiancé left town never to return. Gwen's mother said the embarrassment of the whole thing had given Julia a bad outlook on life. It was not necessarily hard to get along with their aunt; it was just that she was opinionated and not afraid to speak her mind. If she thought someone was out of line, she wasn't afraid to straighten them out, whether it was a family member or a clerk in the store. It made no difference to Aunt Julia. Wrong was wrong.

Aunt Julia backed into the room and gestured for them to come in. Gwen wrapped her arms around the old woman and gave her a big hug. Gwen never quite knew if Julia's gentle pats on the back during the hugs was a show of affection, but she loved Aunt Julia, who had spent lots of time in Gwen's home while she was growing up. As a child, Gwen's deportment must not have met her aunt's expectations because Aunt Julia always called her Baby Gwendolyn; but she promised to call her Lady Gwendolyn when and if she learned to behave.

Julia motioned for them to sit on the couch while she lowered herself into her recliner. Without preamble she got right to the point. "Now, I want you young people to tell me what all this talk around town is about."

Gwen glanced at Harold and then replied, "What talk do you mean, Aunt Julia?"

"You two have apparently gone off the deep end and bought one of those motor scooter things and are riding all over God's green acres on it!"

"Well, Aunt Julia . . ." Gwen looked toward Harold for support. He was clenching his mouth tightly, attempting to hold in laughter. She continued, "Harold has always wanted a motorcycle. Now that he's retired we thought he should get one and enjoy it while he's able." Trying to placate, she added, "It isn't a new one; it's a used one, so it didn't cost much." Gwen looked over at Harold again as if to say, "Say something man, don't just leave me hanging by myself!"

They both waited for Aunt Julia to let go with both barrels about how they should have known better. To their surprise, Aunt Julia slapped her knee and proclaimed, "I wondered when somebody in this family was going to hop to it and do something exciting!"

She looked at them in turn and gave them a rare smile. She slapped her knee for a second time, jumped out of her chair and said, "Take me for a ride on that thing, Harold! I've always wanted to ride on one of those contraptions!"

Gwen and Harold gawked, their mouths hanging open, hardly recognizing this new Julia. They stuttered around before Gwen spoke. "It's pretty dark out there, Aunt Julia. What if Harold came by another day when it's warmer and gave you a ride?"

Julia's demeanor changed, and she replied, "No, I would like to go now. If I don't go, I'll lie awake all night wondering how it would feel to ride on one of those things, and I'm not worth anything the next day if I don't get my sleep."

Harold was grinning from ear to ear. "Well then, let's go!"

Gwen interrupted with "Aunt Julia, do you have a pair of slacks? It might make it easier for you to ride on the bike."

Her aunt turned around, and her face suggested just how out of line Gwen's advice seemed to her. Her answer came immediately. "Young lady, have you ever seen me in a pair of pants? Pants on women are another sign that the women of this world are going to rack and ruin! No, what I have on will do fine!"

Harold raised his eyebrows at Gwen as if to say, "So there." He opened the door to let the older lady precede him outside. Gwen was certain they were about to witness the eighth wonder of the world. She ran after them, holding her sweater out and calling, "Here, put this on so you don't get chilly."

The riders were behind the tree as they mounted the machine. Gwen winced as she thought about that skirt, then grinned and thought, "Go get 'em, Aunt Julia!" She hoped the old-fashioned, halfway-to-the-knee bloomers she remembered from the clothesline were still a part of her aunt's wardrobe!

The engine started, and the unlikely couple took off like a shot. Gwen winced, as it sounded like Harold was going faster than was necessary. She made herself comfortable on the porch swing to wait for the riders' return. She hoped the ride would be everything her old aunt wanted it to be. Gwen thought Aunt Julia needed and deserved a minute or two of excitement in her life.

The two riders headed down the street at a quick pace. Harold saw a bump coming too late to slow down without throwing his passenger to the curb. He hit the bump head on, and both wheels of the cycle went up in the air before landing. Harold felt himself lift off the seat as he also felt his passenger lift from her seat. Uh oh, I'm in for it now, he thought. But instead, he heard Julia laugh as she plopped back in her seat, never loosening her grip on Harold's waist.

She yelled in Harold's ear, "Turn here! Let's ride past Mildred's place. She usually sits on her front porch this time of night." With so little warning Harold had to turn the corner fast to get on Mildred's street, but Julia held on. They continued at a faster pace than he would have driven if he had been by himself. He loved hearing her squeal like a delighted child.

They drove on, and Harold wondered about his passenger's skirt. The skirt lay no higher than a pair of shorts, but this was a ninety-year-old. She was always so prim and proper, and they were close to her friend's house. But he decided not to mention it. This was a new side of Julia they had never known. At any rate, exposed thighs going past her friend's house was Julia's problem. He knew if any flack came up the next week, Julia could handle it. He'd best stay out of it.

As they approached their target, Harold saw someone under the porch light. Julia leaned forward, almost screaming so Harold could hear her over the motor, "Slow down when you get to Mildred's place, but make this thing roar a little." Right before Mildred's house, Harold revved the motor and slowed almost to a stop.

Julia pulled her helmet off and yelled, "Hey there, Mildred. You ought to try this sometime and live a little!" She patted him on the shoulder and said, "Go! Go!" He heard her chuckling behind him as she crammed the helmet back on her head.

Mildred, rising from her chair, threw her arms in the air as if she didn't know whether to keep looking or shut her eyes against such immodesty. Harold guffawed as he revved the motor again and sped off towards Julia's house. What a precious old gal Julia was! He guessed no one had ever truly gotten to know her.

The riders returned, and Aunt Julia looked a little wind-blown, but the smile hadn't vanished. As she dismounted, she said, "I'd ask you to stay for lemonade, but it's way past my bedtime." Gwen figured it would be difficult to top that, so she and Harold said their goodbyes and turned to leave. As they headed out the door, Aunt Julia reached up and gave Harold a heretofore unheard-of hug. Until now, according to her aunt, embraces were only between women. If necessary, women could shake a man's hand.

As they headed home, Gwen laid her head against Harold's back. Her anxiety before the visit had worn her out, and so had the excitement of how her aunt had received them. She wanted to collapse into bed when they got home. During the entire return trip, Gwen thought about how smooth and relaxing the ride was.

She opened her eyes and realized they were turning onto their street. "Just as I was getting the hang of this riding business, we're home," she thought. But she was happy to put both feet down on her own driveway. She sent up a quiet prayer that God would help her to adjust to this new fad of Harold's. After all, she knew she had God to thank for getting them together all those years ago. She'd have to keep trusting.

* * *

Gwen entered the kitchen where Harold sat reading the newspaper. Harold noticed her dress out of the corner of his eye and asked, "Off to play cards with the Magnificent Seven?"

"What gave it away?" Gwen chuckled as she twirled in her dress.

"You know, you look mighty fine in a dress."

"Well, thank you, but I would rather wear pants. I understand wearing a dress to church, but it does bug me to have to wear one to these card games."

"Well, then wear pants. Who's stopping you?"

As Gwen looked for the keys in her purse, she glanced at Harold. "Oh, you have no idea. I have worn slacks to play with these ladies before. Nice slacks too. But everyone else was wearing a dress, and I noticed a few looking me up and down when I came in. Those ladies have a silent dress code."

Harold laid his paper on the table and seemed deep in thought. "Hmm. Well, I don't know what to tell you."

"Why is this town always so concerned with what everyone is wearing? Clothes are the outer shell. The real person is on the inside."

"You tell 'em, honey! You should show up one time wearing your new leather pants. That would teach 'em!" Harold held one fist in the air, the universal sign of triumph.

"Oh, that would not go over well at all. I'm sure they will find out about your motorcycle sooner or later though. Maybe I could throw a pair of slacks on here or there and ease them into it." Gwen smiled and kissed Harold on the top of his head. "It is what it is. I have to go with the flow." She smiled and headed for the door.

Harold chuckled and added, "I'll let you know if your nose gets too far in the air after socializing with them."

When Harold heard the garage door close, he stretched and yawned. Between their move, the motorcycle, convincing Gwen, and even convincing himself, he was worn out.

"I want to sit in my living room and do nothing," he thought. He fiddled with the TV remote and ran through the programs, but nothing interested him. Then he saw a book on the coffee table. Gwen's brother, Kurt, a prolific reader, had dropped it off for Harold a couple of weeks back and told him it was packed with action and he thought Harold would like it.

Harold picked up the book and inspected it, a mild look

of interest on his face. A Western written by Louis L'Amour. Harold reading books was very rare. But maybe retirees lived at a different pace and he should give it a shot. Kurt wouldn't have recommended it if he didn't think Harold would like it. He opened the book and was immediately captivated. Had anyone told him he would enjoy reading about the Old West and Indians, he would have said that person was wrong.

Chapter 7

The ladies were ready to begin their card game, and as they drew their table seating numbers and waited for Lettie to arrive, Frances bellowed, "I have an announcement. My name is now Sissy Fullerton, so you must all call me that."

Tess looked at Bess and then asked, "Why are you changing your name, Fran—I mean Sissy?"

The new Sissy responded. "I am tired of making a call, saying 'this is Frances Fullerton' and having the other person ask, 'How can I help you, Mr. Fullerton?'" She shook her head and said, "My sister called me Sissy when I was little so that name will do fine! They won't mix that name up," she said with fire in her eyes.

Then Betty posed a question. "But didn't your family make a fuss about the name change after all these years?"

"Yes, they did," answered Sissy, "but it was nothing compared to the fuss the bank made! I finally had to tell them in no uncertain terms to give me the papers to sign because it was my name and my money. After that, no one mentioned it again!" Few people were up to arguing with the old Frances, and it seemed the same rang true about the new Sissy.

Mary Alice, Agnes, and Sissy were at Gwen's table today. After a short lull in a conversation about Lettie's latest doctor's appointment, Gwen took the bull by the horns. "Do you think it is alright for women to wear slacks?"

Mary Alice looked at Agnes, but it was Sissy who spoke in her low authoritative voice. "My dear, why would someone like you, who looks so nice in a dress, put on pants? They look so coarse . . . I mean on some people."

Agnes blushed and chimed right in with "But you always look so nice in whatever you wear, dear. We don't want to criticize you in the least!"

Gwen had been right when she thought they disapproved of her wearing pants. She made a mental note to always wear a dress on Dirty Queens day. The ladies were such a sweet group and had been such good friends to her mom. She could give up pants for them every once in a while.

As the conversation moved to Sissy's medications, Mary Alice and Agnes looked at Gwen and smiled. Agnes reached over to pat Gwen's hand, and both older women looked at each other in a knowing way. Gwen wondered if those two had heard something they hadn't shared with the rest of the group. Had Mrs. Peabody been talking? She was even more sure when the two gave her hugs at the end of the day's card game.

When Gwen arrived home she stood in the living room door, looking at Harold in a strange way. "Are you OK? You're reading. I've never seen you reading before. Have you been sitting in here with that book for three hours?"

Harold held up the book and said, "Remember when Kurt left this book for me? I didn't think I would like reading, but this is some good stuff." He thumbed through some pages until he found a certain spot. "These cowboys are riding towards a town to meet a stagecoach. Some Indians are going through the same country and spy the cowboys. Now the Indians are hiding and getting ready to jump them! Gwen, this book is great. You ought to read it!"

Gwen laughed. Harold was more of a hands-on kind of guy. Yet he seemed so captivated by the book. "You had better come get some supper and let those Indians lie in wait a while longer." Harold lowered the book to the end table, trying to read until the moment the book lay closed on the table. He followed her into the kitchen.

"I even made you a rhubarb cream pie this morning. We will cut it after we finish our spaghetti." While they ate, Harold continued giving Gwen the play-by-play plot of his new book. Gwen shook her head. Here was yet another side of her husband that had taken her over forty years to discover. Their conversation eventually drifted from cowboys and Indians to their motorcycle. They talked about future trips and scenic routes.

Usually they watched the birds and squirrels through their kitchen window during dinner. But Harold's mind and eyes turned in a different direction tonight. As they talked he looked at his new motorcycle through the open door to the garage. Gwen loved seeing the smile on her husband's face. It was obvious what his main interest was today. The action in the yard had fallen lower in the "interesting" category; way below his new wheels. He had been convincing when he talked of riding in the open air and being fancy-free. Was this what people meant when they spoke of wanderlust? Whatever it was, Harold had a full-blown case. And, with the inklings she was feeling lately, Gwen decided she might be catching it too.

Talking about traveling on that two-wheeled monster made Harold happy. When he was happy, Gwen was happy too.

Over the forty plus years since their wedding, Harold and Gwen had gotten to the place where they seemed to think alike. They could order for each other at restaurants, and Gwen always knew what stories Harold would tell others next. Yes, if all this nonsense about motorcycles made him happy, then so be it. Looking at his smiling face she laughed. "I don't think I've ever seen a gray-haired lady on the back of a motorcycle. Maybe I should become a blonde!"

"No, you're perfect the way you are. We're turning a new page in our lives, but we are still the same old us. In this new life I might wish for a ponytail too, but I couldn't gather enough hair on this bald head to make one. Nah, we're good! I can see us now, heading out on little jaunts and longer trips. We need to do these things now while we are able to enjoy them."

Gwen chuckled as she raised her coffee cup. "You know, you didn't look like a Harold when you were sitting on your new machine. What should we call the new you?" She gazed at him, turning her head this way and that. She suggested "Bubba" or "Chub." She paused, puzzling over the thought. "No, those names are too ordinary. You need one that implies your fearless wanderlust for adventure! Something with an edge to it!" Harold and Gwen both leaned forward, goofy grins on their faces as their creativity whirred.

"I want a real macho name to go with my new persona," he mused. "'Dude' is too common." He grinned and added, "And 'Buck' is too."

Gwen took a sip of coffee, put her elbow on the table, and rested her chin in her hand. Without warning she got off her chair and went to the garage, returning with their new helmets. She put the blue one on Harold's head. Its design looked like a row of little spikes that ran from the neck to a point at the top of the helmet. She put on the ruby-red one, her favorite color.

For a few minutes they sat there in their helmets, feeling wild and free and a bit silly all at once. Gwen tilted her head to one side, trying out names for Harold in her mind. As she considered his look, it came to her. "I think I have it! 'Spike'! Somehow it suits you."

The new Spike grinned, slapped his open hand on the tabletop and agreed, "Yeah, it fits! I like it. I do feel like a Spike in this helmet!" He took off his helmet and turned it around and around before putting it back on. Then he looked at Gwen. "If I get a new name you have to have one too. What are we going to call you?"

Gwen sat back in her chair and looked upward in thought. "I always wished Mom had named me Phoebe. I've always liked that name. What do you think?"

Spike tapped his chin with his finger. After a few seconds he said, "Nah, Phoebe doesn't sound right for a lady biker in a red helmet and black leather pants. It's more for tea parties and church meetings. We're going on the road, honey, and you need a roadworthy name!" He tilted his chair back on its back legs, his usual thinking position, still looking at her. Righting his chair and reaching his arms out in front of him, he pronounced, "I've got it! I'm going to call you 'Babe'! Yes, ma'am! You're my biker babe! That fits you."

She sat back, contemplating this new name. Then, straightening her helmet, she rose from her chair and struck a pose. "Believe it or not, I feel like a Babe in this helmet!" Her new Spike was right. She had well-padded hips, and hair edging toward white, but when he called her Babe it sounded right.

They both laughed. This whole new concept of Spike and Babe was invigorating and exciting. Maybe their life had been dull. Somehow it seemed the sun was a little brighter as it came in the windows this morning, and the same old kitchen now held excitement.

Walking around the kitchen in her new helmet, hands on her hips, the new Babe spoke out with gusto. "I know at the time I bought my leather pants I did it to show Mrs. Peabody and to make you laugh. But now I think we need leather pants for you and jackets for both of us. This adventure calls for a new look. If we're going to do this thing, let's do it right. Tomorrow let's go shopping. I don't care if we have muffin tops or wide hips or whatever. We are going to look the part. There are heftier motorcyclists in the world than us, but we may be the happiest."

As they were going to bed that night, Spike emptied his pocket change into the jar by the bed and left the bedroom. Babe heard the door to the garage open. A minute later, as she was climbing into bed, she heard a loud roar coming from the garage. The sound was new to her but she knew what it was the instant she heard it. My goodness, he was revving *Hog Wild*. Four loud bursts broke through the quiet night, and then the ruckus stopped. The neighborhood seemed even quieter than it had before. She heard the garage door go down, and the kitchen door close, and Spike appeared in the bedroom doorway holding his new book. He was grinning from ear to ear.

"Can't wait to get that baby on the road! It's every bit as good-looking as those high priced ones we looked at. It's beautiful, Babe! Did you hear it? Doesn't it sound great! It makes me want to climb on and take off for parts unknown right now!"

"Of course I heard it, and I don't doubt half the town heard it!" answered Babe with a tight look on her face. They lived in a small town, and those who hadn't actually heard the sound would soon hear about it, Babe thought.

At that moment the phone rang. Babe picked up the receiver, said hello, and listened for a few moments. Looking at Spike, she pointed to the north side of the bedroom while silently mouthing "Mrs. Kline from next door." Babe looked toward the ceiling as she listened. She then placed her hand to her forehead, rolling her eyes at Spike in desperation.

"No, nothing is amiss, Mrs. Kline. Everything is OK here," Babe said into the phone. She listened again and then replied, "We are both OK. It was Harold starting a motor in the garage." She paused, listening, and then answered, "No, a stranger did not break in over here. Our neighborhood is perfectly safe. Yes, thanks for checking, Mrs. Kline. Everything is fine." A pause and then, "I'm glad you keep your doors locked. Yes, that's a good idea." Listening again, Babe said, "Wait a minute and I'll check for you." Walking to the north window with the phone still at her ear, she reported, "No, I don't see anyone lurking in your backyard. I don't see anyone at all around outside. Yes, I'll be sure to." She paused again, listening. "Yes, they call them motion lights. I'll talk to Harold and see if he thinks we need to install them." She listened yet again and then responded with, "I will. Yes, everything is fine here, and your place looks OK too. It was good of you to check on us. Good night, Mrs. Kline."

Babe put the phone down and flopped onto the bed, sighing in relief. She looked at Spike and asked, "Is there any possible way you can start that thing a bit quieter? Do they make mufflers for them? Are we going to go through this every time you start that thing? We only moved in a few weeks ago, and now all the neighbors are going to assume we are ruffians!"

Spike said, "Don't worry, Mrs. Kline will come around. We may not have known her long, but she is a nice old lady, and the other neighbors will get used to this too."

They went to bed as the dining room clock struck eleven. Sleep came easily after an action-packed day.

In the early morning hours, Babe awoke to loud shouts. She was so scared she jumped straight up in bed. She looked around. It was Spike. Babe asked, her voice quivering, "Harold, what's wrong?" He was asleep. Sound asleep. What was wrong with him, and why was he yelling like that?

Flat on the mattress again, she all but yelled, "Harold, what in the world is the matter with you? You could wake the dead yelling like that!" She didn't know if she was more frightened or mad!

Spike, sitting up in bed, looked a little sheepish as he said "I'm sorry, honey," and then he chuckled. "It raised you right off the bed. I tried to tell you I was sorry before you came down!"

"It's not funny, Harold! What in the world were you doing yelling like that at three in the morning?"

"I guess I was dreaming. We were riding along on our motorcycle and passing some huge boulders. Some Indians on motorcycles roared out from behind the boulders and started chasing us. Their faces were streaked in war paint, and they were wearing these long feather headdresses. They were gaining on us, and I thought for sure they were going to catch us."

Babe's heart was still pounding when she turned over, ready to go back to sleep if sleep would come. "I'm going to tell Kurt no more Louis L'Amour books for you. They aren't good for my health. I'm going back to sleep; and if the phone rings, and Mrs. Kline wants to know if someone broke in again, you can take the call this time to explain!"

Chapter 8

A couple of days later, as Spike was shaving, he noticed his can of shaving cream was almost empty. Usually that would annoy him, but today it gave him a chance to try out his new wheels. To make sure, he rummaged through the bathroom a little before taking a shopping list to Babe.

"Honey, we need to go to the store. I'm almost out of shaving cream, and the shampoo and conditioner are getting low."

Babe looked up from the bread dough she was kneading. Her hands were covered in flour, and there was a dab on her cheek too. She had a quizzical look in her eye as she said, "Is that so? Well, we have some extra shampoo and conditioner in the linen closet. Can the shaving cream you have hold until Friday? I'm planning a trip to the store then."

Spike broke into a smile. "OK, you caught me! I wanted an excuse to take a trip on *Hog Wild*."

"Oh! I knew buying this motorcycle was a good investment. I don't know if you have ever offered to go to the store on a whim before." She wiped her hands on a dish towel. "Well if you are going, then I am going too! Hold on while I put this bread dough in pans to rise and I get my list."

While Babe jotted down a few more things on the list, Spike ran to put on his shoes. He surveyed the several pairs he had in the closet. Brown tasseled church shoes, his old mowing sneakers, unused house shoes, and everyday tennis shoes. He supposed his everyday shoes would be best on a motorcycle, but he wished he had something with more grip to them.

"You ready?" He called out and heard her answer from the back of the house.

"One second!"

He knew that meant he still had a few more minutes. He turned back to the closet and rummaged through his various coats. His closet held different jackets for various levels of weather. He envisioned himself wearing each one on the bike. He tried on a flannel and a denim jacket, feeling his range of motion in each.

Babe came up behind him and reached into the closet for her shoes. "I haven't seen you so indecisive about what to wear in forty years!"

"I'm not sure if any of this is great for riding." He motioned to the jackets and his shoes.

Babe put her hand on his shoulder. "I understand. I bought the leather pants at Second Chances when I went intending to get you a jacket. We should go back over there and see if we can find something comfortable for you to wear while riding."

Spike nodded. "I was kind of thinking about going back to Murry's. I remember seeing a whole clothing and shoe section. I really would like something in leather if they aren't too expensive."

"Oh! I hadn't even thought of that! Let's go—as long as you don't buy a second bike," she said with a chuckle.

Spike and Babe pulled up to Murry's Motorcycles. Spike thought this time they were arriving in style. They got off the bike, and Spike sauntered up to the building as if this was exactly where he belonged. They entered the sliding glass doors and immediately heard a familiar squeaky voice on their left. "Good morning, sir. How can I help you?"

Spike turned and saw Stephen. "Good morning. We are only looking today, thank you."

"For yourself or for someone else?"

"For ourselves. We actually want to look in the clothing department."

"Oh great! Down this way and to the left." Stephen pointed down an aisle toward the back of the store. Babe couldn't help looking over at the big bucks behemoth in the center of the store. It was still foreboding, but this time the whole setup didn't make her head spin.

Spike didn't know where to begin when he arrived at the clothing section. They had everything from earmuffs to underwear. He turned to comment to Babe, but she was already headed to the women's department. Spike turned back and started browsing through what looked to be insurmountable options.

Even though this was for riding his motorcycle, shopping for clothes made him feel the tiniest bit overwhelmed. He was looking for Babe when he heard a booming voice to his right. "Harold Miller! Back already?"

Chuck peeked around a tall display of riding gloves. "So, what can I do for you today? Looking for anything in particular?" The two men shook hands.

"Yeah, I'd like to get some clothes that are better suited for riding." Spike looked down at the denim jacket and tennis shoes he was wearing.

"Harold, my man, you have come to the right place. Are you considering some boots and a jacket, or what?"

"You tell me," Spike said. "I know a lot of bikers have special boots, and I've always pictured leather vests with patches."

"Very true. Now, we have some of the vests, but the patches usually come when you join a biker club."

"A club?"

"Yes, there are several kinds, and they do all sorts of things. Some clubs are based on what kind of bike you own, like the Harley Owners Club. Some are social clubs that respond to disasters or ride in front of funerals as escorts. There are religious clubs, such as the Christian Motorcyclists Association, which focus on ministry. And then there are the one-percenters who aren't chartered, and you probably don't want to ride with them."

Spike opened his mouth to ask a question but paused, arms crossed. Chuck continued. "It is said that 99 percent of the motorcycling community are law abiding citizens." Chuck motioned around the store. Spike saw a large man with a skull-emblazoned bandana tied around his head. Spike wasn't so sure about several of these folks being model citizens. "And then there are motorcyclists who embrace *not* being law abiding citizens. They call themselves the one-percenters."

"I see," said Spike.

Chuck stroked his chin. "You know, unless you wanted to join a biker club right away, I would suggest you get one of these." Chuck led Spike through a few rows of clothes to a wall of leather jackets.

Chuck grabbed one off the rack. It was all black with a couple of thin orange stripes going down the sides. "This jacket is good for the beginning rider. In fact, I wish *all* riders would wear jackets like these. The orange stripes act as reflectors at night. Feel here." Spike reached into the jacket to feel the material and it was hard. Chuck continued, "They have reinforced the material so if you have a nasty fall, it acts as armor and you won't get as badly scraped up. It is especially strong in the arms where you naturally protect yourself during a fall." Chuck held up his arms as if protecting his face.

"Whoa, I never knew they made clothing like this," Spike said as he felt the thick parts around the jacket. The jacket was heavy, yet it moved easier than expected.

When Spike and Babe finally met again, Spike held a new jacket, matching pants, and a pair of black boots.

Spike leaned toward his wife and quietly said, "Babe, you'll never guess what a spendthrift I am! I racked up a thousand dollars on these clothes before I knew what was happening! They are all things I need, but I'm feeling guilty about the total. Getting clothes for riding will be almost as much as the bike." He looked up at her hoping for a sign of approval.

Babe noticed that he was clutching the packages to his chest as if he was afraid she would tell him to return them. Her heart melted. She responded, "A biker needs protection, Spike. You will need those things when you ride. Don't worry; we have the slush fund we can use."

Every night for years the Millers had put all their change in a jar beside the bed. Whenever Babe used a coupon to buy something, she would put the savings in the jar. Spike had asked at various times what she was saving for, and she always gave the same answer: "I don't know. But someday we'll find something we want and the money will be there." They had taken the jar to the bank and refilled it often as the years passed.

Spike grinned, saying, "I always knew I married a smart woman, but at times like this I find out how smart you really are!"

If Spike walked into Murry's feeling as if he belonged, he walked out feeling as if he owned the place. His new clothes were bundled up tight, and even though he wasn't wearing them yet, he sat taller as he mounted his bike. Babe laid the bundle in her lap and held it there with her elbows as they sped off.

Spike and Babe pulled into Snarky's Gas and Groceries on their way home. On a normal day they might have stopped at the town's main grocery store, but Spike was feeling adventurous. There was something about stopping at a gas station on the highway to get their food. It made Spike feel rugged, as if they were living off the road.

"What do you want me to do with your new clothes?" Babe posed as she pulled off her helmet.

Spike hadn't thought of that. "I suppose you could wedge them under the bike. This is a small town, so no one will steal them."

"Are you sure?" She came close and whispered, "It is pretty expensive stuff, you know."

"It'll be fine."

Babe tucked the packages on the ground under their bike, but she wasn't too sure about it. She looked around and saw an unshaven man, dressed in clothes that looked as if they hadn't seen the inside of a washing machine in a long time. The man was leaning against the building eyeing them as he smoked a cigarette. Spike already had started for the door, so she hurried to catch up. As she passed the man, she could feel his eyes following them.

They emerged seventeen minutes later, each with a large brown sack of groceries. Babe's eyes went directly to the man and then to their packages under the bike. They were still there. She breathed a sigh of relief and bent to scoop them up. She stood there with one arm full of groceries and the other with a tight grip on the sacks of Spike's new clothes. Spike put his bag on the ground as he climbed on the bike.

The man leaning against the wall watched them. His eyes moved with their feeble attempts to hold all three bulging packages. Finally, he elbowed himself off the wall and called out, "You shoulda come in your grocery getter."

"Excuse me; in our what?" Spike asked, looking up at the man.

The man took a long drag on his cigarette and exhaled. "Your grocery getter. One of those." The man pointed to a small blue sedan.

"You mean a car?"

"Yep, that's all those things are good for." The man flicked his cigarette onto the pavement and smashed it with his heel. He spat on the ground and walked off. Spike and Babe watched him round the corner and a moment later speed away on a raised handlebar motorcycle.

"A grocery getter. That makes sense," Spike said after a long pause.

"So, how are we going to do this? Without a grocery getter, that is." Babe asked.

"Let me see my new clothes." Babe handed Spike his bundle and he opened it. He put his new jacket over the denim jacket he was already wearing. He took his new pants and jammed them in his jacket pocket. He looked up at a bewildered Babe. "While I am doing this, you start taking all our groceries out of their boxes. Let's see if we can fit it all in one bag." Babe began her task. She removed the bag of cereal from the box and threw the box into the second sack. She opened the pack of razors and dumped the contents into one grocery sack and tossed that box to the other sack. A large woman eating a gas station burrito stopped on the sidewalk in front of them. Spike looked up, and the woman kept staring. She took another bite of her burrito. He said, "We forgot our grocery getter." The woman rolled her eyes and walked off still munching on her burrito.

A few minutes later Spike was dripping with sweat from wearing both jackets. His pockets bulged with his new pants and cans of corn and soup. He wore his new boots after tying the laces of his old tennis shoes together and let them dangle around his neck. As for Babe's efforts, she had fit all the groceries in one sack and was standing next to a second bag of discarded boxes. Her pockets also bulged from stewed tomatoes and evaporated milk. They threw the now unnecessary second bag in the dumpster and climbed on the bike. Spike said, "Who needs a grocery getter anyway," and revved the motor.

Even with one grocery bag, Babe felt nervous. Earlier she had the bundle of Spike's clothes resting in her lap and could lean forward to keep her balance. But now, with an overflowing grocery bag in her lap, she sat about a foot away from Spike. She huddled as close as she could to him and heard crunching and crackling from inside the bag.

A few miles from home two rows of cars were stopped at a red light. Babe looked to her left and saw Mrs. Peabody a car-length ahead in the lane next to them. She cringed and poked Spike, nodding toward Mrs. Peabody. He said, "She must be going home. The parsonage isn't too far from our house." Her window was down, and Babe could hear Christian music over the radio. Mrs. Peabody was singing with the music. Spike edged toward her on the bike.

Babe pinched him hard on the arm. "No! I don't want her to see us. It was bad enough when she caught me in Second Chances! This is too much."

"Come on, Babe," Spike said. "We can't just drive by without acknowledging she's here. If we get close enough, we can just say a friendly hello."

The light turned green, and all the vehicles kicked into motion. As they slowed at the next red light, Spike eased right up next to Mrs. Peabody's window. Babe could hear the sweetest music coming from Mrs. Peabody's car.

Not quite knowing how to engage in an intersection, Spike tapped lightly on the frame of the car and said, "Hey there, Mrs. Peabody!"

Mrs. Peabody's beautiful voice erupted in a bloodcurdling scream as she shrank away from the window. Spike blushed, not realizing how badly they would scare her.

"Whoa, Mrs. Peabody, it's only me, Harold Miller!"

When she saw it was a congregant of her church, she scowled. "Shame on you, Harold Miller! You scared the living daylights out of me!"

Spike said, "I am so sorry, ma'am. We didn't mean to scare you. We just wanted to say hi."

Babe sank deeper against Spike's back and lifted her grocery bag to try to cover her face. It didn't work, and Mrs. Peabody scowled at her. Babe gave a little wave and said, "See you on Sunday."

The light turned green, and all three were glad to move on. It didn't take long to see the humor in how ridiculous they must have looked to their pastor's wife: Spike dripping with sweat from wearing two jackets, with old shoes hanging around his neck, and Babe balancing a large bag on her lap. And all this on their brand new *Hog Wild*. Oh, they must have been quite a sight.

Chapter 9

Babe had promised herself that if she finished her list before lunch she could sit on the front porch swing and relax. Iowa was in full spring mode, and she propped open all the windows in the house as motivation to finish her list. Soon the fridge sparkled, a batch of brownies cooled on the counter, and the first load of wash tumbled in the dryer. She and Spike even had an early lunch.

Babe sank down into the cushions of the swing. Their condo was the last one in a row of four and Babe loved it. Two big elm trees between the curb and the sidewalk swayed lazily in the breeze, shading the porch and the front lawn. A hedge grew between their lot and that of Mrs. Kline. Mrs. Kline had planted a flower garden on her side of the hedge. She was meticulous about its upkeep, always finding new ways to fend off the deer and other animals. Babe often wondered how a woman of her age got down on her hands and knees to weed with such ease.

Babe rocked back and forth, feeling the breeze and listening to the creak of the wooden swing. Out of the corner of her eye, she noticed someone walking down the block towards her. She stopped herself mid-swing and looked again. Why, it was Mrs. Peabody. She didn't seem to be the type who would be out for a stroll. For a split second Babe wondered if she should go inside and avoid any interaction. Especially after the run-in they had on their bike. But instead she smiled at the memory and braced herself for the inevitable. As Mrs. Peabody came nearer, Babe smiled to herself, thinking the pastor's wife should be wearing a hat and gloves. She seemed the type, no matter how out of style or what kind of weather they were having.

As Mrs. Peabody came closer, Babe smiled and gave a little wave. She mentally scolded herself for the unkind things she was thinking. After all, this was the woman who brought them meals when she came home from the hospital after surgery. But Babe was certain she was about to hear something negative about herself or about someone else. "It's probably going to be something about me cleaning up my act," thought Babe. The woman was good-hearted for the most part, and she was effective in her role as the wife of their pastor. But sometimes she set her standards for other people a little higher than necessary.

Mrs. Peabody gave a semblance of a smile as she approached and then turned up the walk to the porch. "I was hoping you would be home, Gwen. I would like to visit with you about something." She came up the steps and stood waiting to be invited to sit.

"It's nice to see you, Mrs. Peabody. Please sit down. It's such a nice day to sit outside."

"It's a lovely day," responded her visitor. Babe thought she looked a little ill at ease. At least she wasn't the only uncomfortable one on the porch.

The pastor's wife walked to the other side of the porch. She dusted off a green plastic lawn chair and sat down, as far from

Babe as she could get and still be seated. When she seemed settled, Babe questioned, "You wanted to talk with me?"

Mrs. Peabody looked down at her clasped hands. She said, "I thought I should bring up this business about the motorcycle. You must realize that gallivanting around town, dressed as you were, isn't a good influence on our young people."

Babe had a strong urge to roll her eyes. Instead, she merely looked at Mrs. Peabody and said, "What bad influence could our riding a motorcycle possibly have on young people?"

Lowering her voice as if she was struggling to keep the conversation between the two of them, the visitor said, "Well, you know. Riding down the street hugging your husband like that. And to make it even worse, that machine is making enough noise to draw attention to you." She paused and then added, "It doesn't seem proper." After another pause she added, "And the wretched names I've heard the two of you called. I heard someone call Harold "Spike," as if he is some kind of demon, and I heard someone called you "Babe," which makes you sound like a floozy!"

Babe got up from the swing and sat down in the chair next to Mrs. Peabody. "My dear," she started, "I'm sure everyone who knows us knows we've been married for a long time and in that time I have hugged Harold many times. That is, if you want to call it hugging when we're on the motorcycle. Actually, I'm hanging on for dear life! And, believe it or not, we gave each other those names."

Babe leaned over and put her hand on Mrs. Peabody's arm. Then she continued, "As for the noise part, a motorcycle makes no more noise than firecrackers! And in a lot of ways that noise keeps us safe. People don't always see motorcycles, so that noise helps them stay aware that we are next to their car."

Mrs. Peabody's face contorted into something near disgust. Babe didn't think she had heard anything past the fact that they had given each other those names. Mrs. Peabody stammered, unsure of how to convince Babe of her folly.

A sudden movement in the hedge beside the house caught Babe's attention. As she shifted her gaze, out popped Mrs. Kline with a fierce look on her face. She stormed up on the porch on a mission. Babe had never seen her neighbor like this.

Babe wondered what had gotten her neighbor in such a snit. Glad for the break in this awkward conversation, Babe quickly introduced the two. "Mrs. Kline, this is Mrs. Peabody, our pastor's wife."

That seemed to pull Mrs. Kline's trigger. She glared at Mrs. Peabody and said, "I was weeding my flower garden and heard what you said about Babe and Spike getting a motorcycle. I don't know that it is any of your business, but these people are the best neighbors I've had in over eighty years. They have worked hard and should be able to spend their money any way they please. They aren't hurting anyone, and they should ride motorcycles if they want to!" That said, the wind seemed to have gone out of Mrs. Kline's sails.

Mrs. Peabody was looking a little nervous, probably wishing she had not come after all. Babe felt sorry for her. In a soft voice she added, not daring to use their new names, "Harold has always wanted a motorcycle, ever since he was a boy. He has worked hard all of his life, and his family always came first before anything for himself. When he retired he bought one. He has earned it, don't you think?"

"But a motorcycle?" chimed in Mrs. Peabody, "and being identified with the kind who ride them?" Babe glanced at Mrs.

Kline, but it appeared she was content to have said her bit.

Babe considered using the argument about 99 percent of riders being good people. She decided not to go into that yet. Giving a little sigh, she tried a new tactic.

"Mrs. Peabody, have you ever wanted something very badly but it never happened or you never got it?"

The woman's eyes flickered as she looked down at her hands and replied, "No, I guess not. I can't think of anything I've really ever wanted that much."

Babe put her hand on Mrs. Peabody's arm and kept looking at her until she raised her head and returned her look. Softly Babe said, "I think everyone has something they've always wanted, and I think you have too."

Mrs. Kline chimed in, "Everyone has a bucket list, Mrs. Peabody. I've always wanted to go on a zip line, but I just haven't had the chance yet! But you can be sure if I ever get a chance I'm going to climb on and go!"

At that Mrs. Peabody give a slight smile. "Well, I guess there is one thing I've always wanted."

"So what is it, and why aren't you doing it?" broke in Mrs. Kline again.

Mrs. Peabody looked at each of the women and then seemed to blush. Oh dear, thought Babe. She hoped they hadn't opened a can of worms here.

"Well," she began, "I've always wanted to sing a solo in church."

That was too much for Mrs. Kline, and she sputtered, "And for goodness sake, why haven't you?"

Babe was thankful her neighbor had thought of something to say, because she was speechless. Indeed, why not? The woman sang in the choir every Sunday. She must have had lots of chances if she'd spoken up.

Mrs. Peabody, looking a little flustered, explained, "When I was in school I sang solos. But I don't want to offer now. That seems too forward somehow. I was taught a Christian should be humble."

Again, that was too much for Mrs. Kline. Words tumbled out, and it seemed she couldn't say them fast enough. "I don't go to your church so I don't know how you do things. I'm a Free Methodist, and we Methodists let anybody and everybody sing, alone or together, and that's the way it should be! My friend Gladys can't sing a note, but she sings straight out and rightly so! It's praise, lady, it's praise! We figure the Lord loves hearing all of us! You sing, lady, because the Lord wants to hear you!"

As Mrs. Kline spoke, Mrs. Peabody's body loosened. She looked as if she was about to hug Mrs. Kline. Her arms started to go up, but she must have given it a second thought because she lowered them immediately. Showing affection was no doubt another no-no in her book. But Mrs. Kline had no such inhibitions. She saw the gesture and threw her arms around the would-be soloist. The hesitant woman's arms shot back up. Babe sighed in relief.

The bright morning rolled by as the three women chatted. After a while Mrs. Kline went back to her weeding but every so often chimed in on the conversation, since she was obviously still eavesdropping from her flower bed.

Meanwhile, on the back porch, Spike savored the spring air. There is something about spring in Iowa that makes you want to get up and head outdoors. He itched to go for a little jaunt somewhere interesting on their bike. Spike looked out at the hanging bird feeders. He needed to go after more finch feed and maybe get another woodpecker block. A downy woodpecker sat in the little tree, looking at him as if to say, "Hey, in there! Did you forget the stuff I like?" Even so, watching the birds didn't seem as interesting as usual today. However, the prospect of travel put some pizzazz back in the picture. He reckoned they had practiced enough on their bike to take an out-of-town trip, hadn't they?

Spike looked up and realized he hadn't seen Babe in a while. He stood and stretched, wanting to find Babe to see what she thought of a trip. "Babe," he yelled into the house, "where are you?" There was no answer. He peeked through the different rooms to no avail. He passed the front door and heard Babe making an odd noise out on the front porch. He went to the window and saw Babe's back and Mrs. Peabody! Was Babe crying?

Spike swung the door open and found Mrs. Peabody and Babe roaring with laughter. He stood there dumbfounded. He never would have expected them to be enjoying each other's company. He silently stepped back into the house and began slowly shutting the door when Babe said to him, "Oh, Spike! Mrs. Peabody was just telling me about the time her choir bus broke down on the way to the Christmas pageant. They had to listen to the service on the radio, and the church where they planned to sing ended up having an open mic talent show!"

Spike stopped in the doorway, unsure what to do.

"Come out here," she continued. "Come sit with us."

Mrs. Peabody looked at her watch and said, "Actually, I had better be going, Brian will be wanting lunch soon. But thank you for the coffee. It was a pleasure talking with you."

The two women stood and hugged. Spike looked amazed as Mrs. Peabody stepped off the porch and headed back toward the parsonage.

"What in the world was that all about?" Spike asked when Mrs. Peabody was out of earshot.

"Well, she came to talk about the motorcycle, but we had the loveliest conversation. She really is a wonderful lady. And remind me to hint at the choir director at church about getting Mrs. Peabody to sing a solo sometime soon."

"Oh, OK. Sure."

"So what is it you wanted?"

Spike's eyes lit up like a Christmas tree. "Alright, I've been thinking." He rocked the swing back and forth. "Over the last few weeks we've ridden all over town and Shelby County, and it might be time for a little longer jaunt. We could even stay overnight. What do you think about Omaha?"

Somewhat taken aback, Babe hesitated, noting the excited look on Spike's face. He wasn't kidding about this. He was planning on going hell's bells down Interstate 80, in and out between trucks from every state while she hung on for dear life. Omaha was in another state and was more than an hour away by car. As Babe sat there trying to analyze this new suggestion, they heard a voice chime in from over the hedge. "I think you two should go for it!"

Spike was taken aback. His eyes grew wide, and he looked towards the hedge. Babe motioned for them to go inside and yelled towards the hedge, "Thanks, Mrs. Kline." She closed the door and told Spike, "Mrs. Kline must have heard what you said about this trip and thinks we should go for it!" To give herself some thinking-it-over time, she headed for the utility room, saying, "Wait a minute, I have to start the washing machine."

As Babe added detergent to the load, she shook her head

in amazement. Until now they had only ridden around the county on less traveled roads. They had recently even tried graveled country roads and had a great time. She'd packed a lunch one day when they went out to the little country church cemetery where her grandparents were buried. Spike had laughed and said he hoped none of his friends drove by. He would be mortified if they saw him sitting on a silly blanket eating a sandwich.

Babe drew a deep breath. Now he was talking about going out into the real world, armed with only helmets and leather to protect against hard cement and crazy drivers. She entered the kitchen where Spike eyed her with concern.

"Are you having second thoughts about all this, Babe?"

"No," she replied. "We're having fun on that machine, and we are having fun together. That's what pleases me the most about all this. I never believed I'd actually enjoy riding, but I do! It's so different from what our friends consider a good time. Sometimes I feel guilty for enjoying it so much. But the idea is growing on me. I'm OK riding around on easy roads, but now you throw in talk about taking a good two-hour ride. I wonder if we're ready."

"Babe," he replied, "we're ready! That thing handles exactly the way Chuck said it would. I'm a novice biker, but I'm confident driving it. I would be the first to say if I weren't."

"Can we get there by going on back roads and avoid the interstate?"

Spike put his arm around Babe's shoulders, laid his forehead on hers, and said, "We can't avoid traffic going that far, and we would eventually have traffic in Omaha anyway. But riding a motorcycle in traffic isn't much different than driving a car. If you drive sensibly and keep your eyes on the road and other drivers, it's the same as being in a car."

Babe looked up at him, smiled weakly, and replied, "Yes, but without any armor around you!" She let out a deep sigh and added, "You're a good driver; I trust your instincts, plus I would miss you too much while you rode all over creation without me! What is the old saying, 'United we stand and divided we fall'? When do we leave?"

Spike raised his fist in the air and proclaimed, "Attagirl!"

"One more thing, Spike. If you want to go overnight, you're going to have to figure out how I can take a change of underwear and an extra shirt. I draw the line on two-day underwear. My leather pants fit so tight I couldn't even tuck a penny inside, say nothing of an extra pair of underwear. And you wouldn't be the best company without a change for yourself. And how about toothbrushes?"

Spike laughed and countered, "You leave the logistics to me, Babe. They have saddlebags that fit onto the bike. Chuck will help us find what we need."

"While I'm out getting the bird seed," he continued, "why don't you look up different things to see in Omaha. This afternoon I'll plot out the route we should take, and we'll be ready for our first real adventure. It may take me a little longer because I need to stop at Murry's and check on those saddlebag things." Chuckling, he added, "Wouldn't want to ride around with someone wearing yesterday's underwear!"

Chapter 10

Babe combed through the Google search results for "Omaha, Nebraska." Somewhere on the fifth page she found a site dedicated to Fort Omaha. A picture of the fort appeared on the screen. It was an old army fort used in the 1880s when the United States was busy fighting Native Americans. Indians had always interested her; plus the traffic in the northern part of Omaha was lighter. If Spike found a cautious route, she was all in. She thought, "I'm going to dwell on how much fun we'll have because we should go while we can." Babe was thankful God had blessed them with good health and each other. Hanging on to Spike while traveling down the highway was togetherness at its best.

As Babe searched for Omaha with her iPad, the phone rang, breaking the silence of the quiet afternoon.

"Hello."

"Mom?"

"Matt? Why aren't you at work? Is something wrong?"

"Mom, I talked to John. There are some weird rumors floating around about you and Dad. According to those rumors, apparently Dad has bought a motorcycle and is giving rides to Great-aunt Julia. I can't even comprehend that happening. So I wanted to call and check with you to see what is really going on."

Babe smiled and shook her head. The kids had to find out eventually. "Yep, that's right. Your dad bought a really nice, refurbished motorcycle at a local bike shop here in town. It looks so nice that you would never know it was a used one. Your dad loves it!"

The other end of the line was silent for a moment. Babe could imagine her eldest son putting his forehead in his hand, not sure what to say next. "Mom, are you sure Dad can ride one of those things? He's over sixty, and his reaction times aren't what they used to be. Motorcycles are dangerous out on the road. He doesn't know anything about them and might get hurt or even hurt someone else. We thought you and Dad were into playing cards and bowling now that you're retired. You have to talk some sense into him."

Babe smiled to herself. What goes around comes around. How often had Spike gotten down to the nitty-gritty with Matt and his brothers about being responsible? Now it seemed roles were changing.

"Matt, your Dad is the most responsible man I know, and he isn't anywhere as near his dotage as you seem to think. Did he ever tell you how much he had always wanted a motorcycle? Now is his chance to get one while he can enjoy it."

"But Mom! He'll be off riding by himself, and that leaves you at home alone. What if he wrecks somewhere and there is no one around?"

"Matt, what makes you think Dad will be riding by himself?"

"Oh, no. Has he joined one of those biker groups? They will eat him alive! He should stay away from those guys!" He hesitated a few moments, then added, "I can't imagine Dad doing something like this . . . it's so unlike him!"

Babe heard the panic in Matt's voice. She wasn't sure if she should feel sympathy or find it humorous their son was trying to protect his parents. Trying to encourage him, she said, "Matt, honey, I'm going to ride with him. We are doing this together, the way we've always done things. We've already been out riding around the area, and it's the most fun we've had in years. Now don't worry about us. We are as sensible as we always were." She hesitated and then thought of something. "Do you remember when you were a senior in high school? You and Mark and Tim wanted to go out East, just the three of you, and hike the Appalachian Trail for two weeks."

"Yeah . . ." replied her son, seeming to know where this story was headed.

"Do you also remember how we tried every angle to talk you out of it, but you were so sure you would be OK? You had never gone off like that on your own before."

"Yeah."

"The kind of concern you feel now is how we felt then. But we knew you had always tried to make good decisions, had researched and planned the trip, and were raring to go. This is somewhat the same. You worry about us, but we aren't jumping into anything. I must admit I was a little leery about this motorcycle business at first too. But your Dad was so enthusiastic about it that I decided to try. You know the old saying, 'Try it, you'll like it'? Well, that's what happened with me."

Babe heard a big sigh on the other end of the line, which told her she had won round one but that he still had his reservations. Then he said, "I'd better call the other three and let them know everything. Promise to be careful, Mom. Tell Dad hi, and I love you two."

Babe grinned to herself as she wondered if their sons would lay awake at night worrying about them. Thank goodness they didn't live in town or they might feel compelled to wait up until Spike and Babe got home from their outings.

It touched her that all four sons were concerned, even if they had no reason to be. She and Spike had sweat plenty over various antics while those boys were teenagers. It wouldn't hurt them to sweat a little. If nothing else, it would help them cope when their children reached the teenage years.

Babe went back to her iPad and googled Omaha. There was plenty of interesting sites to see there. Her earlier reservations lingered, but the talk with Matt had bolstered her resolve. While she was convincing him, she had somehow further convinced herself. She was enjoying their short trips, so why not try a longer one.

When Spike and Babe were first married, Babe read the maps and guided Spike as he drove. Then came the day when she led them three hours in the wrong direction. Spike hadn't stopped asking her to look at the map, but now he always asked her to show him the map to be sure. Babe thought one little mistake didn't mean she wasn't able to read a map.

She went to a drawer in the living room, took out a large folded map of Iowa, and spread it across the table. It came to her that she would also need one for Nebraska. There wasn't one in the drawer, so she went to the car. Sure enough, there was the map she was looking for in the glove compartment. She went back to the table and folded the Iowa map in half so it only showed the western side of the state. She then folded the Nebraska map so it showed the eastern side of that state and laid it beside the Iowa map. She lined the two maps up by Interstate 80. The Nebraska map was a slightly different scale, but she didn't notice.

Babe stood looking down at the different routes they could take. She shuddered as she stared at I-80. It showed up in dark blue, edged in red, and looked ominous to her. Then she spotted a little red line to the south that looked to her like a smaller highway that also went into Omaha. It seemed that it meandered through scenic terrain and might be tamer than I-80.

Babe searched another drawer and found a couple of pens and some highlighters. She spread them out across the map and marked routes. She used different colors to highlight the different routes. She drew circles around the little towns where they might like to stop and eat or just rest.

At one point Spike walked in where she was working. "What's for lunch?"

Highlighter in hand, but her focus still on the maps, she replied. "Not right now. Give me thirty more minutes."

Spike stood behind her and viewed her progress. Green lines, pink lines, blue lines. The two maps had been taped together to form a master map. "Why don't you just use your phone? Nobody uses paper maps anymore. They are no longer efficient; plus they are cumbersome, especially to carry on the motorcycle."

Babe twisted around to look at him. "I can read the paper maps better with my helmet on, and I wanted to mark our routes and save them as a keepsake. When we get back from our trip I will note the actual route we ended up taking and put it in a scrapbook I'm making called 'Motorcycle Trips.'"

Spike rolled his eyes but continued on his way without another word.

The Saturday of their Omaha excursion arrived, and they

both awoke before the alarm. Spike had spent the night mentally weaving through trucks. Babe lay awake wondering how long the muscles in her arms could hold onto Spike's waist. The couple donned their leather gear, and both felt confident about the day's journey. As she packed their sack lunches, and he revisited the map one more time, they heard a clap of thunder.

Their heads snapped toward the window. Spike rose from the kitchen table and peered out the window. Burly, gray storm clouds had crept into town. Babe put down her butter knife and the jar of peanut butter and checked the weather app on her phone.

"Well, what do you think, Babe?" Spike asked, squinting as he peered outside. They heard the first splash of unexpected rain against the window.

"I think we had better wait it out. I don't like the idea of zooming down the highway in this kind of weather."

"Yep. I suppose not." Spike paused, deep in thought.

Almost instinctively Babe shrugged and said, "If you still want to go to Omaha today, we could take the car." Spike looked up at her as if she had politely asked him to throw *Hog Wild* into the trash.

"No, I guess you are right." Babe continued with a little chuckle. "Suppose we head out tomorrow after church? Assuming the rain has stopped."

"But if we leave after church, we won't get to Omaha until way after lunch," Spike said.

"Spike, it is one thing to be gone all weekend and miss church; it is another entirely to miss church because you are driving away from it on a motorcycle."

Spike grinned and nodded. "Can we leave straight from

church? I mean not come back home? We would backtrack if we came home, so why not get a head start?"

Babe put one hand on her hip and pointed at Spike. "If you're suggesting I wear my motorcycle garb to the Lord's house," Babe said in a sarcastic tone, "you need to rethink. There is no way I am going to go to church in anything other than my Sunday best."

Spike chuckled. "No argument there. Let's bring our riding clothes along to church and change before we head out. That way we'll still get a late lunch in Omaha!"

It was settled. The peanut butter sandwiches turned into peanut buttered toast for breakfast, and they reset everything to get ready for the next day. They would begin their adventure directly after church.

Their adventure started the next morning before church. The saddlebags were packed with riding clothes, overnight necessities, and everything else they needed for the trip. To save room they would use the Bibles in the pews instead of bringing their own along. Spike wore his favorite gray suit and maroon tie, while Babe wore a new brown dress, matching heels, and a necklace and bracelet she had received as a gift. The sun was out, and they were as ready as they would ever be.

Ready, until Babe approached the bike. Spike got on, tucked his tie in his coat and waited for Babe.

"How am I supposed to get on this thing?"

"What do you mean? Same way you always do." Spike looked over his shoulder as he put on his helmet.

"But how do I get on in a dress?"

Spike turned all the way around now and looked at her from head to foot. He remembered his escapade with Aunt Julia, but he hadn't wanted to turn around to see how the aunt fared in the dress department. He thought about it for a second or two, but the dynamics escaped him. He shrugged and said "I don't know," and turned back to fiddle with the bike controls.

Babe checked her watch. They should have left five minutes ago, and she hated being late. She lifted the dress a little and tried to swing her leg across. The dress would have to come way higher if she was going to get her leg over the machine, so she halted. She turned around and tried to sit sidesaddle, but riding that way was completely out of the question.

She checked her watch again. Was there enough time to change into a pantsuit? No, not if she still wanted to get there in time for Sunday school. Then she thought, if Aunt Julia had done it, she could too.

She lifted her dress once again, this time much higher, and straddled the bike. She rested her dark brown heels on the saddlebags.

"You ready?" Spike asked and revved the engine.

"No! Not yet—my dress is clear up to my waist!" Babe tugged on the material until she had the dress to the place she considered decently covering her thighs. That would have to do. She would imagine she was wearing shorts. She put on her helmet, grabbed Spike's waist, and they were off.

Soon things got worse. The wind was whipping around them as the bike sped along the road. Babe's dress flapped and waved with the wind. She was not comfortable enough with riding yet to let go of Spike, so she was trying to hold the flapping dress down with her elbows. She was doing a halfway decent job when a blast of wind lifted her skirt way up. Her instincts kicked in, and she let go of Spike and grabbed at the dress. She lurched backward almost falling off. Her sudden motion caused Spike to swerve, thinking Babe was actually falling off the bike. She then lurched forward and grabbed hold of his waist again. In her struggle, her legs kicked one too many times and her right heel went flying. The shoe whizzed away from the bike, bouncing and rolling all over the road.

"Stop! My shoe!"

"What?!"

"My shoe!"

"You did what?"

"STOP!"

Spike rolled to a stop on the side of the road. "What did you say?"

Babe pressed her helmet close to his. "My shoe went flying off; we have to go back! I lost my shoe!" She lifted her bare foot for him to see.

Spike looked down at her feet and then turned to look back down the road. He strained and squinted and finally said, "I don't see it. Where did you lose it?"

"Back there! Hurry, we have to go find it!"

As slow as they could go on the highway, they headed back in the direction they had come. Both scanned the road for the overboard shoe. Finally Babe pointed to a small brown lump on the side of the road and they parked the bike. When the road was clear of traffic, Spike trotted over to the lump, grabbed it, and trotted back. He held out a dirtied brown lunch bag. "Want it?" He grinned.

"Gross! We have to find my shoe! Hurry!"

They rode back and forth a few more times scanning for anything that resembled a brown shoe, but no luck. After twelve minutes of slow back and forth searching, they finally spotted it in the ditch.

"Thank goodness no one ran over it!" remarked Babe as she fitted the shoe back on.

When they pulled up to their church, Sunday school was half over.

"Better late than never," Babe told herself as she patted down her helmet hair and tried to believe what she had just said.

Spike and Babe tiptoed into the building. They quietly approached the classroom door, looked in, and were surprised. Every person in the class, including the teacher, was at the window, peeking through the blinds. When they cracked open the door, they heard someone muttering to the class, "No wonder they are late!" That got a couple of chuckles. The chuckles stopped as one by one the people at the window noticed the bikers by the door.

Chapter 11

"Sorry we were late this morning; we had a little trouble getting here," Babe explained. As the class awkwardly retook their seats, she looked around to see how deep their embarrassment should be. Several men were smiling as they shook Spike's hand while commenting on the motorcycle. Spike kept his cool and said, as he gave Babe a glance, "I always wanted one, and the boss said I should give it a try."

Al Parsons, the Bible study leader for the day, was smiling as he went back to the podium and picked up his notes. "As you know, our lesson today comes from Matthew 7:1-2, which reads, "Judge not, that you be not judged.""

So far, so good, thought Babe as she took a seat beside Spike. Then she glanced at the women returning to their seats. There were a few who avoided her eyes; but Nancy, a fairly new lady to their class, reached over, patted Babe on the wrist, and whispered in her ear, "And I was starting to think this group was kind of stodgy. Learning to ride a motorcycle is great, Babe!"

There were others who smiled, and Eloise asked if she was still planning on having the church group at her house next week. At least she hadn't fallen so far they wouldn't come to her house, thought Babe.

After class, before going into the sanctuary for the morning service, Evie and Mabel came up to her. Evie, holding on to Mabel's arm, quietly asked, "Is it fun, Gwen? Aren't you afraid you will fall off?"

Mabel broke in, saying, "My folks wouldn't let me keep company with a fellow who once came to call riding on his motorcycle. I always wanted to at least go for a ride."

Babe patted her on the shoulder and offered, "Harold will be happy to give you a ride when you are ready to try it."

During the service, Spike and Babe were overwhelmed when they heard the choir sing "Softly and Tenderly Jesus Is Calling." As the solo part was approaching, Mrs. Peabody stepped forward to sing. Her beautiful voice rang through the sanctuary. As she sang, Babe looked around the room. The congregation was so still; no one fidgeted in their seats or read the bulletin. It was a moment Babe wouldn't have missed for the world. The combined voices of the choir swelled as they joined the final chorus of the song, and Babe breathed a sigh of contentment. With tears in her eyes she turned to Spike and mouthed, "Wonderful."

After the song, announcements were given, reminding everyone of the garage sale to be held that next Saturday in the church parking lot. All proceeds would go to the church's Vacation Bible School. But Babe couldn't stop thinking about Mrs. Peabody's solo.

After the service Spike went out to the motorcycle to get their traveling clothes. While Babe waited for Spike, she stood outside the choir robe room. Mrs. Peabody noticed them right away and gave a small wave. Babe ran up and threw her arms around the blushing woman as others came up to compliment the soloist. Mrs. Peabody whispered in Babe's ear, "Please tell

Mrs. Kline thank you for giving me the courage to do this."

"I will, I will tell her. I only wish she could have heard you herself. Maybe we can bring her along next time you sing."

Babe went into the ladies' room, and Spike headed for the men's. Just as Babe was about to enter, she turned to Spike and said, "We can't take our church clothes with us in the saddlebags. There isn't enough room for them. Why don't we leave them here and pick them up tomorrow on our way back?"

"Good idea," responded Spike as he shut the door.

Babe took off her brown dress. She loved this dress; it had cost a little more than she liked to pay, but it was her favorite. She put on her leathers and carefully folded her dress and slip, putting them in a pile. She put her new necklace and matching bracelet on top of the pile. One of her sons, Mark, and his family had given the set to her for Christmas, and it went perfectly with the dress. Lastly she added her brown heels to the pile, thankful the roll across the pavement hadn't done irreparable damage. The few scuffs would buff out.

Babe opened the door, and Spike was standing there with his suit pants, coat, tie, and shirt over one arm. She took his pile, folded the things neatly and added them to the stack of her things.

Spike got on *Hog Wild* and waited for Babe to climb on. Boy, this was lots easier than when she was wearing a dress, she thought. Losing no more time, Spike left the parking lot and entered the highway. They were off to Omaha.

It is amazing what you miss driving in a car and what you see on a motorcycle. As Spike sped down the road toward Omaha, he was in awe at the sights around him. The sky was a rich, creamy blue, accentuated by fluffy, white clouds.

He could hardly believe the clouds were real, they were so picturesque. The rolling hills of green met the blue skyline all around. Spike wondered if they could have picked a more wonderful day to make this ride. Creation was bursting over every inch of the countryside.

"Thank you, Lord, for such a beautiful drive today," Spike prayed under his breath. "Thank you, Lord, for this bike and my amazing wife who will ride through the countryside with me, and for a day like this." Sunday driving along these country roads, Spike felt beloved by his Savior.

As Spike and Babe continued on their journey, Spike reflected on that morning's Sunday school lesson, "Judge not, that you be not judged," from Matthew 7:1-2. How often had he judged the barrenness of these highways? But God was giving him a glimpse of grandeur of the world around him.

They made quick stops at diverse places along the road. It was all interesting, but a little Danish shop was the place Babe loved best. Each item had been imported from Denmark. There were any number of dishes, figurines, and table linens.

Before climbing back on the bike, Babe said, "I found a spot in Omaha called Old Market Passageway. I'd like to go see it. They said it was full of little shops you don't find in other cities. Do you think we can find it and just drive through? The brochure said it was on Howard Street, north of the downtown area." As she spoke, she pulled out the two maps taped together. It was all Spike could do not to roll his eyes, but he stood silently as she got them unfolded. Spike decided not to mention anything about past misreading or misdirecting. He was so thankful she would ride with him, what did a wrong turn or two matter?

Babe refolded the map so only the corner with Omaha

showed. "See how easy it is?" she asked as she climbed back on the bike. "You just drive and I'll direct you."

Biting his tongue, Spike said, "Let's head out and see if we can find it. We're looking for Howard Street, right?" Spike took off, making a couple of turns until they were heading north. There was less traffic now as they came into Omaha, for which Babe was thankful.

They kept a relaxed pace until Spike called over his shoulder, "What did you say the name of the street was where we turn? We may have gone too far north." Babe let go of Spike's waist with one hand and reached into her pocket for her precious map. Unfolding a map with one hand in the breeze generated by the traveling bike wasn't a simple matter. The car behind kept too close for comfort. He moved one way and then the other attempting to pass. The whole time his bumper hugged the rear of their bike. The pickup ahead of them signaled at the last minute and slowed to turn right, forcing Spike to swerve in a hurry. As he turned, the bike swayed a little, and Babe had to grab onto his waist with both hands. The map went flying.

Still hanging on with both hands, Babe cried, "Ohhh, my map!" as she turned her head to see where it landed. "Can we go back and get it, Spike?"

He could see the map in his rearview mirror. It was in the middle of the highway, flapping around in traffic. "Sorry, Babe, but it wouldn't be safe to go back. Even if we could turn back, we would still have to walk over to the opposite lane to pick it up," he said, as he thought, Good riddance!

Spike pulled over when he had a chance. "I think we've gone too far," he muttered. He almost pulled out his phone, but he didn't want to push the whole map thing too far. He could go by guess or by gosh for a while still. They took off again, and he turned east, trying to go back south by a different route.

Spike slowed as they breezed down a tree-canopied street. He put his leg out to balance the motorcycle as it stopped in front of a large, redbrick house. A sign on the lawn announced they were looking at the former home of General George Crook. He had been a Union general in the Civil War and had also fought in the Indian Wars during the late 1800s. His home had been restored and was now a museum. There were cars lining the street and in a driveway close to the house.

"Well," Spike glanced back at Babe, "this looks open. We seem to have missed your market, but how about going in and learning about things in the 1800s?"

Looking at all the cars, Babe responded, "Looks like a popular place. Let's go." Spike wedged the machine between two expensive-looking cars. He marveled at how much easier it was to park a motorcycle than the van. They tucked their helmets under their arms and headed to the front door.

The foyer was teeming with people chatting. Several looked up at the newcomers and smiled, then resumed their conversations. Babe and Spike found space in the crowded entry. This general must have had quite a history to draw this large a crowd, on a Sunday afternoon no less.

Babe glanced around and noticed there were several fur coats and lots of dressy high heels. Not unusual she supposed for the big city of Omaha. She felt no qualms about what they were wearing. After all, no one looked twice at them as they entered in their motorcycle leathers. It goes to show you, she thought, almost everywhere you go these days, there is a diverse mode of dress. Even with that thought, she reached up to straighten the red bandana in her hair.

A woman and a man appeared through the French doors at the top of the stairs. The crowd fell silent, and the man spoke, "To those of you I haven't met yet, I am Alexander Kissinger, curator of Crook Museum, and this is my wife, Linda. We are so pleased to welcome you here this afternoon. Much hard work has gone into this museum thanks to you, and I am pleased to show you the updated exhibits. Take all the time you need to view all the exhibits. When you have finished your tour, we will gather in the dining room for a light supper. Find the seat assigned to you by the place card with your name."

Place cards? The curator paused, making sure he smiled at everyone present. His gaze passed Spike and Babe, giving them the same welcoming smile everyone received.

The curator continued, "We are especially pleased that you are the first to see the additions we have made. I would like to visit with each of you personally to thank you for your generous donations to this project. You were generous beyond our expectations. It is because of your donations we were able to develop this museum into one of the finest in the Midwest. Without the generosity of each of you, none of this would have been possible."

A light bulb went off simultaneously for both Spike and Babe. These were big money people—donors. They turned in unison, and their eyes met. Then, as if their heads were on the same swivel, they glanced at the door. It was tempting to put their helmets on to cover their faces, but then no one here knew them anyway. The door was close by, and they had to whisper, "Excuse us, please," only twice as they headed towards the door so they could escape.

Spike revved the engine. Before he took off he looked back over at Babe. "We left so fast I didn't even remember to leave a couple of bucks for admission. Then we could have been donors too!" They burst out laughing as they mounted *Hog Wild* and drove away.

They sped down the road, impulse guiding them through the town of Omaha. As the afternoon wound down, Spike said, "We're going to need gas. I don't want to chance leaving town without a full tank. Let's fill up tonight so we can leave first thing in the morning. We passed a motel when we were coming into town; and if I remember right, there's a gas station next door. Why don't we fill up and then get a room at that motel? It looked like a decent place to spend the night."

Spike put the bike in gear and announced, "Here we go. Hang on!"

Babe laid her head against Spike's back. In that moment she realized she might have been wrong about this cycle business. Spike's enthusiasm had spread to her like a virus during this trip. And since they were out riding more, she wasn't baking as usual, which also meant not snacking as much. The result was that her leather pants didn't seem as tight as they once did. The front button and back seam of her leather pants no longer was a real concern.

Spike slowed as he spotted the gas station at the end of the block. The motel was on the other side with a sign that flashed "Vacancy." Spike pulled up to a pump and stopped. Taking off his helmet, he turned to Babe and asked, "Why don't you go in and get us a couple of bottles of water while I fill up?"

Happy to walk around a little, Babe entered the store while Spike was busy filling the gas tank. As he was about to finish, Babe appeared in the door of the station and called, "They make pizza here. Should we get one to take to the motel?" Spike gave her a wink and a thumbs-up.

Spike put the lid on the gas tank, got on the bike, and parked outside the station door while he waited for Babe. As he sat waiting, an animal strolled up to within five feet of him. He wasn't sure what it was until it got close and he saw it was a large cat. It was so dirty he couldn't be sure it even had all its hair. This cat was either sick or was leading a hard life, thought Spike. He kicked in its direction, trying to shoo it away.

"Go on, get!" The cat took a couple steps back and narrowed its eyes at Spike.

The store door opened and Babe appeared, carrying a square box that smelled heavenly. She was climbing on the bike when she spotted the cat. "Ooh," she cooed as she got back off the bike.

"Spike, look at that poor thing! I can see every bone in his body and he is filthy!" Her voice told Spike that a remedy was coming. He rubbed his eyebrows and shook his head. She put the pizza box on the seat and slowly approached the cat. The cat sat watching and then backed up. He didn't seem to be a trusting fellow.

Babe stood still and watched the cat. He sat back down and watched Babe. Turning to Spike, she said in what Spike called her pitiful voice, "Can't I go in and see if they sell cat food or at least get something for the poor thing to eat?"

Spike realized it was fruitless to argue, so he gave a wry smile and another thumbs-up. Away she went on her humanitarian mission. She soon returned with a small, flat can of cat food with a pull tab opener. Babe opened the can, immediately smelling the fishy meat. The cat's nose twitched at the smell, but he held his ground. Distance was safety. He hadn't made a sound. He sat and watched as Babe kept talking to him. She approached him, but he immediately got to his feet. Babe stopped, bent over, and put the opened can down on the driveway; all the while telling him he was a good kitty and not to be afraid of her.

As Babe stood beside the can, the cat stayed in his safety zone looking at her. It was clear she still wasn't trustworthy. Then she knelt down and put a tiny bit of the food on her index finger and held it towards the cat. He still sat, not even licking his chops. Babe took a small step forward and stopped. No reaction. She took another small step with the same results. She was near the cat now but was afraid if she approached closer he would run. Still talking softly, she put the speck of food on the driveway. She then backed up, passing the can to stand where Spike sat watching on *Hog Wild*.

Once Babe was standing by Spike at a distance, the real action started. The cat bounded the short distance to the nibble she'd left on the driveway and made fast work of that bite. He then went to the can and gobbled the contents as if he hadn't eaten for a week. Every bite or two he would look up at his benefactor. Once he confirmed she wasn't sneaking toward him, he went back to eating.

Satisfied the poor cat was getting a good meal, Spike and Babe rode to the adjacent motel parking lot. The cat was forgotten, and the two got off the bike. Spike headed for the motel office. Babe picked a few things out of her side of the saddlebag. She unlatched Spike's side of the bag and called out, "What do you need for the night?"

"I already got what I need."

The bag holding their toiletries slipped from her grasp. She reached to pick it up and headed for the motel.

A few minutes later the couple entered their room and

fell onto the bed, exhausted. The rest of the evening they reminisced about Mrs. Peabody, the scenery, and rubbing shoulders with big donors.

Chapter 12

A wimpy breakfast greeted Spike and Babe in the lounge the next morning. Babe remarked to Spike she couldn't tell if a mob had wolfed everything down or if the motel hadn't yet supplied a new breakfast from the morning before.

Rain had swept through the area during the night, and they were glad it hadn't lasted into the morning. Although, with breakfast so scant and them so ready to go home, even Babe might have been willing to ride in the rain. After Babe had a glass of orange juice, and Spike ate a stale muffin, they were ready to head home.

The bike roared to life as they lurched out of their parking spot. Spike pumped the brake and asked, "Did you hear that?"

"I didn't hear anything," Babe said over the soft putter of the engine. Spike inched across the motel parking lot to the street, listening for the noise again. Satisfied it had stopped, he pulled onto the street.

A few minutes later he heard it again. It doesn't sound like motor trouble, Spike mused. Maybe a tire? No . . . they look OK. The sound must have come from somewhere around us.

It felt good to cross the state line into Iowa again. Maybe because it meant they were close to home and would sleep in their own bed tonight. Their thoughts wandered as they motored through the gentle hills of Western Iowa. Suddenly, they heard a muffled moaning noise.

Babe leaned forward, placing her head near Spike's ear. "What is that? Did we run over something?" she asked, her voice a little panicky.

"I thought it was you!" answered Spike. After a minute he added, "It almost sounded like what I think a mountain lion would sound like from a distance!"

"Are there mountain lions in Iowa?" questioned Babe, hanging onto Spike's waist a little tighter.

He slowed a little. "We are going through farm country, and I suppose it is some farm animal that sounds different from a distance," said Spike as he picked up speed.

The bike ate up the miles as the sun rose higher in the sky. The wind was coming up but wasn't strong enough to be uncomfortable. They heard another moan. It was even louder than before. Spike gave a little jolt. "What in the world!" he muttered.

"Is there something following us?" she asked, looking over her shoulder. Home was only a few miles away. Spike tried to think of what could be making that kind of noise. The sound made Babe think of a scene out of some horror movie. She smiled at that and told herself she didn't believe in ghosts or spooks.

The motion light above their garage door came on as they drove into their driveway. Babe went to the front door, unlocked it, and went through the kitchen to open the garage door. Even though their home wasn't opulent by any means, it was their home and she was so thankful for it. It was true that home is where the heart is.

Babe hit the garage door button and it opened. Spike

drove the bike into its slot beside their car, dismounted, and stretched his arms in the air. Babe reached over to the saddlebag on the left side of the bike and retrieved her things. Spike leaned down to his side of the saddlebags to retrieve his things when he noticed the clasp on his side was not fastened. Thank goodness he hadn't put anything valuable in there. About all he would have lost going full tilt down the road was old underwear and a pair of dirty jeans. Everything in there was replaceable.

He lifted the flap and stepped back in a hurry! There was a loud, "Yeeoow," as a bundle of fur jumped up at him.

Spike let out a short, "Ahh!" and Babe squealed as a response to Spike's sudden move. Spike backed toward Babe. As he backed, he recognized the mangy cat from the day before at the gas station. The cat jumped out of the saddlebag with his back arched and stood in front of Spike, glaring at him as it growled and hissed.

Instinctively, Spike reached toward Babe to shield her from this possibly rabid animal. The cat sprang again, this time landing between Spike and Babe. He was looking directly at Spike, his back still arched, his tail up, and the few remaining hairs on his back standing straight up.

Spike yanked his helmet off and swung at the crazed cat, yelling, "Get out of here, you mangy thing! Out the door with you!" The cat held his ground, back still arched and tail still straight in the air.

"Babe, go inside before it attacks you!" ordered Spike.

"For goodness sake! Will you stop yelling at the poor baby! He's scared, Spike. How would you feel trapped in a saddlebag for the whole time? And he probably hasn't eaten since I fed him yesterday."

"Maybe," said Spike, "but either way, take my things and go on inside until I get it out of the garage." As he stepped toward Babe, the cat let out another howl. The closer Spike got to Babe, the louder the cat howled. Spike stopped. The cat stopped. Both waited as they watched each other. Everything was still while the antagonists took stock of one another. Suddenly the cat turned toward Babe, walked to her, and calmly rubbed his back on her leg.

Spike thought, "That deranged cat is protecting Babe. But dogs protect people—not cats!" Trying again, Spike reached toward Babe. Immediately the cat arched his back and gave another, "Yeeoow!"

"That cat thinks I'm going to hurt you!"

Babe giggled. "He sure does! I've got a knight in shining armor protecting me." Still laughing she added, "You had better watch out, Spike, or I'll sic Sir Galahad here on you!"

That brought a smile to Spike's face as he savored the conflicting image of this mangy cat being knighted.

"Spike, before we go in, please go down to the store and get a couple of cans of cat food. We don't have anything in the house for him to eat, and I can't stand letting him go hungry." Realizing the uselessness of arguing with Babe, Spike put on his helmet, climbed on the cycle, and took off—still shaking his head at how Babe was treating the mangy thing like royalty.

Babe turned to go in the house and the cat followed her. "No, Sir Galahad, you can't come in." She carefully opened the back door and slipped in, closing the door behind her. She spoke through the screen, "Spike will bring you some food, but you can't come in." With that she turned and left the cat meowing and scratching the screen door.

Spike returned and parked the bike in its spot in the garage.

He retrieved a sack from the saddlebag and pulled out a small can. He tugged at the pull tab and put the open can under the bushes at the side of the house. "There," he said to the cat, which was following him at a safe distance. "Have some supper, and then hightail it out of here and find yourself a new home."

The cat arched his back and hissed as Spike passed him heading back towards the garage. Only when Spike was out of sight did the cat start to eat.

The next day Spike and Babe went to their front porch to relax in the beautiful weather. Babe craned her neck trying to see the cat. She called out a few times with no luck. Cats are silly creatures, Babe thought. Begging to come inside one day and disappearing the next.

Spike sat in one of the porch chairs while Babe took her usual seat on the swing. After a few minutes of watching the birds, Babe asked, "Spike, why don't we go over and tell Mrs. Kline about Mrs. Peabody singing the solo in church and how beautiful it was? I know she'll be pleased to hear Mrs. Peabody's thank you. Mrs. Kline's encouragement was just what Mrs. Peabody needed."

"OK, let's go see if she's home." They walked down the driveway to the gate in the hedge. Walking through, Babe said, "I think she's sitting on her back porch." Mrs. Kline was sitting quietly, enjoying looking around her backyard while softly stroking something sitting in her lap.

Babe exclaimed, "I think it's Sir Galahad!"

They got a little closer and Spike noted, "I think you're right. It sure looks like the beast that stole a ride home with us on *Hog Wild*. It's the right color, but it couldn't be the same cat. There's no way that cat would sit on someone's lap."

When Spike and Babe got within ten feet of the porch, the cat sat up and gave a "Yeeoow!" It was the hitchhiker cat after all.

"Mrs. Kline, when did you get that cat?" asked Spike.

"I was eating dinner last night, and he jumped straight through my open kitchen window onto my lap. He seemed to like it here, so he stayed, at least for now." she answered.

Spike stopped at the foot of the steps onto the porch, but Babe climbed the two steps and stood next to the quiet couple. Spike went toward the steps, but the cat sprang to the floor, arched his back with his tail straight up, and gave his signature snarl. Spike stopped in his tracks. Why did this cat hate him so?

Babe stepped closer. The cat leisurely rubbed against her leg. "Come on up, Spike," called Mrs. Kline. "The cat won't hurt you."

As if to show Mrs. Kline he was in charge here, the cat again let out a loud "Yeeoow."

"Cat, you stop that right now!" said Mrs. Kline, raising her voice. "I won't have that kind of nonsense from you!"

A fat lot of good that will do, thought Spike, but the cat immediately settled back down by Mrs. Kline's chair and licked himself. Spike dared a step closer, carefully watching the cat. The cat stopped his grooming, watched Spike, and then carried on. He didn't seem the least bit aggressive after the scolding.

Mrs. Kline brought out lemonade and cookies. Babe told Mrs. Kline about the service the Sunday before and Mrs. Peabody singing her solo.

"It was about time someone straightened her out about church music," she answered.

"Well," challenged Babe, "she never would have gotten up the courage to do it on her own. You said the right words at the right time to make her see what was possible."

"Oh, I don't know about that," answered Mrs. Kline. "I know I'm outspoken, but sometimes I can't understand why others don't see things as I do." She smiled and added, "I'm over eighty years old, and if I don't say it now, I may not get to say it at all. Strike while the iron is hot, they always say."

When it was time to head home, Spike rose from his chair and offered his hand to help Babe out of her chair. The cat hissed, but Mrs. Kline stopped him with a stern "Cat! Stop that!" and the cat ceased voicing his objections.

They headed back home as Spike ventured, "What did I ever do to that cat to make him react to me like that? I was the one who went to get food for him after he hitchhiked to our house uninvited!" Babe laughed and grabbed hold of his hand as they came to their own porch.

"You're just not a cat person, Spike. But you're still my kind of person!" she added with a grin and reached over and patted his shoulder with her other hand.

* * *

Agnes Bolton's condo was the location of the Dirty Queens card game this week. It was a small condo, but Agnes said it was just the size she liked. One group had to play at the kitchen table, and the other table was in the living room. A certain protocol was always followed: players drew lots for specific table seats as they entered. Today it appeared things were different. As Babe walked in, Agnes handed her a number. She heard Sissy give a humph and mutter under her breath something about changing things. Evidently, today, all seat positions were handed out and not drawn. Babe thought it best to ignore it and wait to see what played out.

Lettie, Sissy, Tess, and Bess sat at the table in the living room. That left Agnes, Mary Alice, Betty, and Babe in the kitchen. Agnes was smiling even more than usual and glancing at Mary Alice and Betty off and on. It was like the three were joining forces about something.

Between hands Betty said quietly enough to be inaudible to the table in the living room, "It's good when people break away from what everyone believes they ought to do. That means they are their own person." Mary Alice and Agnes kept looking at their cards but nodded in agreement. It wasn't so much what Betty said as the way she said it. Babe thought this was some type of message; but for the life of her, she didn't know what it meant.

Agnes, still looking down at her cards, said quietly, "It's good to try out your wings once in a while." The others, again, kept looking at their cards but nodded in agreement. Then Mary Alice said, "Live and let live," with a sense of wonder in her voice.

Babe was a little relieved when Tess called from the living room, asking everyone what they were donating to the garage sale this weekend. She remarked what a good idea it was to raise money for Vacation Bible School. Babe, having packed so many boxes for the sale, was interested in what the others planned to contribute. Plus, it relieved any possible tension about all this live and let live business.

Agnes replied immediately, "As you may know, I love mystery novels. I know I should be reading something more enlightening, but I simply can't get over my mystery addiction.

It's as if I become a detective and have to solve the mystery after the first twenty pages. I plan to put the books I've read in the sale; but if anyone asks, please tell them you don't know who donated them."

Betty piped up with what her donation would be. "When my tenant moved out she left a bunch of canning jars and new lids still in the box she bought them in. Canning is becoming popular again—kind of a reawakening thing. I'm going to put them in the sale."

Sissy cleared her throat and added to the conversation. "I just had my bathroom repainted, and I splurged and got new bath towels and hand towels. Then I thought I might as well get new throw rugs. You've heard of the woman who got a new doorknob and had to build a new house around it so it would look right?" Sissy laughed and added, "I guess that's what happened to me! I'm going to put all my old towels and rugs in the sale. They are still in good condition."

Tess looked at Bess and said, "We are going to make a couple of kinds of bread for the sale. If we have time and can find some fresh strawberries, we'll add strawberry bread too."

Not wanting to be left behind, Mary Alice broke in, saying, "I'm going through all my old jewelry and putting the things I don't wear anymore in the sale. Jewelry always sells well at garage sales.

Lettie chimed in, "I have been going through my knitting patterns, and there are many I won't use again. And I think I have some skeins of yarn that I won't use. Do you think those would be alright to put in the sale?"

There was a chorus reply, "Of course!"

Babe said, "I was going through my closets and cupboards and putting things I haven't used in the past year in a box for the sale. I had no idea I had so much I wasn't using—things that someone else might need and can put to good use."

The conversation went back and forth with the others thinking of more things they could add to their donation boxes. The three at Babe's table never seemed to hint towards anything else for the remainder of the time, much to Babe's relief.

When Babe got home Spike asked, "How were The Seven today?"

"Well, the church should have quite a sale if other church members are donating to the garage sale the way they are." Then she shook her head and said, "I'm not sure, but they may be losing it. Either that or I'm not getting the message they were trying to tell me when I first got there!"

Chapter 13

Since Spike and Babe had been preoccupied by the strange noise on the way home from Omaha, not to mention being glad to be nearing home, they had forgotten to stop at the church on the way back to pick up their clothes. Spike had been concerned about the bike. One day turned to two, and as these things go, they hadn't picked up their clothes all week.

Babe was going through closets and cupboards gathering more things for the garage sale at church. She found some boxes in the garage that had never been unpacked from their move a few months earlier. Sure enough, she found several items for the sale. Then she went to their closet, and things they hadn't worn in a long time went in the garage sale pile. She was finding more than she ever thought. The last area to go through was the kitchen. Same drill. With only a few exceptions, if she hadn't used it in a while, it went in a box for the church.

This sale was a good idea. When her sons were younger and going to Vacation Bible School, she had been a teacher. She remembered how she had to dig into her own pocket for supplies when there wasn't enough in the church budget to cover necessary items. All church members were digging deep to help fund VBS this year.

Spike suggested they go to the church early Saturday morning to put their donations out instead of going Friday because so many people would be adding things that day. The sale was to start at nine o'clock Saturday morning, so if they were there by eight, they would have plenty of time to add their things to the display tables and also pick up their Sunday clothes. Babe put price stickers on each item before they left home. They were marked with amounts she considered garage sale prices—high enough to make money, but not so high that things wouldn't sell.

On Saturday morning Spike loaded the boxes in the car. As Babe got in, she stopped and said, "I think I'll go back and get some hangers for our good clothes we left there last week. I folded them thinking we would pick them up the next night, so they are probably wrinkled by now. I'll hang them on hangers in the car." She returned carrying a wooden suit hanger and wire hangers for her dress and Spike's shirt.

As they drove into the church parking lot, they were surprised to see so many people already there. Others must have had the same idea of marking at home and coming early Saturday instead of Friday. Spike drove as close as he could get to the display tables and took the boxes out of the car. Carefully placing her items next to items in similar categories, Babe finally emptied her boxes. The tables were loaded. Everyone had been generous with their donations, and it promised to be a good sale. She saw some things she would like to buy, but that was part of the success of a sale like this. You bring and you buy.

By this time the early bird shoppers were already speeding off to their next sale, and new shoppers were arriving to fill up the parking lot. Church members went about welcoming people from the neighborhood who had come to shop. Things were going fast. Babe wished she had taken time to browse a little before it got this busy.

The sale had been advertised from nine to five; and, after a busy day, it was nearing closing time. Spike had been asked to man the cashbox. One person added up the purchases for a customer, another sacked the purchases, and Spike took payment. The process ran smoothly. They had run out of sacks, so Spike asked Babe to go home and bring back the grocery sacks they always saved. The sale was a huge success, judging by what little was left on the tables. Closing time came, and May was busy gathering everything that remained. The committee had decided that donating to Second Chances was the best way to get rid of everything that was left. Those proceeds would still go to a good cause.

Several men from the church took down the display tables and carried them back into the church. It was then that Babe remembered their clothes. She headed for the bench in the hall where they had left them on Sunday. She stood there looking at the empty bench and wondering who moved them. She went to look for Ralph and Rose, the church custodians, in the crowd. They had probably moved their clothes out of the way before the sale. She approached Ralph and asked if they had seen a suit and dress folded in a pile on the end of the bench by the side door.

Ralph replied, "When we were here yesterday to get the tables out, that whole bench was full of things for the sale. I can't remember what all was on it, but lots of people were helping mark prices and putting them on the tables. When we got finished, and all the donated clothes were on tables, Rose put a few items she didn't think would sell somewhere else. I can't remember what all was in that pile, but I think Rose put it under that bench at the end."

Babe went to the end of the bench and looked beneath. What she saw was a ripped pair of jeans, a coffee-stained purse, and a pair of brown shoes. Her brown shoes.

As she was retrieving them, Rose approached and said, "I didn't think those shoes would sell because one of them is scuffed up something awful. You can have them if you can find a use for them. Otherwise I'll just throw them away."

Well, thought Babe. I can fix these up to almost new with a little buffing. She picked up the wounded shoes and went to look for Spike.

It was clear. Their good clothes had gone in the sale with everything else. Babe grimaced as she told Spike when they were alone, "I found my shoes, but all our other stuff went in the sale. That was my favorite dress!" She clutched the shoes closer as she said, "I can save these shoes. The scuffs should come off if I work with them a little. But I bought them specifically to go with the dress!"

Spike said, "What about my suit? It might have been six years old, but I only wore it for church and to funerals. It still had lots of good years in it, and I hate to lose something good like that."

"Oh, Spike!" moaned Babe as she put both her hands up to her mouth. "What about my necklace and the matching bracelet? Mark's family gave the set to me for Christmas, and I just loved it! Now where is it? This gets worse all the time!" Dejectedly they headed for their car. What was done was done. No use dwelling on it.

The next morning Babe entered the kitchen a little later than usual. Spike was at his place at the table with the morning paper spread out before him. "I thought maybe you were going to sleep all day. The garage sale yesterday threw me off too. I woke up and figured I had been at church all day yesterday, so today must be Monday." He tossed the paper onto the table and stood up. Then he looked up at his wife. He froze. "What's the matter, Babe? Don't you feel well?"

Babe's face was pale, and there was no sign of her usual banter. She slumped into her chair and looked him in the eye. "I was in the shower this morning, and I found a lump in my breast. But don't worry; lots of women have them and they turn out to be nothing at all." Her words tried to convince him it was nothing to worry about, but her face told a different story. She hadn't even convinced herself.

Spike knelt beside her chair. He laid his arm around her shoulders, and looking in her eyes, said, "Well, we're going to check on this. You're right; we're not going to worry. We're going to pray about it and have your doctor take a look."

"No, Spike," she answered. "It may be nothing, and I don't want to rush into something. I'm going to wait a couple of weeks and see if it goes away. They say sometimes lumps disappear. If it's still there after that, I'll have it checked."

Spike looked stern as he replied, "No, we aren't going to wait. Babe, I'm putting my foot down. This affects both of us. We are a team; *we* have a lump. We are having it checked as soon as the doctor can get you in. It's not wise to wait with something like this. If it disappears or is nothing, then we will thank God and be glad we checked."

The uncertainty of the situation weighed heavily on their minds throughout Sunday school. But there was no better place for them to be on a morning so dark. After Sunday school they were standing in the foyer when Spike did a double take. Walking up the steps to the church was Wendell Long, one of his fellow workers at Cromwell Heating.

Spike stuck out his hand in welcome as Wendell and his wife entered the church. "It is really good to see you here, Wendell. We'd like to have you and your family to become members.

Wendell blushed, looked around to see if anyone was listening, and leaned closer to Spike. "I never thought I could come before, Spike. We didn't have the clothes for church, but I found this suit at the garage sale Saturday." He stood straighter and pulled the jacket down a little. It was a little tight, but it looked good on Wendell. "How does it look?" he asked.

Spike did another double take. The suit . . . was his suit.

"You look good, Wendell," Spike sputtered, "and we're happy you are here. We'll look forward to seeing you every Sunday. You should come earlier for Sunday school, too, if you can." With that the couple, trailed by their two little ones, went into the sanctuary.

Babe came out of the restroom and noticed Spike looking a little bewildered. It was time for church to start, so they headed for their usual seats, four rows from the front, left side.

As they walked down the aisle, Spike leaned over and whispered, "Did you see Wendell Long and his wife here?"

Babe nodded yes. Then Spike added, "Did you notice his suit?" Babe shook her head no. Before they said more, the choir stood and the service began. The entire choir sang the first verse of the opening hymn; and, as the second verse began, Mrs. Peabody stepped forward to sing as the choir hummed in harmony.

Spike heard a sudden intake of breath from Babe. He looked

117

over and saw she was looking at the choir. She looked at Spike and lightly touched her neck, then touched her wrist, and lifted her hand back to her neck. She was trying to signal him about something.

Mrs. Peabody sang beautifully. It was as beautiful as last time, if not more so. Spike looked back at Babe, and again she touched her neck and then her wrist. Spike looked back at the singer. Then he saw it. She was wearing Babe's Christmas necklace and bracelet. She must have found it at the garage sale too. As Mrs. Peabody completed the solo, she reached her hand up to lightly touch the necklace. She seemed as pleased by her jewelry as the former owner had been.

It was a quiet ride home. Each was thinking about their lost items and if there was any chance of getting them back. Babe remarked, "I can't ask Mrs. Peabody to give me back the necklace and bracelet or even buy them back. She seemed so proud of them and she needs all the confidence builders she can get."

Spike shook his head before adding, "Wendell told me that they wanted to come to church but didn't have the proper clothes for church. He was so proud of that suit. And he did look good in it."

Babe paused and then remarked, "Where did all this 'what we wear to church' nonsense come from? I don't think God gives a hoot about what we wear. Somewhere along the way the emphasis has been centered on the outer self. It's gotten all out of line."

"Preach it, Babe. It's not what's on the outside but what's on the inside—what's in our hearts."

Spike rounded the last corner onto their street. "I suppose we shouldn't be so attached to our things that we can't rejoice if those same things bring happiness to others or bring them to worship. I once had a teacher who told me, 'Get in the habit of giving things away.' I guess we're just practicing our good habits today."

Babe chuckled, adding, "Now I'm beginning to wonder if my dress is off somewhere doing good things too!"

Spike laughed, "We may never know."

* * *

Time moved slowly as the day of Babe's doctor appointment drew close. They made several little trips on the motorcycle, and neither of them talked about what the outcome might be. Whenever the tests were mentioned, they reminded each other that God was in charge and repeated their favorite Bible verse, Philippians 4:6-7: "Be anxious for nothing, but in everything by prayer and supplication, with thanksgiving, let your requests be made known to God; and the peace of God, which surpasses all understanding, will guard your hearts and minds through Christ Jesus."

Babe thought of the appointment as her day of reckoning. Spike drove her to the doctor's office. where a nurse led her to the examining room, another nurse took her vitals, and the doctor came in and examined her before the nurse took her to get an X-ray. Afterward the doctor told Babe he would contact her with the test results. He patted her on the shoulder and told her not to worry; no matter the diagnosis, modern science could handle it.

The doctor was right about modern science, but Babe knew prayer was the first line of defense to a medical or any other problem. Thank you, Lord.

On their way home Babe asked, "Are you sure you don't mind postponing the trip you were planning?"

"There is no rush to go on trips, Babe. You rest and recuperate. There is plenty for me to do around here. Maybe now is the time I should fix that slope in the backyard that has bothered me. As far as trips go, this will give us more time to select places and plan."

Spike reached over and wiped away a tear falling down her cheek. "Babe, think of what you are going through as a hurdle. You are my other half. We belong together, and we handle things as a team. Don't ever forget that, honey!"

"I keep telling myself not to worry about anything I've prayed about, as hard as that is sometimes." Babe looked at Spike and added, "I need to be thankful for the tough times in life, no matter how bad they are. They should open our eyes to the good things that happen all the time when we aren't paying attention."

Spike looked at her and replied, "That's the way to look at it, Babe. I'm proud of you. You concentrate on healing, and I'll concentrate on the loose ends I need to get done around here. Why don't you come out on the patio and help me decide the best way to spruce up the backyard?"

They took glasses of iced tea to the patio and got comfortable. Then Spike said, "I like surveying our estate, don't you, Babe? It's small, but it is ours." He pondered for a few minutes and then ventured, "I talked with the condo board, and they gave me the go-ahead to bring in some dirt to level off that slope. They even offered to pay for the dirt and hauling if I would do the leveling and seeding part. So maybe if we got a load or two of black dirt and leveled it out it would look better."

"Oh, Spike, that sounds nice."

The couple talked about how far the renovations would go and what Spike thought it would take to do the job. Spike wasn't one to hold back and overthink a project. As soon as he made up his mind *how*, it was only a matter of *when*. Sitting on the porch was a nice break from such a dismal day, and they talked well into the evening.

Chapter 14

A few days later, Spike's two loads of black topsoil arrived. He no sooner had it in the backyard than he started distributing it with a rake. As he raked he noticed a little boy watching from the corner of the lot. Spike figured he was due for a rest, so he leaned his rake against the big oak and sat on the patio. The little boy's eyes followed Spike through the yard. Spike made eye contact with the little guy and smiled. That's all it took. The boy raced toward Spike. His running engaged his entire body, the run a toddler does before he learns how to really do it. His little legs stopped short at the edge of the patio, staring at Spike.

"Why don't you sit up here by me?"

The boy jumped towards the seat near Spike and plopped himself down. He sat proper with his hands folded in his lap for about a second and then raised his arms on the armrests and settled back into the chair.

"What's your name?" Spike asked.

"Kenneth. My mom calls me Kenny, except when I do something I'm not supposed to do. Then she calls me Kenneth Lucas Welch. I'm almost seven."

"Well, nice to meet you Kenny. You live around here?"

Kenny nodded and pointed at the house on the corner

explaining, "Me and my mom live there." Then he looked back at Spike and asked, "Do I have to call you 'mister'?"

"No," responded Spike. "All my friends call me Spike, and you and I are friends."

"What are you doing, Spike?" asked Kenny.

"I'm working," said Spike. "A big truck brought some dirt and dumped it out right here; now I have to get it all level. It's a lot of hard work."

"You know what? I am a real good worker. Can I help you work?"

Spike's heart melted at this little fellow who seemed hungry for male companionship. Spike suggested Kenny go tell his mom where he was and ask if it was OK for him to help. Kenny took off like a shot. Spike went back to his raking and shoveling, but Kenny soon returned with his mom in tow. He had a tight grip on her hand, dragging the poor woman behind him. It was as if Kenny worried Spike might finish the job before he got back to help.

Mrs. Welch introduced herself, and Spike explained that Kenny had suggested he might need a good worker to help him.

"Are you sure he won't be a bother?"

"Oh, no. I imagine we will get along fine."

"If Kenny ever gets in the way, please send him home."

Spike agreed. Kenny's mother thanked Spike profusely and headed back down toward the corner lot.

The new worker had laid claim to the rake while Spike was talking to his mom and was busy moving dirt around as best his short arms allowed. Spike went to the garage to find a leaf rake that would be easier for him to handle. About an hour and a half later, Spike explained that Babe needed to go for some appointments so they would have to cut their work short.

The next morning the doorbell rang as Spike and Babe were finishing their coffee after breakfast. Babe went to the door, and there stood Kenny looking up at her expectantly.

"Can Spike come out and work?"

The lawn work went well, and Kenny was right there whenever Spike went outside. The two worked in a somewhat mismatched tandem to level the dirt pile, making the slope less steep and more pleasing to the eye.

That afternoon Spike and Kenny leaned on their rakes and surveyed their handiwork. Spike took out his handkerchief and wiped his brow; then he looked down at Kenny and said, "We got it all leveled, Kenny. Looks good, doesn't it?"

Kenny, who had watched and copied Spike for the past days, reached in his pocket and pulled out what looked to be one of his mom's old dishcloths and wiped his brow too. "It looks good, Spike!"

Looking up at Spike, Kenny said, "We worked good, didn't we, Spike? I'm going home and tell my mom all about it." He shot off. A few minutes later, here came Kenny with his mother in tow again.

After Spike chatted with Kenny's mother for a few minutes, he returned to the kitchen for a glass of iced tea. The project was a job well done, and it had been fun having little Kenny help. One gift about this whole surgery business and retirement was that Spike could be home with Babe during her difficult time, and he could be a light to a kid in need.

The next day when the phone rang, Babe bit her lip as Spike answered. She heard his greeting and held her breath. "Yes, this afternoon sounds fine," he said and hung up. He looked at Babe. "The doc wants us to talk with the surgeon this afternoon." He put his arms around her and said, "God's in charge, Babe. We won't think about how big this problem is; we'll think about how big our God is! Whatever happens, God will be with us as we deal with it."

* * *

A week later the surgeon came out of the operating room after the mastectomy and told Spike all had gone well. Babe could go home the next day, and six weeks of chemo were prescribed. The doctor reiterated that things looked good for a full recovery and it was fortunate they took action when they did.

On the way home Babe looked around and thought she had never appreciated the blessing of their home enough. Spike helped her into a chair and told her he was chief, cook, and bottle washer for the next couple of weeks. It flashed through Babe's mind she had probably never appreciated Spike enough either.

Later that day Spike returned to where Babe was sitting looking out the front window. He saw tears running down her face and knelt beside her chair. "What's the matter, Babe?"

"I thank God that everything came out the way it did. Sometimes I catch myself in tears for no reason."

The next day, as Spike was cleaning the breakfast dishes, the doorbell rang. I'll bet I know who that is, Babe thought as she went to the door. "Well, good morning, Mr. Kenny. Come in!"

With his head tilted a little sideways, Kenny looked up at her and said, "Babe, you don't have to call me 'mister' because all my friends call me Kenny and we're friends."

Nodding in agreement, while trying to hide a smile, Babe stepped aside, and Kenny walked past her to the kitchen. "Do we have some work to do today, Spike?" he asked.

"Let's go to the garage, Kenny. I'll need you to pull the harrow for me. Are you strong enough to do that?"

"I don't know how to howl, but I am really, really strong!" he said as he put both arms up so Spike could see his muscles.

Entering the garage, Spike dug around in a stack of used lumber and found a two-foot piece of a one by twelve. He rummaged around in some plastic jars until he found the one he wanted. He drilled a hole in both ends of the board. "Come on, Kenny, let's go outside. You bring that jar of nails, and I'll carry the board and the hammer."

Outside, Spike laid the board down on the ground. "Kenny, hand me a nail, please?" The nails were produced, one by one, and Spike hammered them into the board in two long rows. The job might have been completed sooner, but the close observation over his shoulder slowed things. Even so, it tickled Spike to have the little guy around. Who could turn down help from someone so enthusiastic?

The board was finished, and Spike flipped it over. Two neat rows of nails were protruding out about an inch through the bottom of the board.

"Kenny, will you please go in the garage and get me that bunch of yellow rope over by the bench?" Spike had hardly finished the question when the rope was on the ground beside him. He took out his pocket knife and cut off a length a little over ten feet long. Putting one end through a hole in the board, he tied a knot. He put the other end of the rope through the corresponding hole at the other end of the board and tied another knot.

Standing up, Spike proclaimed, "That's a harrow, Kenny, and it is your job to pull it over the dirt. Point the nails in the dirt so it breaks up any clods. It's a hard job. Do you think you can to do it?"

The little would-be farmer jumped up and down and yelled, "I can, Spike, I really can! Will you show me how to howl?"

Laughing, Spike said, "Kenny, it's *harrow*," and he put the middle of the rope over Kenny's head and down to his waist. He instructed Kenny to walk forward slowly, pulling the crude apparatus along behind at a safe five-foot distance. Spike stood at the end of each row to help with accuracy and then got the "machine" safely turned to head back down the next row.

The next step was to seed the area. Spike spread grass seed evenly while Kenny stood and watched. The little guy fidgeted, impatient to help, but obediently stayed where Spike told him to stand.

Later, the two friends sat on the porch, each holding a glass of lemonade and surveying a job well done. Spike looked down at Kenny and said, "You are a good worker, Kenny. Thanks for helping me." The little boy smiled in agreement, and his chest seemed to expand a smidgen as he crossed his little arms over it.

"Are we going to work tomorrow, Spike?" he asked hopefully.

"Well," said Spike, "this job is done, but now we have to keep the ground watered if it doesn't rain. If the grass seeds don't have water they won't grow."

"I'm going to go home and check the weather, Spike!" said Kenny as he sprinted towards home. Spike thought, "That kid is turning into a regular farmer."

Spike was finishing his second cup of coffee a few days later when Kenny knocked at the door. When Spike answered, Kenny looked up at him and said, "I looked at our birdbath this morning and it didn't rain last night, Spike. I think we need to water or the seeds won't grow."

The kid was a sharp student, Spike thought. Giving Babe a little wave goodbye, he led the way toward the yard. They stood in the open doorway studying their handiwork. "See those tiny green shoots, Kenny? That's the grass coming up. Isn't it beautiful?"

Crouching down to get a closer look, the youngster proudly proclaimed, "We work good, Spike." They walked out into the yard where the dirt had been spread. "Where are we going to water today?"

"I think right here today."

Kenny stared at the spot as if burning it into his memory. He then ran off to find the hose. When Spike caught up, he found Kenny tugging at the hose with all his might. Spike divided up the coils into two bunches, and the duo dragged the larger bunch across the lawn towards the spout. Spike stooped and connected the hose to the faucet, an eager face looking over his shoulder. The watering team backed up and watched as the hose came to life, sprinkling the thirsty seeds.

About a week later, as Spike and Babe we're getting ready to go to Sunday services, Spike looked out the kitchen window and remarked, "It's looking good, Babe. We'll have a nice lawn in no time!"

The couple left for church and entered their Sunday school classroom to greetings. Later in the service they especially enjoyed hearing the choir lead the congregation in their favorite hymn, "Borning Cry" after the pastor's message. Following the service they stopped a few times on their way out of the church to visit with friends before heading for their car.

"I made a pineapple ham casserole for lunch today, so it won't take me long to heat it up when we get home," said Babe. All was well as they drove into the garage and got out of the car. Spike stopped before closing the car door and remarked, "I think I hear water running."

Spike and Babe went inside and straight to the kitchen window. Looking out they saw the water ring spraying water at full blast. The running water had made small gullies down the newly gentled slope. Spike ran out the back door and turned off the faucet.

Spike was laughing as he returned to the kitchen. "I guess my hired man looked at his birdbath this morning and decided it hadn't rained. He's getting to be a self-starter and that will take him far. I think this lawn will be the best lawn we've ever had!" He stood looking at the green shoots of grass. It was coming along, and the gullies would soon disappear. "However, I think I'd better hang the hose close to the garage ceiling or we may have a creek at the back next time we come home!"

That afternoon, Babe filled her watering can, adding fertilizer and watering her houseplants. Her plants looked neglected; not because they were actually neglected but because, as she often explained to people, "I was born without a green thumb." But she felt she should have an *A* for at least trying, and she loved having plants inside her home.

Spike came into the kitchen from the garage with a magazine in his hand. Babe saw the pages were all dog-eared, and it appeared to have been read repeatedly. In his other hand he held an atlas. Spike must have something up his sleeve. She pretended she didn't notice anything, waiting for Spike to bring up whatever it was. She did not have to wait long. "Babe," he began, "I saw Chuck from Murry's at the gas station yesterday. He said he and his wife planned to go to the Sturgis rally this year with another couple. Something came up and the other couple can't go now. He was wondering if we would like to go with them. They have booked two rooms for the first week of the rally. They have had these rooms booked for at least a year now."

"What is Sturgis, and what kind of a rally are you talking about?"

"Sturgis, South Dakota. It's where motorcyclists from all over the United States gather every year the first part of August. It started in 1938 and has been a yearly event since then, except during World War II when gas was rationed. It started with racing and stunt riding and has morphed into a time when all cyclists, white-collar and blue-collar, get together for all kinds of runs and races. It's a big deal. A year or so ago more than 700,000 people attended. You can read all about it in this magazine."

"Why in the world would you want to go to something that crowded, Spike?"

"To see it and to see all the different kinds of motorcycles. They say some people ride their bikes to Sturgis, but others fly in from all over and have their bikes trucked in. Chuck said they have been there before and loved it."

"But I don't even know Chuck's wife. And how long a ride is that?"

"Maybe we should have Chuck and his wife come over some evening to talk about it. Then we could meet her and find out if this rally is really something we want to see."

Spike made the call to Chuck, and invited Chuck and his wife to come over the next night.

Chapter 15

About eight o'clock the next evening, Spike and Babe heard the roar of two motorcycles coming up the drive.

Chuck introduced his wife, Jenny, and Babe liked her instantly. She was tall with hair that had enough white strands winding through to make it look like an expensive salon job. Jenny had gathered her hair nonchalantly into a bun at the back of her head. She and Chuck both had infectious smiles, and Babe felt at ease with them right away.

Chuck got down to the nitty-gritty immediately. He began by reiterating all the things to do and see that Spike had shown Babe in the magazine. He talked about the hill climbs and motocross races. Often Jenny would chime in with, "Oh, you two have to go with us!" Chuck would continue, thinking of something else to tell them about, and Jenny would, again, enthusiastically encourage them to come along.

"How long a trip is it to Sturgis?" asked Babe.

"It's about 550 miles from here," answered Chuck. "I figure it would take us two days of easy riding to get there. Since you haven't made a trip like this one on your bike before, we would go about 300 miles the first day. We could also take a break every 100 miles or so for a stretch or to grab something to eat."

Babe glanced at Spike and noted that he was all ears. She thought that in Spike's mind he was on his way, cruising at sixty miles per hour, happy as a flea on a dog. It sounded like fun to her too.

As Chuck and Jenny finished their spiel on Sturgis, Spike asked, "Have you always been in the motorcycle business?"

Chuck laughed. "No, I worked in the loan department of a bank most of my working years. During that time a couple of my sons bought old motorcycles that needed constant repairs. I was born on a farm, and anything mechanical interests me. My Dad taught me a lot, and I soon found that I could figure out how to fix nearly anything. So when my boys starting having problems with their bikes, I spent a lot of time tinkering with them in the garage. One thing led to another; and before I knew it, their friends were coming to our house to have their bikes repaired too. Then strangers from surrounding areas started coming for maintenance. Word got around, and my boys and I decided we might as well be making a little money from something we loved to do."

"Repairs like that must have taken lots of time," interjected Spike.

"I guess I didn't really notice until one night when I came home, Jenny met me at the door and asked me to introduce myself. Between my bank job and my motorcycle repair jobs I had spent very little time with her. I figured I needed to quit one of my jobs. So I retired from the bank and established a repair shop in my garage. It was great because I had enough work to keep food on the table, plus I could work from home. Soon broken motorcycles were filling the garage, spilling all over the driveway and onto the front and back lawns. We needed a bigger place for the business. That was six years ago."

Babe piped up, "Jenny, what do you think of all this? Are you as interested in motorcycles?"

Jenny nodded. "All those years, and I didn't have a clue about what I was missing. When we finally bought the store, I still had never ridden. But I figured if we owned an actual motorcycle shop I should learn! And I fell in love with the whole thing. Two years ago I finally got my own bike, but we still ride together when we go on trips."

Chuck asked, "Do you think you would be interested in going with us to Sturgis? Three couples will be joining us when we get to Sioux City. We met them several years ago up there. They have made their own room reservations. We have the two rooms reserved in a good hotel, and finding food while we are there is no problem."

"How long do you plan to stay? I wouldn't want to be gone longer than a few days," said Babe.

Chuck replied, "The two of us thought we would spend three days in Sturgis and then tour the surrounding area for a few days where there is a lot of history. If you decided not to stay that long, you could always head back home taking the route we came. That way you would be familiar with the road."

Jenny added, "If we leave home on a Monday I think we would miss much of the weekend traffic, and it would bring us into Sturgis on Tuesday afternoon, ready to see the sights. Even if you left midday on Friday, you would be home in time for church on Sunday.

Spike looked over at Babe, and judging by her facial expression he could see she was for the adventure. He answered, "You've sold us! We will be road-ready next Monday morning, bright and early."

Spike and Babe spent the next couple of days getting ready. They needed to put the mail on hold at the post office, halt the newspaper for a few days, and let Mrs. Kline know they would be gone. This was the first long trip they had taken, and they would be covering territory they had never traveled.

Babe had to take time off from the preparations for the monthly Dirty Queens game. She knew there would be too many explanations if she called and said she and Spike were busy getting ready to go out of town for a few days. In quiet rebellion she put on a pair of slacks and a short-sleeved top, and she went off to play with the Magnificent Seven.

Babe arrived at Mary Alice's home where they were to play. She parked her car and noticed the others had already arrived. Oh dear, thought Babe as she checked her watch. Punctuality was a must with this group, so she hoped she wasn't late. She walked up to the glass door. She was surprised to see that all seven ladies were sitting or standing around one table with their heads huddled together. Babe wondered what was up, but that was part of what made them all so interesting. You could never guess.

As she rang the doorbell the ladies scattered as if they had seen a mouse. They all rushed to seats and sat looking at her as Mary Alice opened the door. She was the last to arrive, so she took the empty seat.

Mary Alice was at her table with Tess and Bess. The three of them kept glancing at each other. Funny, Babe thought. Mary Alice asked who would like a glass of iced tea and went to the kitchen to get glasses and the tea pitcher. As she came back, she passed the other table; and someone, Babe wasn't sure who, whispered loudly, "Did you ask her?" Mary Alice shook her head, poured tea for those who wanted it, and sat down again.

Tess spoke in little more than a whisper, "Gwen, are people calling you Babe?"

Bess lowered her head and quietly added, "We've seen you riding on that motorcycle around town!"

Babe smiled to herself and wondered how long it had taken this group to approach her about the motorcycle. It was obvious it was not a new subject for them, but it had finally gotten to the place where they were bursting at the seams for information. They needed to know all about it. She decided to tell them everything—to clear the slate. The conversation at the other table was not the usual, and Babe knew all ears were perked to hear what was being said at her table. This was colorful stuff to these ladies who lived quiet lives.

Babe raised her voice enough so the other table could hear too. "When Spike was young he wanted a motorcycle more than anything else. His father died when he was in high school, and he felt responsible to see that his mother and younger siblings had what they needed."

This was almost too much for the oldsters, who took turns muttering, "Oh my, how sweet!"

Babe continued. "When we got married Spike took his responsibility as husband and father just as seriously. What his family needed always came first. This didn't mean he no longer wished for a motorcycle; it just meant he had other priorities. I didn't know anything about his wish for a motorcycle until this year because he never mentioned it.

"Then he retired, and one day he mentioned his yearning. We laughed about it at first, but I soon saw he really did want one. We went to Murry's, that motorcycle shop here in town, and it was like showing candy to a little kid."

By this time the ladies at the other table had moved to Babe's table, and some had even brought along their chairs. They crowded in close; and when one of them spoke it was in an elevated whisper, almost as if they were afraid someone outside of the room would get ahold of the prized information before they did. They weren't about to miss one iota of information. All eyes were on Babe.

Babe, feeling a little crowded by such an appreciative audience, knew she had to continue with the whole story. "You've probably all heard that some people call us Spike and Babe. We actually gave those names to each other for fun, and now some people call us that. While riding, we even wear leather pants and jackets because we are riding in all kinds of weather. And that's the whole story. I was a little leery about riding on that thing; but, you know, it's kind of fun, and the best part is that we are doing it together."

All of the ladies were smiling; and Sissy, of all people, was even wiping a little tear from one eye. Then the questions started coming about holding on, what if they fell, was gas cheaper for a bike than a car, did the noise hurt her ears, and on it went. The ladies were definitely enjoying this developing situation more than playing cards. Several leaned over and patted her on her shoulder. But the big change was that they now called her Babe. Babe felt more accepted by this sometimes haughty group than she ever had. She could hardly wait to tell Spike.

* * *

At 5:30 on Monday morning, all systems were go at the Miller house. Anticipation had kept both Babe and Spike from sleeping well during the night, so they were up and ready early. They were only to be gone for a few days, but both looked around the house to see if there was anything they had forgotten to do. They had cereal and toast for breakfast, and those dishes were washed and put away. Babe had cleaned out the fridge last night and taken a half loaf of bread, a piece of leftover meatloaf, some lettuce, and a tomato over to Mrs. Kline. Yes, they were ready. The saddlebags were packed with their necessities, and all that was left to do before takeoff was to gas up *Hog Wild* for the first leg of the journey.

As Spike and Babe sat at their kitchen table, Spike bowed his head and prayed, "Dear Lord, we thank you for loving, blessing, and guiding us this far in our lives. Be with us as we travel, not only to keep us safe, but to use us to reflect your love to all we meet—for your glory, Lord. We ask that you protect us, guide us, and bring us safely home. In Jesus' name we pray. Amen."

Babe, head bowed, echoed, "Amen."

"It's time to mount up, Babe," said Spike. "Thanks for joining me in this. It wouldn't be any fun without you." The garage door closed behind them as they rode down the driveway and on their way to their first motorcycle rally.

As they neared the gas station, they saw Chuck and Jenny pulling in. Jenny let go of Chuck's waist and waved both arms at the Millers. As the riders got off, the men shook hands, and the women gave each other a welcome hug. Excitement was in the air.

"I'll take the lead, and we'll stop about every hour or so if we can find a safe place to pull over and stretch our legs for a few minutes. We'll go north into Sioux City. I told you about the couples from Omaha and Lincoln who will join us there. It is safer to travel interstates with more than two bikes because a group is easier for cars and trucks to see. You will ride behind me. I'll be on the left side of the lane. You follow on the right side of the lane. The other three bikes will follow, each taking an opposite side of the lane than the bike ahead of them so we're all staggered. We'll keep going north to Sioux Falls where we will head west toward Sturgis. Tonight, if all goes as I think it will, we'll stop at a little motel we've stayed in before where we have reservations for tonight.

Chuck got on his bike. "Well, let's get going! Climb aboard, folks! We don't have all day," he called as the wives climbed onto their seats behind their husbands.

Babe didn't have to see Spike's face to know it was all smiles, just as hers was. He was right about doing exciting things in their retirement. If she hadn't been sold before, she was now. The day was beautiful. There was a light breeze, and they were with people they liked, doing what they all enjoyed. She would recommend this retirement business to anyone!

They saw multiple motorcycles on their route, probably all headed toward Sturgis too, she thought. When they stopped in Sioux City, the other three couples joined them. Babe thought they seemed to be the kind of people she and Spike would like for friends. They were all of retirement age, and motorcycling was fairly new to two of the couples. The other couple had been riding for years.

As the couple from Lincoln got off their bike, they introduced themselves as Lance and Lacey Ludwig. Babe noticed a bulge in Lacey's leather jacket. Before heading for the cafe, Lacy unzipped her jacket and took out a small dog. She placed the dog in a small basket hooked to the underside of her seat.

"Stay!" she said and walked to the cafe. Babe looked back and saw that the dog was sitting there quietly, looking around.

"Will he stay there until you get back?" asked Babe.

Lacey replied, "Yes, he won't move, and if anyone approaches the bike he will growl and carry on like a Saint Bernard!"

"He is so cute," Babe said. "What's his name?"

"We call him Brutus because even though he is a Chihuahua, he thinks he is six feet tall and tough."

One half of the two couples from Omaha were sisters who had bought their motorcycles after retirement. As widows they had met their current husbands at a local bike race two years ago and were all members of the Christian Motorcyclists Association. Their patch on the back of their jackets was a gold triangle surrounding a Bible, embossed with a gold cross. Banners at the top and bottom of the triangle announced, "Riding for the Son." They parked their bikes close to the Ludwigs', explaining that if anyone got overly interested in their bikes, Brutus would let them know in a flash. He seemed to know which bikes belonged to friends.

When it was time to hit the road again, Chuck took the lead with Babe and Spike following. The bikers from Omaha followed the Millers, and the Ludwigs and Brutus brought up the rear. As they went down the interstate, Spike rode behind Chuck in the opposite side of the lane. The other bikes followed them on staggered sides of the lane, with the Ludwigs again acting as rear guard. Chuck was right about safety in numbers. They were more visible to other drivers as a group.

The troop traveled toward Sioux Falls in beautiful weather with little wind. They stopped to stretch their legs as necessary, and the miles sped by. As they approached Interstate 90 on the outskirts of Sioux Falls, they moved into single file at Chuck's prearranged signal. The group turned west toward their destination and then positioned themselves back into their staggered formation.

Chapter 16

Traffic was heavier on the interstate, so when the group arrived at their motel for the night, they all were ready to hit the sack. It had been a good day for riding, and they were happy to see a small shop selling Maid-Rite sandwiches. It was nothing fancy, but it was all they wanted after a long day.

When Spike and Babe got to their room, Babe flopped down on the bed and commented, "We are going to have another expense if I'm to keep being your back warmer on these jaunts!"

Spike gave her a quizzical look, and asked, "What expense will that be, Babe?"

"When we get to Sturgis, Chuck says there will be all kinds of stalls selling everything from soup to helmets. We are going to find one that has extra-padded motorcycle seats! All this time I thought I was overly padded in that department! Today proved how wrong I was!"

Spike laughed and said, "It's the first thing we'll do when we get there, Babe."

The group met the next morning at 6:00 a.m. as planned. Chuck looked at them and asked, "Everyone still with the program?"

Babe put her hand in the air and asked, "Is it normal for new bikers on long rides to have cushion problems involving the back side of their lap?" There was a chorus of "Yes, yes," and Babe added, "Well, I won't be complaining anymore, but the Millers will be making seating changes in the near future!"

"You will have plenty of choices when we reach our destination," Chuck interjected. They mounted their bikes and headed out on the highway, searching for the first place that looked to be serving breakfast.

By late afternoon the group reached Sturgis. Spike and Babe stared in awe at how many people and bikes were there already. How in the world could a small town such as this one hold all these people? There were few cars visible, as motorcycles of every kind, size, and color crowded both sides of the street. Chuck led them to the hotel, and they checked in, thankful that Chuck's friends had provided them with a reservation. Their room was not fancy, but it was comfortable. Spike tried the bed and pronounced it more than adequate.

Arrangements had been made by the group to meet the next morning for breakfast. Then each couple would go their own way until dinnertime that night when they would all meet at a favorite restaurant.

After breakfast they parted ways. At first Babe wanted to just sit and people watch, but Spike reminded her of the long ride home and the condition of the back side of her lap, as she had phrased it. Chuck had mentioned several brands they should look for, so they went off to check the different booths and stores. After a thorough investigation, Babe chose the softest seat cover in the store. Spike offered to carry the package for her, but she said she would carry it herself because she didn't trust that he wouldn't lose it. She even mentioned that losing this new necessity might be a vow-breaker, but she was laughing when she said it.

When they convened for dinner, everyone had different stories to tell and things they recommended the others see the next day. The Ludwigs had heard that a choir made up of motorcyclists was going to perform that night in a park close by. They all decided to see what that was all about. After asking the concierge for directions to the park, the group roared off. They were pleasantly surprised when they got there. On a stage ringed by torches stood about fifty men in leathers. The crowd hushed immediately as the choir sang "The Battle Hymn of the Republic." The harmony was magnificent, and Spike and Babe were enthralled. As the song finished, the crowd roared and clapped their approval. The choir went on with their concert with even greater approval. The last song was "God Bless America," and the crowd was encouraged to join in. The beauty of hundreds of voices almost brought tears to their eyes. Chuck and Jenny stood with Babe and Spike after the concert was over talking about how wonderful it was. Most of the audience had left by the time the group headed back to their hotel for the night. It had been a wonderful first day.

They were strolling past some park benches when Babe stopped short. Spike turned to see what had stopped her. Babe put her hand over her mouth and was speechless as she pointed off into the crowd.

"What are you pointing at?" asked Spike.

"I don't believe it!" answered Babe. "I don't believe it!"

Spike, still in the dark, strained to see where Babe was pointing. Chuck and Jenny had stopped up ahead and turned to come back where Spike and Babe were standing. They saw that something had really spooked Babe.

Babe ran to a small bench and began hugging two women. Spike, Chuck, and Jenny followed her to the bench. Babe turned to them and introduced Agnes and Mary Alice, explaining that they were members of her Dirty Queens card club back home. Spike couldn't believe it either—not only that these two older women were sitting on a park bench in Sturgis, but also that Babe had spotted them among the hundreds of thousands of people swarming around them.

"Why are you here in Sturgis? How in the world did you get here?" asked Babe.

Agnes sat up straighter and said, "We came by bus this afternoon. After you told us about getting a motorcycle, we saw an article on Sturgis. We decided to come see what it's all about."

It was getting dark, and Babe asked where they were staying. Agnes looked at Mary Alice, and she replied, "We didn't know it would be so crowded. We have checked everywhere, but there are no rooms to be had."

Then Agnes spoke up and staunchly added, "You know, this is going to be quite an adventure. We've decided that we can just stay here in the park on this bench and be perfectly fine! We'll get back on the bus for home tomorrow."

Spike looked at Babe and knew without a doubt what was coming. Sure enough, Babe replied, "No, you are not sleeping on a park bench. We have a small room that you can have, and we will find something else." Chuck started to say something, but Jenny gave him a nudge to keep him quiet. "Now come along, both of you, and we'll take you to the motel," she said with authority. They each had a little pull-along suitcase that Spike picked up as they headed to the motel.

Chuck sidled over to Spike and whispered, "Do you realize

you are not going to be able to find somewhere now, especially at this time of night?" Spike just looked back at him, raised a suitcase in each arm, and shrugged. Chuck had never had to deal with Babe when she was in one of her humanitarian modes.

They got the two elderly ladies settled in their room and ordered clean towels for them. They told them they would pick them up at 8:00 a.m. for breakfast and take them to the bus in a taxi. If they took *Hog Wild* it would take two trips, and they would lose their parking spot. It was all settled, except for the small problem of Spike and Babe not having a bed for the night. Chuck came to the door of his room as they were leaving saying they wished they had a couch or something for them to sleep on. Spike told them they had been having a lucky streak lately. He laughed and added that he was sure it wasn't over yet.

Babe and Spike each held a backpack with their necessities. They looked at each other and started down the hall when a hotel maid passed them with towels for their room. Spike stopped her and told her what happened; then he asked, "You don't happen to know of an available room anywhere, do you?" The woman just shook her head and turned to continue down the hall. Halfway down the hall she stopped and turned, calling to the retreating Millers, "It's not much, but we have an extra room at home. My little girls still want to sleep in the same room, so this one is empty until they decide they want rooms of their own. It's yours for the night if you want it."

Spike looked at Babe as if a miracle had just happened and then turned to the maid and asked, "How much?" Then he held up his hand and added, "I don't care how much, we'll take it."

"The maid laughed and thought for a moment. Then she said, "I don't know how much . . . how does twenty dollars sound?"

"We'll give you forty dollars," countered Spike. She gave them the directions to her house and said she would call her husband, who was at home with her three little girls, to tell him they were coming.

It was nearly 11:00 p.m. when the taxi arrived at the address they had been given. The neighborhood didn't look that bad; all neatly keep small houses. They walked up the sidewalk to the little porch, and as they approached, the door opened. A young fellow was standing there holding the door open for them. He said quietly, "My girls are all in bed, and I was afraid the doorbell would wake them. No telling when they would go back to sleep." Then he added with a smile, "I hope she told you the room isn't much. But I did get the bedding changed and put clean towels and washcloths in the bathroom for you. It's the only bathroom we have, so I hope you aren't disappointed."

Spike put his hand on the fellow's shoulder and replied, "You don't know how much we appreciate your opening your home to us at this late notice. I told your wife we would pay her forty dollars. Is that enough?"

The young man answered with a smile, "It's more than enough. Betsy told me you gave up your room to two old ladies. I think what goes around comes around, don't you?"

The bed was smaller than the hotel room, but under the circumstances they were thankful to have it. And with such a nice family to boot. They were both tired, and sleep came quickly.

Babe woke first and had to think about where they were and

why. The house was quiet as she opened one eye. Just inches from her head was a pair of blue eyes looking directly into hers. She turned her head slightly, and two more sets of blue eyes were staring intently at them. "Hello," Babe whispered.

The closest set of blue eyes blinked and then whispered back, "This is my Gamma's bed and you aren't my Gamma!"

"Your mom let us use this bed for the night." Babe smiled and asked, "What is your name?"

The little girl thought for a moment and said, "I'm not supposed to talk to strangers."

"Oh, that's right. Well, my name is Babe."

"You're too old to be a baby!" the little girl squealed. Then, "Who is that over there?" as she pointed to Spike.

"That's my husband, Spike."

The chief questioner turned to the other two pairs of identical eyes and whispered, "Daddy said them could sleep in Grandma's bed last night, but one is a baby and one is a dog. I like them." The other two pushed closer for a better look at the impostors. The little girls looked like three peas in a pod, and all three faces were framed by blond ringlets. The only difference was that they were like stairsteps in height.

The youngest stepped forward and asked, "Does you have dirls?"

The oldest sister interpreted. "She wants to know if you have girls at your house."

Suddenly a call came from downstairs. "Girls, time to get up!" Babe peeked out of the bedroom door as the three little girls left the room in single file. Their mother's face went stricken as she watched her daughters come out of their guests' bedroom.

Babe was quick to assure her they hadn't been a problem,

only curious that the lady in the bed wasn't their grandmother. Then Babe added, "We can't tell you how much your gracious offer of the room meant to us. We are so grateful." As they left the house to return to the hotel for breakfast, Spike handed Betsy a fifty dollar bill.

As they approached what once was their hotel, Babe looked at Spike and said, "Maybe we should ask Agnes and Mary Alice if they want to have breakfast with the other couples."

Spike gave her a thumbs-up and replied, "The other guys will love them."

Chapter 17

As the group sat down at an oblong table that held all twelve of them, Spike introduced the crew to the two oldsters.

Agnes, not the least bit embarrassed about being found at a motorcycle rally, explained why they were there. "I was very young when I got married, and I had no skills to go to work. But that was fine with both my husband and me because we badly wanted a family. However that was not to happen. We couldn't have children; and then to make matters worse, my husband died of a congenital heart condition. So I went back to school, got my teaching degree, and taught until I retired thirty years ago.

"After retirement I made a bucket list and started doing everything on the list. I marked off the Grand Canyon and the Statue of Liberty, and I rode the mountain train through the High Rockies. Getting a pet was the next thing on the list. The dog was a mistake, but I marked it off the list and found a good home for him. I then went with a group to see the pyramids in Egypt and took a cruise to Alaska. I went to Denmark to see where my mother was born and even tried to play the slot machines in Vegas. Now, that was a mistake too. I must have put it on the list in a weak moment."

Agnes looked around at those at the table, who were hanging

on her every word, and continued, "Everything on my bucket list was crossed off before my ninetieth birthday, which was my goal. Then we heard rumors that Harold and Gwen Miller had invested in a motorcycle. We only knew Gwen through the card club, but we all loved her. I decided if she wanted to ride a motorcycle, maybe I should try it too.

"That was when I made the addition to my bucket list—riding a motorcycle. I told Mary Alice about it, and she agreed I should try it. We kept talking, and before we knew it, we had talked ourselves into buying one. But how do two women know what they want or need unless they check things out? We thought if we came to Sturgis and looked around we could find one of those three-wheeler deals, and no one at home would be the wiser. Mary Alice said if I bought it she would drive me around, so we came here on the bus yesterday. We had no idea there would be so many people here, but we did get to see a motorcycle just like we want."

Chuck entered the conversation at this point, saying, "If you're interested in a three-wheeled motorcycle, you come and see me when I get home. We'll get you fixed up with what you want."

Agnes responded with a smile, adding, "I think we have seen what we want, Chuck. I'll give you a call next week, but you need to keep this quiet. We have friends who think riding on a motorcycle is only for young boys."

Spike and Babe put the two ladies in a taxi and climbed in beside them. Babe had never seen the two women smile more. Mary Alice boarded the bus first. When Agnes got to the top step, she turned and climbed back down to where Spike and Babe stood. She reached up and gave them both big hugs, thanking them again. Spike and Babe stayed at the bus station until the bus left and waved at the smiling pair as they headed back to Iowa.

Babe turned to Spike and said, "Losing our room wasn't bad at all. It just added another exciting chapter to our retirement book." They spent the rest of the day looking around town. They watched races and marveled at the stunts the cyclists were doing on their bikes. They got to stay in their hotel room that night after having dinner with Chuck and Jenny as well as their new friends from Omaha and Lincoln.

The next morning they said their goodbyes to the gang and took off toward home. It had been a long day, but they had been through this territory on their way to Sturgis. As with all of these new trips, it had been fun and they had been together.

Although their traveling crew had gone home another way, Spike and Babe did not feel alone as they drove south out of Sturgis. Motorcyclists peppered the highways coming to and leaving Sturgis. Around lunchtime on the second day of driving toward home, Spike's stomach began rumbling. He saw a long line of motorcycles exiting a ramp, so he filed into line and exited with them. He hoped these bikers would lead him to a good spot for food.

Sure enough, a little way off the highway, a food truck sat in the middle of an enormous parking lot. The parking lot held no cars but instead was filled with picnic tables and motorcycles. As the Millers pulled into the lot, Babe read the sign out loud, "Iron Horse Hitching Post—BBQ and Beer." The line at the food truck wasn't too long, so Spike parked the bike, and they headed to the truck. As they walked, Spike noticed small diamond-shaped patches on some bikers' shoulders that said, "1%," in white lettering. Spike got in line, and Babe said, "Honey, I'll take the chicken and potato salad. Will you order it for me? I'm going to go find a bathroom. I saw some portable restrooms over there."

Spike placed their food order. While he waited he had time to survey the scenery. This was an isolated place. He could see a gas station sign about a mile down the road, but other than that there was nothing in sight but cornfields. But when this many hungry people come passing through, there are bound to be entrepreneurs popping up to meet the demand. Too bad they didn't have a trunk full of Babe's pies; they could have made a fortune here.

Spike got the food and looked around for Babe. Where was she? He looked around for the portable toilets, too, and finally located them in the back corner of the lot. He headed that direction, looking for an empty table where they could eat. He found a table where no one was sitting and decided to sit and wait for her. The table was covered in trash, but Spike carried most of it to a nearby trash can and sat down. It is amazing what slobs some people can be, he thought to himself. As he waited for Babe, keeping an eye on the portable toilets, he loosened his boots. He pulled his foot out of one boot to let it breathe. The day had been warm, and his feet were hot.

A hand grabbed his shoulder and almost yanked him off the bench. "What are you doing? You're sitting at our table!" Spike's heart froze as he whipped his head around to face the yeller. "And where's our food?"

Spike opened his mouth in an attempt to answer. "I thought this table was free; I put it all—"

"Get off!" The man's friends all drew closer. Spike could smell the strong stench of alcohol floating around them. "Get out of here!"

Spike was not a man prone to running from an altercation,

but in the present circumstances he did not see the point in standing up to a gang of drunken bikers. He stood up, grabbed the food he had put on the table, and stepped away. As soon as he stepped away he remembered his boot was still under the table, and he reached down to grab it as the men were taking their places at the table. The main instigator took this as a threatening action and stood back up. As Spike grabbed the boot, the drunken man shoved him to the ground. The food went flying; and as Spike fell, his hand twisted hard as he tried to catch himself. He scrambled up in a flash and said, "OK, just let me get my boot." The man looked to the ground and laughed. He kicked the boot in Spike's direction, and Spike grabbed it in a flash and walked away. This was not a fight he was willing to continue.

Boot in one hand and the other hand still throbbing, Spike took a few steps when a sharp pain shot up his foot. He yelped in pain and quickly knelt on the ground. He could hear the drunken men roaring with laughter. He hopped to the closest bench and inspected the wound. A nail was protruding from his right foot. With the hand that wasn't throbbing with pain, he pulled the nail out. A good half inch of nail came out painfully slow. His eyes watered, and he bit his lip hard. He saw blood on the underside of his foot and removed his sock. He then used the sock to wrap around his foot, trying to put as much pressure on the wound as possible to stop the bleeding.

At that moment Babe rushed over to Spike and screamed, "What happened!" She knelt by his bleeding foot.

Through gritted teeth he said, "I stepped on a nail. And I think I sprained my wrist."

"Why in the world were you walking around barefoot? What were you thinking?"

"Just help me over to the bike. Let's get out of here."

Babe knew she would get answers, but not at the moment. She put his good arm around her shoulders and helped him hobble toward their bike. As Spike hobbled he tucked his injured wrist close to his body. Suddenly a man in an apron ran up to them. "I saw everything. Stuff like that happens from time to time; but when I saw your wife, I figured you weren't one of those guys." The man offered to help Spike hobble to a bench. Babe's head was spinning. She left Spike alone for three minutes, and here is some stranger saying he saw whatever had happened and Spike wasn't one of those guys. What did it all mean?

The man helped Spike to a bench by the food truck. He ran inside for a moment and came back with two bags of ice and some iodine. He asked them what food they had ordered and brought them a new batch, at no charge. Spike didn't want to eat at first; but as the adrenaline wore down, he realized he was starving.

While scarfing down his chili pie, he told Babe what had happened. As he talked, she kept huffing and puffing. She would gasp and then look over Spike's shoulders to where the ruffians were sitting. A couple of times she slapped her hands on the table like she wanted to get up to teach those guys a lesson. Spike brought his saga to a climax, really getting into the telling of it now that he had the sympathy of his wife. The man from the food truck came back with a plate that held a massive funnel cake.

"Now, I tell ya, ma'am," the man said to Babe as she sat next to Spike, "this guy is as tough as nails." Babe was almost in tears, but Spike cracked a sly smile. "And he is a lot calmer than I would have been. I would have stood up swinging and probably would have ended up in a hospital. But your man here," he slapped Spike on the shoulder, "he had some sense and walked away fine."

"That's right, I am." Spike squeezed Babe's hand reassuringly. She was proud of him, staying so calm and collected in a tense situation. Once again, as in other times through their many years together, she was glad Spike was her husband and her champion.

Spike bent down and removed the ice pack from the bottom of his foot. The bleeding had stopped after he applied the iodine. He figured he would walk away from this. He checked the ground for nails or anything else he might step on. Then he placed his foot tenderly on the ground and gently began to rise to his feet. It wasn't so bad, he first thought. "Oh!" Spike plopped back onto the bench, pain shooting up through his leg. Babe's face told Spike she was feeling the pain with him.

"Buddy, I hope you've got your tetanus shot."

"Yes, he does. We're all caught up," Babe spoke up for him.

"Well that's good. And I hope you don't have to walk or stand much for work because it doesn't look like you will be doing much standing for a day or two. Well, good luck. I've got to get back to my truck."

Spike didn't know what to do. They were hundreds of miles from home, and their only mode of transportation was *Hog Wild*. If he couldn't even stand, how could he drive the thing? Without ice his foot throbbed and made it hard to concentrate, much less drive. But here was the real deal breaker: Spike took the ice off his wrist and tried to move it. The pain was unbearable.

Babe looked at Spike with concern in her eyes. She sat confused and hurt. How could anyone be so mean to her

156

Spike, the sweetest man she had ever known? She could see he was in pain, and she was already calculating how best to help him on the way home. She would encourage him to stop every time his ice melted to get more. She would hold a cooler of fresh ice in her lap if she needed to. Sure, she didn't like carrying large things when on the motorcycle, but she would do anything for him.

"Babe, honey. You have to drive us home."

Chapter 18

"What? Drive us home! No! That is not happening—what has gotten into you?"

"Babe, I can't do it. I can barely stand, and that alone would make it hard for me to drive. And with my wrist . . . how can I maneuver or change gears or brake or do anything without a hand and without a foot?"

"Well, you will have to find a way. I mean, don't people with casts drive motorcycles all the time?"

"I don't know, do they?"

Babe's mind raced. Her drive *Hog Wild*? She had no license. She had no training. She had nothing. All she had was an injured husband, a hero of a husband, who was looking at her with vulnerability and tears in his eyes. She knew this was difficult for him to ask of her. But was it even possible?

Babe sat on the bike—the front of the bike where it had never entered her mind to sit before. Spike, injured and iced, sat behind her, where he had never imagined sitting before.

"OK, turn on the engine."

"How?"

"Shift into first gear, right there," he said pointing, "and let the clutch out at the same time you pull back on the throttle." He said all this with limp hand motions on either side of Babe's face. She did as Spike told her, and the bike began rolling forward. But it did so with a grating scratch. "Stop! You forgot to put up the kickstand!" Spike yelled.

Her mind brimming with too many new instructions, Babe stopped the bike and yelled, "I didn't forget it; I never knew to do it in the first place!"

Spike regrouped. He calmly showed Babe the kickstand, and she put it up. "Now try turning it on again. You did great the first time, so you can do it again."

She turned on the engine, and the bike rolled forward. It stalled. They tried again and again until Babe had them rolling forward.

"I'll show you when to change gears, but the driving should be natural. You steer with the handlebars. You should be a pro at this because you have been riding on the back of the bike for months now. When I first started I had never driven one before so it took longer for me to get the feel of it. But you know how it feels to turn and things like that. Your body should know how to drive somewhat, so just do what feels natural."

They drove back and forth inside the parking lot for a while until Babe felt that she was ready for the highway.

Luckily, this was an isolated spot. Other than the hundreds of bikers, the food truck, and the gas station, there was nothing for miles but straight highway. Babe inched along the shoulder of the highway towards the gas station. It was slow moving, but that would have to be fine for now. As they moved, Spike kept pointing things out. He had to admit, she was a quick learner.

When they were almost to the gas station, Spike asked, "Do you want to take a break or keep going?"

Babe was too focused to respond. She could not believe she was doing this. She had never ever done anything like this. This was supposed to be Spike's dream, not hers. Why did they have to stop at that food truck? They could have come to this gas station right here to get what they needed. They would have been well on their way by now if it wasn't for that one stop. Those men who started the fight with Spike should have been arrested. She should have called the police. In fact, if she saw a police officer she would just tell him about those men back there.

That thought stopped her cold. If he asked for her license, she didn't have one, and, therefore, she was breaking the law.

Babe swerved a little under the impact of this thought. Spike instinctively reached out his injured foot to steady them on the ground, and she could tell that action had hurt. His entire body tensed, and he held on tighter to her waist.

She had to keep going. She had to. It was up to her to get them home.

There was nothing around them except the occasional passing vehicle. Other than that, there was only a straight highway and acres of cornfields. Babe appreciated straight highways and minimal traffic. As the miles passed, she felt more and more comfortable. She slowly sped up until she was able to go the full speed limit. Even that made her nervous, but she was getting the hang of this. She made a game with herself. If she saw tar spots on the road ahead, she attempted to weave through them. One on the right, one on the left, a version of weaving cones she had seen Spike do during his license training.

License. Her mind kept circling back to a license. Her stomach knotted, and without thinking she slowed again.

Why was this happening? Because of those boozed-up troublemakers at the barbecue place. The food truck really shouldn't have served drinks. She boiled as she thought about that whole experience. How could they escape running into drunken people going to an event like Sturgis? They were just asking for trouble with thousands of people coming to a small town. It was a miracle they had survived as well as they had. And to think that sweet Mary Alice and Agnes were sliding down this slippery slope. She needed to do her duty and put out the motorcycle fire within them as soon as possible. Those poor, defenseless ladies. What would they have done if a bunch of drunken ruffians had tried to push them around?

The longer Babe stewed, the more the recent incident spoiled her adventures on the motorcycle. Her mind went back. Murry's. The motorcycle. These leather pants. She had half a mind to stop at the next town and throw these filthy pants in the nearest dumpster. She had jeans in her bag. She felt foolish wearing biker clothes. Maybe their son had been right.

As they crested a knoll on the otherwise flat highway, Babe saw flashing lights up ahead. Her heart jumped into her throat. The police would stop her for sure and arrest her. Who knows in what kind of small-town jail they would throw her. She slowed, checked her speed, and rechecked her speed. Did she need a blinker on? Anything?

She drove past the officer twenty-three miles slower than the speed limit. As they passed, she saw the officer had pulled over a couple on a motorcycle. She began to sweat.

Four miles later they crossed the city limits into a small town. It was a quaint town where an old fashioned barber shop probably still thrived and people didn't lock their doors.

As Babe drove through town she saw a police car ahead and coming towards them. She panicked and without thinking took a sharp right turn onto a neighborhood street.

Spike picked up his head a ways and tapped on her shoulder. He pointed back to the road, and she could hear him asking, "Where are you going?"

She felt silly and was about to turn back to the highway when the officer turned down the same street. Without thinking, she made a sharp right again. Spike tapped harder, and his questions got louder. She was a couple of blocks ahead of the officer, so before he reached that last intersection, she turned into the Our Lady of Grace Catholic Church parking lot. She picked up speed until she was around the corner of the church and stopped under the shadow of the steeple. Babe peeked around the corner and saw the officer drive on past the church.

Spike ripped off his helmet. "What in the world are you doing?"

Babe laughed. She lifted off her helmet and burst into laughter that brought tears to her eyes. She said, "You know Spike, I think I've turned. Just now I flat out ran from the police! Now I think I've done everything! Here I am thinking about getting those ruffians from the last stop arrested, and then I run from the cops!"

As Babe told him the story, Spike lifted himself off the bike. He tested his foot on the ground and immediately regretted it. It hurt badly even when he wasn't standing on it. The pain almost knocked him out when he had put pressure on the foot. He then tried to move his stiff wrist. Instant pain. He had hoped a short rest would put him back in the saddle, but it looked as if Babe was the pilot a while longer.

The couple headed back to the highway. Spike was proud that Babe started the bike again without stalling once. Forty-five minutes from the small town and the terrain looked familiar. A wave of relief swept over Spike. Finally he could go home, rest, and put ice on his elevated foot. They passed Spike's old office, the Cromwell Heating and Air Conditioning building. He gave a slight smile. How he had changed since his retirement. He craned his neck to see if any of his buddies might be there. For an instant he considered stopping by at least to say hi; the guys would get a good laugh out of the incident at the Iron Horse food truck. But he knew he would have to come back another time. There was no way he would let his buddies see him riding on the back of a motorcycle with his wife driving. He would never hear the end of it.

Spike and Babe pulled into their driveway and both sighed in relief. Spike was the first off. Despite his injuries, he wanted to make sure no one in the neighborhood saw him riding on the back. That and he wanted to lie down. Babe sat on the bike for a moment longer, soaking in what she had accomplished. She had driven *Hog Wild*. Never in her wildest dreams had she expected to drive the beast. She looked over at Mrs. Kline's house, half wanting to see their neighbor peeking out the window. Now that the police were no longer an issue, she wanted to be seen driving. She got off and helped Spike into the house, then went back to the bike to get the rest of their things.

They hadn't been home more than an hour when the phone rang. It had taken about that long to get Spike comfortable and cleaned up. Babe answered. It was Agnes, who Babe thought must have either been watching for them or had a spy keeping track of when they arrived home. She listened for a moment and handed the phone to her husband. "Spike, it's for you."

Agnes wasted no time. "Spike, I want you to take me down to see Chuck as soon as you can," she said without greeting or preamble. "Do you think I can trust him? I only do business with people I can trust."

Spike grinned to himself and thought he had risen to new heights in the recommending business. "Yes, Agnes, you can trust what he says, and he will tell you if he thinks you are making the wrong decision. Babe and I can come by with the car and pick you up."

"Do you have to bring the car? I'd much rather ride on your motorcycle," Agnes answered.

Spike, a little surprised, countered. "Sure, I can bring the bike, but you know it's hard to ride on a motorcycle in a skirt."

"Not to worry," came her answer. "I have that part all figured out."

"Alright. It may be a couple of days before I can take you on the bike. Will you have time this Tuesday?"

"Of course I have time. I'm retired! What time shall we go?"

"How does 10:00 a.m. sound?"

"See you out in front at 10:00 a.m. Try not to be late. Now, let me talk to Babe."

Spike dutifully handed the phone back to his wife.

"Sure. I'll be right over." Babe hung up the phone and picked up her car keys. "The ladies want me to come visit them. I'll be back in a little bit."

As Babe headed out the door, Spike adjusted to a more comfortable position and picked up his newest book. He opened it but stared out the window. Agnes buying a motorcycle. Who would have ever thought this would happen? You think you know people, and then you find out you're off by miles.

He picked the book back up and looked for his spot but then put it down again. He figured with some good rest he would be back on the bike in no time. Having a motorcycle appointment in a few days gave him a deadline to be functional, and he intended to be well by then. He was only hurt this morning, but was ready for things to get back to normal. His wrist and foot still throbbed, but his mind sped to what their next trip could be. He couldn't wait to be the one driving again with Babe on the back. That is how it should be, he thought.

Babe parked her car at Agnes's condo, wondering what this call was all about.

"Hope we didn't interrupt anything you were busy with at home," Agnes began.

"Oh, no, you didn't," Babe assured her.

"Come on in the house," Agnes said with a twinkle in her eye.

Babe saw that Agnes had put coffee cups and a plate of cookies on the table. "She's going to try to sell me on something," thought Babe as she sat down in the chair where Agnes was pointing. Mary Alice and Agnes also took a chair.

"Where did you get your license? We need to know before we get our bike."

Babe was taken aback slightly, both because of her venture this morning and because of their assumption she already had it. "Well, actually, I don't have a license."

The two women's eyes widened and they leaned in. "At all?" Agnes asked. "But Mrs. Kline told us you were driving when you pulled in on the motorcycle today."

Babe was so surprised she didn't know what to say at first. First, these ladies had spies working for them; and second,

Mrs. Kline actually had been peeking out when they got home. She was almost happy to have been discovered; that way she could answer their questions about her adventure, and it wouldn't sound like bragging. She launched into the story about coming home and Spike's clash with the men at the table, while all the time painting him as a gentle hero, full of self-control and incredible strength. She told about how she had been forced to drive, stepping up to get them home safely. She laughed about the police following them when she had to go into a church parking lot to hide. Both Agnes and Mary Alice were spellbound and careful to not miss one word. They gasped and laughed along with Babe as the story unfolded.

When the story was finished, Agnes asked Babe, "Why don't you get your license so you can ride with us sometimes?"

Babe hesitated as she thought about the possibility and then said, "I don't know how Spike would feel about that. He likes to do the driving, even when we're in the car. I guess men just like to be in charge."

Agnes straightened in her chair and cleared her throat, reminding Babe of the times Agnes wanted to have her say at card games. Then Agnes said, "But you should be ready in case something happens when you and Spike are on your trips, as it did coming back from Sturgis. Why don't you get your license along with Mary Alice. She would appreciate the company, and you really need yours, too, just in case."

Interesting, thought Babe. "I'll think about it. Thanks for asking, and I'll get back to you." Babe was in a dither when she got in her car and headed home. She did like driving after she tried it and caught on to how the machine reacted. It might be fun to have her own license so she could ride with the ladies when they were going on their little jaunts. She wondered what Spike would think of the idea.

Spike was sitting at the kitchen table when she went in the house. He said, "So, how was it? Did you talk about the motorcycle they want to get?"

Babe hesitated, wondering how she should approach this. She decided to jump in with both feet and tell it like it was.

Chapter 19

"Agnes suggested I get my motorcycle license along with Mary Alice. She said it would be wise in case we ever have something happen again like it did coming home from Sturgis. You would have to agree, it would be best if I had my license for such situations."

Spike was taken by surprise. He sputtered around and then said, "You told them about what happened?" His pride looked slightly wounded, and Babe was almost going to apologize for telling if he didn't want the story out when he burst out, "That's not going to happen again, and I don't see any reason why you should need your license."

He said it with a little too much gusto for Babe's comfort. She said, "Well we needed it coming home. And what makes you so sure something like that couldn't happen again?"

He sat there thinking and then answered, "I just want to do the driving. It bothered me to have to sit behind you while you drove, even when I knew we didn't have a choice."

"Well," countered Babe, "It couldn't have bothered you any more than it did me to be driving and see that cop turn that corner and follow us. Plus, I would like to take the bike by myself sometimes and go riding with Agnes and Mary Alice. Jenny has her license and even has her own bike. I can drive a car, so I don't see what's wrong with me driving a motorcycle. I hope you're not saying you don't think I should be driving a motorcycle!" So there, she thought. That's my line in the sand.

Spike seemed to realize they had somehow come to the final hurdle on this license thing. He had always prided himself in never sweating the little things. Maybe this was the time to remember that. Anyway, what could it hurt if she wanted to do this? "I guess it might be smart, and it would be fun for you to ride with your friends." He just wished his heart was more into the idea.

* * *

Agnes felt rather like a crew chief. She wasn't going to get her license, but she thought she needed to spearhead the drive to get Mary Alice and Babe theirs. Sometimes these younger people needed guidance in such matters to get things done. She telephoned Chuck about the licensing process. He suggested that his employee, Stephen, give them driving lessons in Murry's parking lot before their actual license class. The more familiar they became with a bike's operation, the better off everyone would be. Agnes insisted she pay Stephen's wages while he was instructing, but that fact was to be between Chuck and Agnes and not mentioned to the new drivers.

Lesson times were established, and Chuck furnished the bikes that Mary Alice and Babe would use for learning. The idea was to start on smaller bikes to get the feel of driving and then to graduate to their own machines. Agnes insisted on picking them up in her car on lesson mornings. Babe wondered if Agnes feared either she or Mary Alice would renege at the last minute. Actually, Agnes got a lot of satisfaction out of others learning something new and she wanted to watch. For Babe's part, she had asked that the lessons take place in the early mornings. Her thinking was that earlier meant fewer witnesses.

When the students arrived the first morning, Stephen was busy placing pylons in a staggered line between the two sidewalks. Two bikes stood to the side—one a small three-wheeler and one similar to *Hog Wild*, but not as big. Mary Alice and Babe walked over to where Stephen was waiting for them.

As Stephen was ready to start, Agnes called, "Stephen, would you be so kind as to help me get my lawn chair out of my trunk? I want to be where I can watch." Stephen ran over to the car and retrieved the chair. He tried to help Agnes get seated, but she brushed him off saying, "Get along over there, boy." Then she added, pointing to Babe and Mary Alice, "Those are the two who need the help."

Babe mostly had the knack from the get-go. But Agnes could tell the lessons weren't going well with Mary Alice because Stephen kept smacking his hand against his forehead. However, Chuck's directions must have been explicit because Stephen didn't give up and walk away. It was when he started giving encouragement and quit smacking his forehead that things got better. Their speed and Mary Alice's stability picked up as their confidence built. Eventually Stephen stood to the side as the students gained the know-how they needed, and they soon were going through the pylons in fine style.

On the last day of practice before their actual licensing, Mary Alice lost control of the bike she was riding. She blast past Stephen, knocking down pylons at an alarming rate. She passed Babe and looked as if she was going to let go of the handlebars when she passed Agnes watching from her lawn chair. "Use the brakes, you fool! Brake!" yelled Agnes. That seemed to bring Mary Alice to her senses, and she brought the machine to a screeching halt. Agnes, a little more frightened than she cared to admit, added, "Please don't kill me before I've had a chance to ride on this bike at least a few times!"

On Thursday morning Spike called Chuck to advise him to get his ducks in a row because the ladies would be arriving about 10:00 a.m. to do some serious bike shopping. He hoped Chuck had experience in dealing with women of advanced age.

Spike was outside of Agnes's condo at 9:55 a.m., quietly biding his time until his passenger appeared. Agnes appeared on her porch, locked her door, and put the key in her purse. Then she stopped and looked at her purse. She took the key and her billfold back out of her purse, unlocked her door, threw her purse back inside, relocked her door, and put her billfold and key in her pocket. It only took seconds as Spike watched, marveling at a women in her late eighties making snap decisions. Then he noticed what she was wearing. Agnes was attired in a black pullover, long-sleeved blouse and a gray, full, mid-calf-length skirt. He had driven one lady of advanced age on his cycle who was wearing a skirt, but that was after dusk. Well, he thought to himself, she'll be behind me so I won't be able to witness any immodesty.

Agnes approached the motorcycle, halted beside it, and said, "You know, I'm going to have to hold onto your waist to stay on this thing, don't you?"

Spike responded, "Of course I know that. That's the only way to ride safely." He handed her Babe's helmet.

"I wanted to be sure you didn't think I was getting fresh!" she answered with a spry smile and plopped the helmet on her head.

Agnes wasted no more time. Spike thought it was appropriate to look straight ahead as she climbed on. She swung her leg over the passenger seat and put her arms around Spike. When he felt she was seated he pulled away from the curb and headed for Murry's.

Spike and Agnes arrived at Murry's in record time. Chuck was standing at the front door waiting to welcome them. Spike parked the bike directly in front of the store and waited for Agnes to get herself off as modestly as possible. She climbed off but stopped Spike from getting off by putting her hand on his shoulder. She said, "Would you mind going over to pick up Mary Alice? She really should be here when we make these big decisions."

"Does she know I'm coming?" questioned Spike.

"She will be waiting for you," answered Agnes, giving him the address.

Chuck came out and took Agnes by the elbow, leading her into the store. He turned and winked at Spike as he rode away to retrieve Mary Alice.

When Spike arrived, Mary Alice came outside and down the sidewalk. Funny, he thought. She was wearing the identical gray, calf-length skirt that Agnes had been wearing. But, he thought, what do men know about women's clothes?

Stephen held the door open for Spike and Mary Alice when they arrived at Murry's. He smiled and told them that Chuck and Mrs. Bolton were waiting for them in Chuck's office.

When they came to the office door, Chuck was standing behind his desk and pointed to a chair for Mary Alice beside

Agnes. He motioned for Spike to take a chair beside his desk. There were several pictures of three-wheeler motorcycles laid out on the desk. He explained to the women the benefits of each but said they were limited in their selection if they insisted that both would ride on the same machine.

Rising from her chair, Agnes announced, "That's the kind we want." She pointed to a picture of a green machine and took her seat again. Mary Alice nodded in agreement. Agnes rose to her feet again to get a better view of the remaining pictures. "I think this is the exact one we looked at in Sturgis, isn't it Mary Alice?" Mary Alice again nodded in agreement.

Chuck laughed as he said, "You really know how to pick them, ladies. You have very good taste. This is what is called the *Tri Glide Ultra*. It has a two-up seat with a deep rider bucket and a passenger seat with armrests. It also has what we call a large tour-pack with a roomy trunk for traveling. It is the most expensive one of the bunch. You can save at least $1,000 if you choose this one," he said as he pointed at another machine. Then he pointed at the third picture and said, "And you can save $1,500 if you choose this one."

Agnes shook her head and repeated, "No, this is the one we want! We tried sitting on one in Sturgis and we both fit; plus it is Mary Alice's favorite color—green."

Chuck sat back and sighed, then took out another book and flipped through several pages. He drew a circle around an amount and showed it to Agnes. "This is the price of that cycle. Even with the discount I'm giving you, it is pricey. I can do some research and see if there is a used one available if you have your heart set on this model."

Agnes didn't hesitate a minute before answering. "This is the one we want, and we want a new one. I have my checkbook along, and I'll write you out a check right now."

Chuck and Spike were stunned as they looked at one another and then back at Agnes. They were both thinking maybe she was a little off her game, age and all considered. Where would a schoolteacher get that amount of money to spend on a motorcycle even if she was a serious saver?

Agnes smiled when she saw how perplexed they were and explained. "We had an old man named Jonah who lived down the block from us when I was growing up. He lived in a rickety old house and seemed to have very little; and he looked to be completely alone in the world. It was just my mother and me, and Mother was afraid Jonah wasn't getting enough to eat. So every day she made a little extra for one meal, and it was my job to take the food to him. It was never much, but when she baked bread she would send along half a loaf with his meal that day.

"We had very little, but Mother was one who helped where she could. I asked Jonah one day if he had any children or brothers or sisters, and he told me no; he had grown up an orphan, but he never told me where he was from. We would see him out in the backyard with an old dishpan and a washboard washing his clothes. Mom offered to do his washing with ours, but he wouldn't hear of it. Well, to make a long story short, in his final days he had no one—no wife or children or any friends. We just couldn't stand that he was so alone. Mother and I went to see him in the hospital and just sat and talked with him or read to him during his last months. When he died my Mother and I were the only ones at the funeral home, and there was no funeral service. It was sad."

Spike and Chuck were spellbound by the story. Mary Alice

had heard it before, but she still got tears in her eyes as Agnes was retelling it.

"My mother died a month or so later. I was shocked when an attorney came to my door one day and told me Jonah had left me an inheritance. He handed me an old, well-worn Bible and a note on a piece of paper. All that was written on the note was, 'Do not forget to entertain strangers, for by so doing some have unwittingly entertained angels. Thank you.' I learned later it was a Bible verse from Hebrews 13:2. The lawyer told me that Jonah was indeed an orphan who never knew his family. In fact, he had chosen his own name. Early in his teens he headed for Alaska where there was a gold rush in progress. He met up with an older man there who took him under his wing, and they established a claim and did very well. When the older man died in a mine accident he left what he had to Jonah. And then the lawyer said, 'Now his inheritance is yours.'"

Agnes paused in thought then continued. "I used the money only when I felt someone or a church or charity was in need. If a need came to my attention I went to the bank, got a cashier's check, and had the bank deliver it anonymously to whomever needed the help. I never considered it my money. Now I'm well into the fourth quarter of my life, and I know my days are limited. That money is all just sitting there. Maybe I've suddenly become selfish, but I have decided I want to mark one more thing off my bucket list before I die, something just for myself. I've been thinking about what it should be for a few years, and nothing really got my attention before I met Babe. She inspired me, so I'm going for it even if it's reckless spending."

Chuck and Spike were taking that in when something

pushed on the door. Spike did a double take when a cat strolled in. It saw Spike right away and gave its *yeeoow*. It was the hitchhiking cat from the saddlebag. Spike stood straight up, almost knocking his chair over. "How in the world did that thing get in here?" he yelled, pointing at the cat. Meanwhile, Chuck had started to sneeze and wave his arms, yelling, "Someone come and get this cat! Stephen! I thought I told you to take this cat twenty miles out in the country, throw it out of the car, and then drive back quick!"

"Oh, no!" squealed Mary Alice. "Please don't do that to this cat. Please!"

By this time the cat, who must have known a good thing when he heard it, jumped onto Mary Alice's lap. She put her arms around it and whispered sweet nothings in the cat's ear, assuring him that the aforementioned twenty-mile trip would not happen and he would never be abandoned. At the same time Chuck was still sneezing and wheezing while waving his arms. It even looked as if his eyes were swelling shut. Loud and clear he proclaimed, "Mary Alice, I am giving you this cat if you promise me you won't let it get within two miles of here."

Stephen appeared in the office doorway looking penitent. He grabbed the cat from Mary Alice's lap and started for the door. Chuck started to speak; he sneezed and then gave orders. "Stephen, see that this cat gets to Mrs. Wonder's house. I will be taking her home. Wait with the cat in your car until I leave and then take it to Mrs. Wonder's door!"

"Yes, sir, I'll do it just that way!" he said as he put the cat under his arm and left the office. As they were passing Spike, the cat let out a final *yeeoow*.

Spike was stunned. "Chuck, how long has that cat been

here?"

Chuck was blowing his nose into a handkerchief. "Since a week before Sturgis—actually, since the day after we had dinner at your house. That night, Jenny and I stopped by the store after dinner, and as soon as we had parked in the garage that blasted thing jumped out of my saddlebag. I've been trying to get rid of it ever since."

Agnes interrupted as if there had been no break in the conversation. "Chuck, I want you to order us one of those Tri Rides, or whatever they call them. Be sure it has a horn on it. And remember, our days are limited so don't be slow in getting it done! When it gets here, gas it up and have it ready!"

Chuck smiled and replied, "Consider it done." The puffiness around his eyes was receding.

"And Chuck," said Agnes, "I want you to organize the whole thing. At our age, we don't have time to be fiddling around." Then she looked long and hard at both Chuck and Spike. "None of this whole deal goes beyond this room. Is that understood?"

Chuck answered, "It's going to be up to you to spread any word that gets spread. As for Spike and me, our lips are sealed!" Spike nodded in agreement.

"It will take about two weeks to get the machine here."

With that, Agnes pulled her checkbook out of her pocket. Spike was awestruck that anyone could sit down and write out a check for that amount of money. Especially for a toy! He had never known anyone who could do that. He hadn't rubbed elbows with many well-heeled people.

"I feel good now that that's done," said Agnes with a smile. "Spike, will you take us back home now? I think we've had enough excitement for today!"

Chuck put his hands in the air and said to the group, "I'll take Mary Alice home, and Spike can take Agnes on his bike." It took only minutes for the ladies to get on the bikes, almost as though they had been getting off and on their entire lives. They headed off in different directions after an afternoon of exciting business.

When Spike got home, Babe met him at the door. She expectantly looked at him, waiting for him to tell all. He raised both his arms in a halt gesture and said, "Don't ask me anything. I'm sworn to secrecy!"

"But I know all about what those two are looking for. I've talked with them about it. Certainly you can tell me the outcome," Babe said.

Spike just shook his head. "My lips are sealed. I promised. How would you like to go against two of the Magnificent Seven? I think they want to be the ones to break the news to that group. They certainly can't be afraid of gossip from anyone else."

Then he went into a strange pantomime. Not looking at Babe, he moved three chairs away from the table. He put two chairs side by side and the third in front of the two, leaving just a little space in the middle of the three. Still not making a sound, he lifted his leg as if he were climbing into the front chair of the three. He squatted and looked over his shoulder as if talking to someone but making no sound. He turned and patted the center of the combined seats of the two chairs behind him. He then turned toward the front again, held his arms out at angles to his body, looked to both sides and made fists like he was holding on to handlebars. That done, without a word he got up, moved the chairs back to where they belonged at the table and started to leave the room. Babe just grinned and promised herself she would say nothing to either Agnes or Mary Alice or to the rest of The Seven. Her lips were sealed, too, but she could keep her eyes and ears open.

"Oh, and one other thing, Babe."

"What's that?"

"That cat is back."

Chapter 20

The afternoon after Mary Alice received her motorcycle license, she drove the new *Tri Glide Ultra* over to Agnes's condo. She parked in the driveway and honked the horn, shuddering at how loud it was. Agnes appeared, all smiles, and was ready for her first ride.

Agnes had a small garage, so they had decided Mary Alice would keep the bike in her larger garage beside her Mini Cooper.

"Let's ride!" Agnes said as she climbed on and inspected the machine from her new perch. It was nearly dusk, but traffic was minimal, so Mary Alice turned around slowly and drove out onto the street.

"Tell me when you are ready to go back home," she told her passenger.

"OK, but can you go just a little bit faster? We're going so slow, I feel as if I should get off and push!" She gave directions to go down a few blocks and turn to pass the church. That might be letting the cat out of the bag, thought Mary Alice. But she did as she was told, hoping choir practice wasn't over yet. Then they went past the library, and Agnes suggested they stop for an ice cream cone. Mary Alice got up her nerve and said maybe they could stop next time because she was ready to head home. She turned down Agnes's street and drove into her driveway with a sigh of relief.

"That's more tiring than I thought it would be," Agnes said as she climbed off the machine, "but I'm glad we have it. People our age should do something exciting now and then just to keep their vitals working at the right speed. Lying around can kill you!" With that she patted Mary Alice on the shoulder and said, "You are a good friend to me, Mary Alice." Then she went inside her house. When Mary Alice saw the lights go on she made a U-turn and headed toward home.

It was getting dark, and Mary Alice noticed that a street light at the corner of Agnes's block was out. She would have to call city hall tomorrow and report it. She felt around for the light switch on the motorcycle. Her fingers fumbled around in the darkness. She slowed and looked down, but the switch still eluded her. Well, there was still enough daylight to find her way home, she thought. She drove a little farther; and, looking around, didn't recognize the houses on her right. As she noticed the houses were getting farther apart, she suddenly realized she was on the wrong street. She looked both ways to see if she recognized any landmarks, craning her neck as she squinted at houses. Bang! The front tire hit the curb and she slammed on the brakes. She tried to get off the bike to check on any damage, but she found she had a pain in her ankle. She must have twisted it in the sudden jolt. What if she had been thrown? Thank goodness for helmets!

Mary Alice stumbled off the bike and sat on the curb trying to think what to do, checking her pockets for her cell phone. She would call Spike to come and check the bike and help her get back on. Where was that phone? She crawled around, feeling in the grass and looking in the street, but no phone.

This was a conundrum if there ever was one. The only good thing about the whole mess was that Agnes was not on the bike with her or she might have fallen.

Still sitting on the curb, Mary Alice rested her elbows on her knees and laid her head in her hands. She closed her eyes and prayed, "I got myself in a pickle here, Lord, and I need help!" As she sat with her head in her lap she heard a whirring noise approaching on the sidewalk. There was still just enough daylight to see a wheelchair coming toward her. A wheelchair, Lord? But she knew she should not question. The wheelchair stopped on the sidewalk, even with where she was perched on the curb.

"Flat tire, Miss?"

"No, I was looking around when I should have had my eyes on the road. It seems I've banged up my ankle, and I can't stand on it. Do you have a cell phone with you?"

"No. Don't believe in them, myself. But I could give you a ride home or take you to find a phone. My name is Edward Walters, and I'm safe and decent."

"It is very nice of you, Mr. Walters, but just how do you propose to give me a ride? Your vehicle doesn't look like it has a ride-along option to me, as kind as it is of you to offer."

"My dear," explained Edward, "it looks to me that we have only one option and that is this: you sit on my lap, and this mechanical machine will take both of us to where we decide to go, with me driving." Then he chuckled and added, "And I am known for keeping my eye on the road while driving."

Mary Alice looked around and realized there were no lights on in the few surrounding houses. Not one car had passed while she had been sitting there. He was probably right. This was her only option. "Alright, Mr. Walters. Please take me to the nearest phone," she said as she tried to get up.

"Just a minute, young lady, I think I can drive this thing closer to you." He worked his hand lever and turned the chair, steering it toward her. He reached her and told her to grab the arm of the chair to pull herself up.

Mary Alice pulled herself to a standing position and just looked at this man. She believed him when he said he was safe and decent. Even if he weren't, she could probably fight him off. But what if someone saw her riding in a wheelchair sitting on a man's lap? Now that was juicy gossip fodder for card clubs anywhere! Her reputation would either be ruined or she would be famous. She would opt for famous if she had a choice. She carefully turned and sat down in his lap.

Edward, working the controls proclaimed, "And . . . we're off!" as the chair purred its way down the sidewalk. As they passed the bike, she reached and grabbed her helmet. If nothing else, she could put it on for some anonymity.

As they puttered down the sidewalk, Mary Alice thought of another problem. She blushed as she asked, "I hope this won't upset your wife!"

"Oh," replied Edward, "she won't be upset. She'll be looking down from heaven and cheering me on. She was quite a lady and was always helping someone."

They had gone a block when Mary Alice turned to face her driver and asked, "Shouldn't we be going the other way back to find a phone? There aren't many houses along here."

Edward patted her shoulder and answered, "There are no houses because we are entering a park. I was on my way to meet some friends who play horseshoes here once a week. I can't play anymore, but I like to watch them."

Mary Alice shuddered to think someone might witness her

mode of transportation, but she hoped they would realize she had no choice and remember that in a storm, it's any port. Maybe someone there would have a phone.

Then Edward chuckled again and added, "I hope you won't mind, but I want that bunch I meet every week to see us. Never in a million years would they believe me if I just told them about how I rescued a damsel in distress!"

Mary Alice thought she must be tired because she began to see the humor in all of it. Here she was, riding down the street in a wheelchair, seated on a man's lap whom she had never met before. She just wished the Dirty Queens group was playing cards tonight and that she had nerve enough to have Edward take her past where they were. They would never believe her either if she told them; that is if she ever dared tell them.

Lights shone up ahead, and Mary Alice heard the clink of the horseshoes as they hit the stakes. Getting closer, she saw a group of men laughing, talking, and having good time.

As Mary Alice and her driver approached the group, Edward hollered, "Hey, fellas, I might be late but I'm here!" The group quieted immediately as they turned to see their friend's wheelchair approaching. They were used to seeing him come and watch them play, but what they saw tonight rendered them speechless. And making this group speechless was quite a feat! Edward was partially hidden by his passenger, a lady also up in years, sitting in his lap! Then one player started to clap; and soon all the players joined in the applause. Another yelled, "Eddy, we had about given up on you coming, but now we can see what held you up!" Another of the men added, "Man, you travel in style!"

A cell phone was quickly produced, and Mary Alice called Spike, who said he would come by the park and pick her up. Edward was quick to insist he would take her the short distance back to her bike and meet Spike there. He gave Spike the approximate address. They waved goodbye as the men were loudly telling her they were honored to meet her. Mary Alice thought this was the only time she remembered getting anywhere close to being the belle of the ball.

Spike hadn't arrived by the time Mary Alice and Edward got back to the stranded bike. Edward insisted she stay seated on his lap until her friend came. Spike rode right up to them, acting as if he saw ladies perched on strangers' laps every day. He checked on the bike and told Mary Alice that Chuck was on his way to pick up the bike and inspect it. He would deliver it to her apartment if it didn't need any repairs.

As Mary Alice got down from her perch, she put her weight gingerly on the foot with the injured ankle. When Edward was sure she could stand by herself, he asked if she would meet him again sometime. Mary Alice said she would like that; but, adding with a laugh, she thought it was her turn to drive if he would give her his address. Spike thanked the new friend and lifted Mary Alice onto his bike. Edward was waving goodbye as they left.

Chapter 21

It had been an eventful and fun summer. Never had Spike expected having a motorcycle would mean this much adventure. He hadn't thought it possible that he and Babe could be closer than ever, but *Hog Wild* had brought them closer. They rehashed the memories of their trips as they sat together throughout the day. Life was good.

When Babe got home she could see immediately that Spike was planning something. "What's up?" she asked as she entered the kitchen.

"I got a call from our grandson. Do you remember the last time we were in Kansas City to see Luke and his family, and little Ben helped me fix their screen door?"

"Yes, and when you were finished he went over to their neighbor and asked if the neighbor had anything he wanted fixed because his grandpa could fix anything." She paused, "You mean Ben called and not his mom or dad?"

Spike laughed. "When I answered the phone, and he was on the line, I asked where his Mom was, and he said she was gone and he had a sitter today. I asked where the sitter was, and he said she was sitting right beside him talking on her phone too."

Babe laughed and said, "I would bet that sitter thought he

was on a play phone."

"Well," continued Spike, "Ben said I needed to come down right away and fix the sliding door on their patio. I asked him if his dad had worked on it, but Ben said Luke couldn't fix it. Then I asked how he knew that for sure. He said because his dad said, 'Oh, rats,' and went in the house. Ben said his dad always says that when he can't get something to work."

By this time they were both laughing. "We haven't been down there for a while, Spike. Let's make the trip on our bike. That way you can fix the sliding door, plus Luke can see that the bike is a great thing for us in our retirement."

"When a grandson asks for help you have to go! Let's call Luke to see if this weekend works for them." Spike called Luke's number at work. When Luke answered, Spike said, "We hear you have an 'Oh, rats,' situation down there." He told him about the call, and Luke said Ben knows he isn't supposed to use the phone except for an emergency. Spike countered, "Evidently, 'Oh, rats' is an emergency to him."

Later that day Spike laid down his book, finally finished. There was something about finishing a good book. He wanted to pick another one up immediately, to start over again. He milled around the house, picking up Babe's books and seeing if anything struck him as interesting. None did. He rifled through the mail and found a motorcycle catalog. Why not, he thought. They had all the equipment they would ever need, but it was fun to just browse and see what was available—kind of like seeing how the other half lives.

As Spike turned the catalog pages he saw lots of bells and whistles that riders could get for their machines. He stopped on a page that featured padded seat covers like the one they had bought for Babe in Sturgis. Maybe he should get one for himself. No, he thought; the more he rode, the softer the seat on his bike felt. He chuckled to himself and thought what an inadvertent money saver it had been to grow his own built-in seat cushion. He had been working on it for years as a do-it-yourself padding project at most meals, blissfully unaware. Now he was reaping the benefits.

He turned the pages in the catalog slowly. Now here's something interesting, he thought. It was a page of tents that were motorcycle portable. Wouldn't it be fun to go camping before cold weather set in? Spike hadn't been camping in years. But he had fond memories of the times he spent in a tent with his Boy Scout troop. He went to the coffeepot for a refill and returned to his chair where he kept turning the pages of the catalog. He wondered how that idea would fly with Babe. They hadn't done anything like this before, and Spike also wondered if there were nice camping spots in the state. He had driven past Lake Okoboji a few times. He googled the lake area and found a secluded camping spot on Loon Lake, north of Okoboji. The website said it was a great place to tent camp on the lake. It had firepits, restrooms, and showers; and it wasn't too crowded.

Next he went to the computer to check what they would need to camp and if their motorcycle could carry everything. The website he found told him all about how much to take and how to efficiently pack supplies to fit everything on the cycle. The information told him if their cycle weighed 580 pounds, and he factored in his and Babe's weight, they could carry an additional 75 pounds in other camping necessities. Spike was energized by all the information. Yes, he was sold on a trip like this!

First on the to-do list would be to convince Babe. He started to list mentally what he considered to be good selling points. He wanted to make his presentation so good that she would want to leave right away.

Babe's days were filled with routine things and social obligations. But she had to admit that *Hog Wild* was a game changer. When Spike was trying to sell her on getting the bike he said they were in a rut and most of the time did nothing really exciting. In retrospect, he had been right, and she was enjoying his new hobby. Actually, it was *their* new hobby. They had found an escape from mundane days. Some days they just dropped what they were doing and took off for a ride. The dusting waited, the laundry waited, everything waited. Life was too short for everyday chores to be more important than spending time with each other.

Spike woke early the next morning. The timing seemed right, and he was ready to approach Babe about the camping idea. He made the coffee and was ready when Babe made her way to the kitchen.

"Coffee! Thanks for making it, Spike."

"Babe, what would you think about going camping?"

"Spike, if you're talking about sleeping in the open, no showers or toilets, and cooking on a camp stove, I'm dead set against it." She must have somehow gotten another clue because she turned and looked at him as if he had gone off his rocker. "Are you talking about taking the bike and going camping?"

He guessed he should have eased her into it; but he had shown his hand, and there was no backing up now. The only way to go was straight ahead. "Babe, think of it this way. Northern Iowa isn't that far. The lake I've found is Loon Lake, close to Lake Okoboji, and there are clean restrooms with showers. We could go there in a day, spend some time there, and make the trip back in one day. I'll get a tent, and we'll put it up by a lake. No one else will be around, just the two of us. It will be so peaceful. Think about how quiet it will be. Or we could take our time coming back from Kansas City and spend some nights out under the stars. If the Loon Lake campsite has showers, I'll bet there are several campsites like it from here to Luke's house. Everything we will need will fit on the bike. I've researched the idea, and lots of bikers do it. We don't need to stay more than a couple of nights if you want to come home. When we get there and put up our tent, I'll go into town and get enough groceries to make breakfast. Hey, I'll even do the cooking!"

Babe sat there, processing the information. "You really mean you will do the cooking?"

Spike put his hand in the air and promised, "Yes. I'll do the cooking and the cleaning up. We can go into town for lunch and bring something back for supper." He got up from his chair and went to get his catalog. "Here is the tent we could get. See what it says? It weighs almost nothing and has enough room for us both, plus room to keep clothing and food supplies."

Babe wasn't showing signs of expedition approval, but she was still listening. So far, so good, he thought. "We can get a five-bar luggage rack to install behind your seat so it will hold the tent and a campfire grate, plus the two sleeping bags. We still have the sleeping bags the boys used in Scouts."

He searched Babe's face to see any sign of interest. He waited for any negative comments so he could counter-attack. He was ready. He was prepared.

"You really mean you'll do the cooking and the cleaning up?"

she asked.

"I promise I will, and you won't even have to ask me to do it. You can just sit and watch."

Babe looked out the window and then thoughtfully committed herself. "OK, let's do it. Can we be ready by the time we go to Luke's house? And what do we have to take?"

Spike's head reeled. He couldn't believe it. He'd sold her on the idea, and it seemed all systems were go. He was getting to be a pro at this convincing game. It took him only forty-odd years to figure it out. He patted himself on the back mentally as he got out the list he'd tucked in the catalog. "Oh, we can be ready; especially if we get on it now. We'll need that old percolator and some coffee in a plastic bag. We can make coffee and heat water in that. We can carry it in one saddlebag along with some heavy foil to use to cook over an open fire. Plastic cups, plates, and silverware should work, and we'll need a spatula. We'll also need a skillet. Do we still have that old iron skillet? We can put the rolled up sleeping bags inside the garbage bags we'll need for garbage. We can get wood for making a fire at the campground."

"Don't forget to add bug spray and a flashlight. Oh, and some matches. You'll need those to light the fire for your cooking," she added with a grin. "How about toiletries and extra clothes?"

Spike had the answer ready. "The article I read said we should each wear a backpack with our extra clothes. The toiletries, packed in a plastic bag, will go in the other saddlebag, along with a towel and washcloth for each of us. They will have to be hung up after use to dry so we can use them again."

"This is sounding more like fun all the time, Spike. Order that tent today and have them ship it overnight. We can charge the extra shipping costs off to not having to stop at motels!"

Spike went to the phone, and Babe went to the garage to find the box with the old percolator. She tried to remember where the boxes were with the boys' old sleeping bags. They hadn't used them for years, and she hoped they were still usable. She thought if she hung them on the patio a couple of days they should be fine.

A few days later the garage looked like they were moving. All the camping stuff was on the floor. Space was at a premium, so Spike had moved the car out of the garage and left it parked in the driveway. He specified that nothing should be piled up so he could see everything and nothing would be forgotten.

With tongue in cheek, Babe asked Spike why *Hog Wild* didn't have to stand out in the weather instead of the car. Spike didn't comment; he just gave her his anti-sarcasm look and kept on checking items off his list. When it was clear he had no time for chitchat, Babe went back in the house to gather their toiletries and towels, plus other incidentals they were taking in their backpacks. When everything was gathered and on the kitchen table, she packed them in the backpacks. Spike still had to put a few incidentals in his bag, but her part in the packing was done, so she ventured back to the garage.

The motorcycle was loaded, and Babe had to admit that it looked impressive. Surprisingly, there was still room for both of them on the bike.

The trip to Kansas City was pleasant with no rain and not much wind, ideal for riding. Babe had called Luke's house when she and Spike were a few miles from arriving and asked to talk to Ben. She told him they would be at his house soon. When they arrived, the four-year-old Ben was waiting on the front porch.

Spike guided the bike into the driveway and came to a stop in front of the garage door. Little Ben ran to them carrying a hammer. "Why are you carrying a hammer, Ben?"

"Well," replied Ben, "If you are going to fix the sliding door you might need it. I thought we could work on it now." His little face was hopeful.

Spike ruffled the little guy's hair and said, "We had better take our things in the house first and say hello to your mom and dad. You can help carry our things in. Oh, I almost forgot. Grandma brought you some chocolate chip cookies. We'll work on the patio door tomorrow."

"But, Grandpa, you didn't bring a suitcase. Did you forget your jammies?"

"Come here and I'll show you," responded Spike as he went to the saddlebags and opened one side. "This is like my suitcase. See, here are all the things I'll need for tomorrow. We have to go home the next day so I don't need much." Spike pulled out a plastic bag that held his toiletries and toothbrush. Then he reached in and got another bag that held a clean shirt, socks, and some underwear.

"I'll carry them for you, Grandpa. Can we fix the door the first thing tomorrow morning?" Evidently there would be no fooling around until the chores were done.

When Spike woke the next morning he got out of bed carefully so he wouldn't wake Babe. He headed out the bedroom door to the bathroom and almost stumbled over Ben sitting outside their closed bedroom door. "Good morning, Ben. Aren't you up a little early this morning?"

"I wanted to help you fix the patio door, and Mom said I couldn't wake you up, so I was waiting for you."

"Why don't we go down and get some breakfast and then

look at the problem door," suggested Spike. It was then he noticed that Ben had the hammer beside him on the floor. The boy rose from his sentry spot, picked up the hammer, and followed Spike downstairs.

It was a good breakfast of sausage and eggs, with good company. Babe had joined them in her robe for breakfast; and, when she had eaten, left the table to go back upstairs to take her shower. Ben had trouble finishing his breakfast and kept looking at Spike. He wanted to ask if Grandpa was finished eating yet, but his mom had said he had to let Grandpa finish his breakfast. When Ben got down off his chair and came over to stand by Spike, he figured he'd had enough coffee. "Guess we'd better get busy and fix that door. What do you think Ben?"

"Come on, Grandpa, let's go!" were the marching orders as Ben headed for the crippled patio door. Somehow the door had come off the track and seemed to be sprung. Spike worked at it and finally got it back in the track, but it still wanted to balk.

Spike sat back on his knees and took another look at the door. "I wish I'd brought my tools."

Little Ben was on his knees right beside his Grandpa. He watched as Spike pushed the door back and forth while shaking his head. "Grandpa," he said as he looked up at Spike, "the next time you come, why don't you put more tools in your motorcycle and leave your toothbrush and underwear at home."

It was always good to be with family, and when that family lived far and you rarely saw them, it was even more special. They had a good visit the rest of the day, and everyone had a ride on the motorcycle. The next morning Babe and Spike said their goodbyes and headed for home. Their trip north was beautiful with all the trees changing colors. They had been on the road only a short time when Babe leaned up and said in Spike's ear, "I enjoy this ride lots more on the bike than I ever did in the car."

It was about time for their second stop when they came through a little town with a small park. Spike pulled over. They got out their water bottles and were relaxing when Babe asked, "Spike, when do I get to drive the bike? There hasn't been much traffic the last few hours."

She could tell her question threw him for a loop because he started to sputter, then gave her his no-nonsense look and said forcefully, "There is no reason you need to drive. If it's an emergency, that's another story."

"We have a fifty-fifty marriage, which means we make joint decisions. I don't want to be just a Band-Aid for emergencies. I think we should take turns being boss since this is not the 1800s anymore. Have you heard women are equal now and that means we can drive, we can work outside the home, and we can vote!"

Boy, Spike thought, I really tripped her trigger! "Babe," he said in a more conciliatory tone, "I don't feel right riding behind while you drive. And there is no reason for you to drive when I can." Now that was said in a nice tone, he thought, and certainly she would understand. Then he noticed by her face that her defenses were going up, so he decided he'd better soften his stand even more. "When we get to our campsite why don't you drive the bike around the campground?"

Babe figured she had pushed his buttons about as far as she could about this, so she replied, "OK, you made that decision, so you are boss today. Tomorrow it is my turn, and I'm going to be boss all day! You will have to wait until the following day to be boss. OK?" He didn't answer, but they got back on the bike and headed north again.

When the pair arrived at their destination they drove around the camping area looking for the perfect place to pitch their tent. Babe wanted it close to the shower and restroom facility, and Spike wanted it close to the lake. They finally found the spot that suited them both and parked.

Babe pointed to a circular ring made of bricks and said, "What is that thing? It's looks like we could stumble over it." The ring of bricks surrounded a hole, and a heavy layer of sand about a foot wide edged the bricks.

"That's the firepit where we can cook. The grate we brought will fit over it," answered Spike.

Babe got an amused look and replied, "I'm glad you will be the one doing the cooking on that thing. I'll take my stove and microwave any day!"

Spike was busy hunting through his saddlebag. "Drat it! Where are they?"

"What are you looking for, Spike?"

"I'm trying to find my Birkenstocks. I know I packed them, and my feet are tired and hot after that long ride! Ah, here they are!" He took off his boots and socks and put on the sandals. He walked over to the nearest tree, sat down with his back against the trunk, wiggled his toes, and sighed with contentment.

"Spike," his wife said after they had rested a while, "it is almost dark. Don't we have to get things unpacked and the tent put up before dark?"

"I guess so. We'd better get at it." He walked over to the bike, changed back into his boots, and started unloading. "Find a nice, smooth place to pitch the tent, Babe. Just be sure there aren't any rocks or tree roots. Let's put it close to the firepit so we can enjoy the firelight from inside the tent; plus, a fire should keep any varmints away."

Babe looked around and then said, "Right here is a level place, and I don't see any obstructions. What do you think?" she asked as she pointed to a place beside the tree and fairly close to the firepit.

"Looks good to me," replied Spike, as he brought the tent over and laid it on the spot. He squared it off on the area and started to pound in stakes. Soon the tent was up, and Spike lit a fire in the pit. They finished unloading the bike, stowed everything in the tent, and rolled out the sleeping bags. The tent was just the right size for everything. If it rained during the night everything was safe inside the waterproof tent.

When dusk came, Spike and Babe sat by the tree and watched the sun go beneath the skyline, eating the sandwiches they had bought in town for their supper. Babe thought, this is everything Spike said it would be! It is so peaceful here.

"Spike, there doesn't seem to be any traffic around. I think I'll take the bike for a little spin."

"If you want to look around the park, I'll take you," answered Spike.

"No, I want to go by myself. If you're pulling your boss thing, I'll wait until tomorrow and drive all the way into town." She knew that would stop him in his tracks.

"OK, off you go; but be careful!" He followed her to the bike and was almost ready to help her get on. She gave him a replica of his own no-nonsense look, and he backed off. She started the motor, made the bike give a few loud vrooms to put him in his place, and took off down the dirt road. She got as far as the entry to the park and turned to go back to their campsite. This driving was fun, and she thought she was pretty good at it too! She slowed as she came to the turn to get to the campsite but must have misjudged her distance. Bang! She scraped against a tree.

Chapter 22

Babe stopped and dismounted. It was dusk, but she could see a wide scratch on the front fender. She knelt down, spit on her index finger and rubbed the scratch, hoping it was just dirt and would come off. No such luck. No amount of rubbing took it off or even made it less noticeable. She would just have to face the music. She remounted and headed for their campsite. Maybe if Spike didn't notice it tonight it would be better to tell him in the morning. After all, she would be boss tomorrow. She parked the bike and went over to Spike, who was sitting by the tree, and talked only about what a nice night it was.

Since it was getting late, Spike and Babe decided it was time to bed down for the night. "Put some more wood on the fire before we go to bed, Spike. If we leave the tent open we'll be able to see it from inside." Spike obligingly went to their small stash of wood and put more on the glowing embers.

"I'll take the sleeping bag closest to the door," said Spike. "You can have the one close to the side of the tent."

Babe crawled over to her assigned place, pulling her sleeping bag along. She arranged it and lay down on top. The temperature was still too warm to crawl inside of it. Spike lay down on his sleeping bag and sighed with contentment. What a great life this was. It was everything he had hoped it would be.

Babe was so tired she fell right to sleep. Spike twisted and turned, trying to get comfortable. He was tired and badly wanted to sleep but just couldn't find the right position. There seemed to be a rock under the floor of the tent. Drat it! He told that woman to find a place that was flat with no rocks or tree roots protruding. You would think she could at least have checked better than this. When twisting and turning didn't help he finally got up on his knees, pulled his sleeping bag over next to Babe's and lay down. There were no rocks here, thank goodness.

Babe woke and mumbled, "What is the matter with you? Why are you over here? Your spot was close to the door, and you have been flopping around like a windmill. Keep still so I can sleep!"

Spike was about to give her a piece of his mind about the dos and don'ts of finding the right place to pitch a tent, but he was too tired to go into that now. Then he realized tent placement might not be her strong suit, but she was still the right companion for him on a trip. He lay down, reached over and gave her a pat on her shoulder, and fell fast asleep.

The next thing Spike knew it was hard to breathe; he was coughing, and he heard Babe coughing too. He looked out the tent door. The wind had changed direction and was blowing smoke from the firepit directly into the tent. What more could keep him from his sleep?

Spike looked through the things in the tent until he found the percolator. He ran to the shower building and filled it with water. Hurrying back to the campsite he poured the contents on the fire. Ash and heavy smoke billowed out of the pit and into the tent until he had made more trips to the shower building. Thankfully the fire was finally out. Spike strode back to the tent where Babe was busy flapping her shirt around, trying to get the smoke out of the tent. She handed Spike his shirt, and they both flapped until the tent was as smoke-free as it could be.

The tent was finally clear enough so they could try to sleep. The weary couple crawled in and once again took their places on their sleeping bags. Spike grimaced as he glanced at his watch, which showed four in the morning. Babe thought he could at least move his sleeping bag back over beside the door and give her more room, but she was just too tired to approach the subject. She figured all's well that ends well.

The next morning was bright and beautiful. Who would have thought they had been up and down most of the night. In the wee hours before she went to sleep, Babe wondered how she could have fallen for Spike's glamorized version of this camping trip in the first place. Give her day trips from now on . . . but then she looked at the bright morning, and it canceled her negative thoughts. She still had to tell Spike about the tree that got in her way last night and show him the scratch.

Spike took out the old skillet, and he fried eggs for breakfast. Before Babe could confess to the scratch, Spike spoke up, trying to have an amiable tone in his voice.

"Babe, maybe for tonight we should move the tent to a level place without any rocks."

"I inspected the space like you told me, and it was free of any rocks or roots. Why? Did you feel some?"

"Well, comfort is a necessity when camping, you know," he said as he loosened the corner stake of the tent.

"I'll show you what I mean," he said as he stuck his hand under the tent. He felt around under the tent and then paused. He slowly brought out an object. "Oops," he said, and in his hand was one of his Birkenstocks.

"Doesn't look like a rock or a tree root to me," Babe commented and then considered she had said enough. She had the good sense to not mention that he hadn't told her to check for Birkenstocks.

Babe went for water in the percolator and made coffee. As they were enjoying the fresh coffee, she told Spike about her mishap and the scratch.

He laughed and leaned over to pull on her earlobe. "I saw the scratch this morning and wondered when you were going to confess. Don't worry, Babe, we don't sweat the little things. What is a little scratch when no one got hurt!"

They spent the rest of the day exploring the area and just sitting around their campsite enjoying the peace and quiet.

On the second night of their stay, the wind was picking up a little as they got their sleeping bags arranged inside the tent for the night. One more night of this would do her for this year for sure. But it had been quiet for the most part, and the scenery was beautiful; it was so peaceful there by the lake. She lay on her sleeping bag and listened to the wind in the trees above the tent. It was a soothing sound that was only interrupted by Spike's soft snoring. It didn't take long for her to fall asleep.

Babe woke thinking she had heard something strange. It sounded like something scratching at the tent. Could it be a tree branch? What if it was a bear or a wolf? With that thought she hopped out of her sleeping bag with all the grace and agility of a stampeding elephant. She lost all sense of direction and couldn't even think of where Spike was lying. Spike only added to the confusion by hollering, "Hey, hey, what's—hey . . . don't!"

Somehow Spike managed to find the flashlight just as Babe grabbed hold of him as if he were the only port in her storm. He moved the beam of the flashlight back and forward, but there was nothing in the tent. Then he heard the strange noise too. It wasn't just the wind in the trees.

"I'll go out and check," Spike said.

"You're not going anywhere without me, Spike. I don't want to stay in this tent by myself."

Spike unfastened the tent flap, and they both stepped outside. Babe kept a good hold on Spike's arm. "I think the noise was coming from that side of the tent," he said and pointed to the left. They took a few steps in that direction and then stopped as if they had hit a brick wall. Directly in front of them stood a tiny black animal the size of a small kitten. Only this black kitty had a white stripe down his back. It was a baby skunk.

"We have to get him away from here. But try not to scare him," Spike said. They stood there waiting for him to turn when they heard a different sound. Looking to their right they saw an adult skunk.

"Good grief! It must be the mama!" muttered Spike. They stood as still as statues, hoping the little guy would head for his mama and she would be so happy to see him that she would forget how to spray. They were standing just around the corner of the tent. Mama stood looking at them like she knew trouble when she saw it. She must have smelled food in the tent because she walked forward, spraying as she came, directly into the tent. Spike and Babe were standing

203

at the corner of the tent directly in her spray line. The smell was overwhelming. After doing her dirty deed, she slowly came out of the tent and walked off with baby following close behind. Spike turned to Babe and asked, "What do we do now? How do we get rid of this stink?" When preparing for this trip they had missed the chapter on how to deal with varmints found around camping sites.

"We'll just have to go take a shower and see if it comes off." Their backpacks were on the motorcycle, so they grabbed their toiletries and a change of clothes and headed for the showers. They scrubbed until their skin was red and almost raw, dressed in fresh clothes, and headed back to their tent. On their way they passed the garbage can and tossed in their skunk-sprayed clothes as unsalvageable.

"You still stink, Spike!"

"So do you!"

The soap had done little or no good to get rid of the smell, but at least they felt cleaner. They were twenty yards away from the tent when the odor hit their noses. The closer they got to the tent the worse it smelled. The tent and everything inside had been hit.

"What now, Grizzly Adams?" Babe asked sarcastically. "I think I've had about all the outdoor living I can take for this year!"

"It's only three o'clock in the morning. Do you suppose we could bring the sleeping bags out and get some sleep under that tree over there?" It was the only solution Spike could see to their problem. It didn't make sense to pack up and leave in the dark. They would just have to make do and decide in the morning.

"Those sleeping bags won't be fit to use," cautioned Babe.

"They probably reek more than we do. No, let's just use our backpacks over under that tree until morning."

Spike held Babe's backpack out to her, and she headed for the big tree. Spike grabbed his, followed her, and laid his backpack beside her under the tree. "See," he said hopefully, "this could be a whole lot worse!" He laid his head on his backpack and promptly went to sleep. Spike being able to fall asleep that fast after what they had gone through irritated Babe, but she didn't have words to phrase her rebuttal nicely. If he thought somehow the situation could have been worse, Babe didn't want to be anywhere near when worse happened.

Sleep did not come as easily for Babe. She kept wondering where the mama skunk was and if she was still mad. Would she come back in retaliation? She heard a faint buzzing around her face, but sleep finally came.

"Wake up, Babe!" It was Spike shaking her. She slowly tried to open her eyes, but the lids didn't seem to want to cooperate. Spike put his arm under her shoulder and helped her get to a sitting position. Her eyes still didn't want to open, but she worked at it until she could finally see Spike.

"Spike, what's wrong with your face? It's all puffy!"

"The same thing that's wrong with yours! I think we were a mosquito buffet during the night!"

"I think I brought some calamine lotion in my backpack. Just don't start to scratch the welts or they won't quit itching!" She found the bottle she was searching for, opened it, and applied the white liquid to Spike's and her own face and neck until they both looked like zombies.

"Well, what do we do next?" asked Babe.

"I'm going into town. There was a gas station with a store right at the edge of town. Maybe they have something that will kill this smell."

"I'm going with you, Spike. You aren't going to leave me alone out here with a riled skunk walking around!" They both climbed on the bike and headed for town. It was only a few miles to the station. It looked to be the only thing open this early in the morning.

They got off the bike and entered the store. As they entered a voice yelled, "Whoa, I can smell what you're after. Don't come in any further! Wait right there and I'll bring you what you need."

Spike and Babe froze where they were, wondering what the man meant. But they waited for him to come to them. When he came down the aisle toward them, he was holding a bottle. He just stood there and laughed. Then he said, "I could tell the minute you came to the door what you were after. You aren't the first victims to come in. You've run into our skunk. And it appears you spent the night outside with our bugs. It's good you had lotion for that. I'm sorry I don't have what you need to get rid of the skunk odor, but I'm out right now. However, this should work almost as well. It's the last bottle I have." He handed Spike the bottle.

"This says it's dog shampoo," said Spike.

"Yes, but it will work. Just use it as you would soap in the shower, but you will need to use it all. Just stay in the shower and wash until the bottle is empty. It will take the entire bottle to rid you of the smell. You aren't the worst case of skunk smell I've had come in, but you aren't the best either! Our skunk is famous around these parts. We call her Jezebel."

Spike gave the clerk a ten dollar bill. As the clerk brought the change back to them as they stood in the doorway, he added, "She is the scourge of that campground, and several around here have tried to hunt her down, but she's a crafty one. She seems bound and determined to halt the camping in this area."

Spike and Babe got back on their bike and headed for the campground. They planned to shower with the dog shampoo, load up what was salvageable, and then "get out of Dodge."

Chapter 23

Upon reaching their camping site, the couple headed straight to the showers. Spike parked the bike outside the shower entrance. The skunk must have done a superb job of scaring off campers, because it seemed they were the only people for miles around.

"We only have one bottle of the stuff," remarked Babe. "There is no one around. Why don't you come in the women's side where there are two stalls so we can pass the bottle back and forth."

Men just don't go into women's bathrooms, Spike thought. He stood there trying to come up with a better plan. Finally his desire to get clean overpowered him, and he realized there was no better quick and workable solution. So they headed for the showers with the blue sign that showed a figure wearing a skirt. They both had their towel and washcloth in hand as they started to undress.

"Do you suppose there is skunk odor on these clothes even if they weren't hit directly? We've worn them since we showered last night," said Babe.

"We should probably air them out while we're showering," answered Spike. "Where can we hang them in here?"

"They won't get aired out in here, Spike. Is there anywhere

could we hang them outside while we shower? There is no one around, and there is a little breeze today that would really help."

"We could just throw them over the bike. Oh, better yet, there is that big bush on the corner of the building. That might work better."

They looked around the area once again to make sure no one was around. It was decided they would disrobe; Spike would wrap himself in his towel and take all the clothes outside to hang them over the bush.

Spike picked up his towel, wishing the towel was a little larger, and wrapped it around his waist. He held the towel tight to him with one hand as he picked up his clothes with the other hand. Babe handed him her clothes as she climbed into one of the shower stalls and started the water.

Spike managed to onehandedly throw the clothes over the bush while tightly clutching his towel in place. After he placed them where each piece could get enough breeze, he headed back to the women's shower room and climbed into the second shower stall. He reached around the shower entrance and asked Babe to hand him the dog shampoo. They washed and scrubbed, passing the bottle back and forth, until there was no shampoo left.

Spike turned off the water and stood sniffing to see if there was any remnant of skunk smell left. I think I got it all, he thought to himself. He went to his shower entrance and called to Babe, "How do you smell, Babe?"

"It seems to be gone. I just hope we weren't so used to it that we can't pick up the scent if it's still with us!"

Spike wrapped his towel around his body again and headed for the door to retrieve their clothes. Just as he started out the door, a little voice piped up and said, "Mister, if your clothes blew away, they landed on that bush." Spike looked and saw a little boy pointing at the clothes that adorned the bush. In a dither, Spike turned and rushed back to the shower room.

Babe, standing there in her towel, had heard the whole thing. "What are we going to do now?" she asked frantically.

Spike was busy looking for a window or some way to see outside. There were a number of three-foot screen-covered vents along the top of the side walls. They were high enough so no one could look in but also too high to see out. Spike spotted a trash can and pulled it over so it was directly under one screen-covered vent. He climbed on top when Babe cried, "Be careful! Don't fall!"

That must have been the last straw for Spike, who was still trying to climb with one hand while tightly clutching his towel with the other. He turned toward Babe and gave her a withering look; and as he tried to get on top of the can, it began to wobble. Babe ran over to help steady it.

After much effort Spike managed somehow to get on top of the can to look out the window. Certainly if there was a little boy out there, his parents weren't too far away. The little boy was still there, looking at the door to the shower room. Spike called to him, "Hey, Fella. Go get your dad. I want to talk to him!"

The little guy just kept looking around trying to find where the voice was coming from. "I'm up here," Spike called, but the little guy just kept looking all around. Finally, Spike said with as much authority in his voice as a man wrapped in a towel could muster, "Go get your dad right away, please." The little boy recognized authority when he heard it and ran off.

It's hard for a man, draped in a towel, to have patience while standing on top of a trash can in a women's restroom, but Spike stayed the course. Finally he saw the little boy coming around the corner of the building tugging on the hand of a man.

"The man said I had to go get you right away," the little guy said, looking up at his dad who looked bewildered.

Spike called, "Sir, sir, I'm up here. I need your help!"

The man looked up and located where the voice was coming from, then looked at the restroom door with the blue sign signifying it was a women's restroom. Then he gave a huff, placed his hands on his hips, and yelled, "You pervert! What are you doing in there? You'd better get out of there before I call the cops!"

"Please, sir, I can explain if you'll just give me a chance! My wife is in here with me."

The guy leaned down to the boy and told him to go back and stay with his mother while he took care of some business. Then he looked up in the direction of Spike's voice and said in a stern voice, "This better be good, man."

"Those are our clothes on that bush. Would you get them for us, and when I'm dressed I'll tell you everything. I promise."

The man went to the bush and gathered all the clothes and came back to the door of the shower room. By that time Spike had crawled down from the garbage can and was standing there ready to grab the clothes. "Please, just wait out there until we get dressed, and I'll come out to talk with you." The man looked a little leery but waited while Spike hurriedly dressed. Babe was dressing just as fast and was ready to go outside with Spike.

As they left the building, Spike stuck his hand out to shake the other man's hand, identified himself, and introduced Babe.

Spike started with the late night visitor of the skunk. Then he told of their only bottle of anti-skunk dog shampoo. With only one bottle, there was no alternative other than using the same shower room. The deeper he got into his saga, the more the man laughed. He shook Spike's hand again and said, "My name is Pete Felter, and your story is just too crazy. You couldn't have made up something this crazy!"

Spike and Babe both thanked Mr. Felter profusely, and the man walked back to his family still laughing and shaking his head. As the man left, Spike called a warning about watching for Jezebel the skunk.

Spike and Babe rode back to their campsite. It was just as they had left it the night before, smell and all. They soon decided nothing could be salvaged and proceeded to take down the tent. They rolled it up with everything in it as best they could and hauled it to the dumpster beside the shower building.

Standing beside their motorcycle, Spike and Babe looked at each other and began to laugh. "Spike, now that we have had our first tent camping experience, please list all the things you think will convince me to make a second trip like this! I don't care how long that list is, I can give you my answer right now. No way! No amount of sweet talk will sway me or change my mind!"

Spike climbed on the motorcycle and still laughing, replied, "Before I make that list, I have to check my catalog to see if they have a skunk-proof tent."

Babe looked at him with chagrin and challenged, "Get rid of that catalog! Throw it in the firepit, and let the next poor sucker find it and convince his wife camping is all moonlight and roses!" Then she climbed on behind him and they left for home. She put her arms around his waist and gave him a little hug, adding, "All this will seem funny next year, and I'll be able to laugh at it, I hope."

Spike and Babe were traveling through a small town when they saw a small but neat looking motel. It had a row of eight rooms, painted a crisp white with shiny green shutters. Window boxes were packed with geraniums and some hanging green vines. The whole operation appeared to have had lots of tender, loving care.

"Maybe we should stop here while it's still light instead of going on," proposed Spike.

"Looks good to me," answered Babe, as Spike slowed the bike to turn in. "Looks like some grandmother is caring for it. A shower with soap for humans will feel good."

Spike parked the bike, noticing only one other car in the parking lot a short distance away. Sure enough, the desk was operated by a grandmotherly-type lady. There were even starched doilies under each lamp in front of the two windows.

When the paperwork was completed, Spike questioned her about a place to get something to eat.

"Oh, there's a little hamburger joint a block over, but it is carryout only. It isn't fancy, and the menu is simple, but you can be sure the food will be tasty and you won't be overcharged," she assured him. Spike left with a key to their assigned room, which the clerk had called the "blue room." Babe was still standing beside *Hog Wild*, her arms holding the meager necessities they had left.

Spike looked at the key before handing it to Babe and pointed to the room they had been assigned. As they were walking to the door, several cars drove in, and their drivers parked and headed for the office.

When the couple entered their room, Babe remarked, "Those newcomers arriving seem to all be about our age. Maybe it takes years of practice to recognize a good motel when you see one."

The room was clean and neat as a pin with curtains, bedspread, towels, and throw rugs, all in shades of blue. There were two easy chairs and a TV between the door and the bed. They each took a chair, and Babe turned on the TV, wondering what the weather would be like tomorrow. They didn't plan to leave too early because they would be traveling east and didn't want to have the sun directly in their eyes.

Spike looked toward Babe and spoke. "I'm getting kind of hungry. Why don't I go pick up something for us? The lady in the office said there was a takeout place close by."

"What are you hungry for?" questioned Babe.

"She said there wasn't much choice, but what they have is good; so why don't I surprise you," he answered.

"I'll take my shower while you're gone so you can take yours after we eat."

"Sounds good," he replied and went out the door.

Spike found the place with no trouble. For a small town there was a surprising number of people either waiting in line in front of the order window or eating at the picnic tables in front of the small building. When his turn came he told the girl at the window he was new in town and asked her what she would recommend.

"Most people order what we call 'the barnyard'," she answered. Noting the look on Spike's face, she smiled and told him, "It's a combination of bacon, pork sausage, and beef made into a big patty served on a bun. We like to think it's the best burger in the county. It comes with fries and a drink. I think you'll like it if you like burgers."

"I'll take two of those with fries and two Sprites if you have it."

"What do you want on those burgers?" she asked.

"Why don't you walk them through the whole garden," he replied with a smile.

She smiled and said, "You got it!" She asked his first name and said, "I'll call your name when your food is ready." Then she clipped his order on the ticket wheel for the kitchen behind her.

Spike looked around for a place to sit while he waited for his order. All the tables were taken, but a fellow sitting with a young family put his arm up and motioned for him to come and sit by them. Apparently that's how the seating worked in this small town.

Spike's order was ready before he got acquainted with the family at the table. Returning to his bike, he put the food in a saddlebag and took off for the motel. The sun had gone down while he was waiting in line, and the weather was pleasant for the short ride back to the motel. This bike is the best purchase I've ever made, he thought to himself for maybe the hundredth time.

When Spike reached the motel parking lot, he carefully removed the sacks from the saddlebag and headed for the door to their room. He juggled both sacks in one hand and tried the door knob. It was locked—of course. He forgot that Babe had said she was going to take a shower. He knocked lightly, thinking she would be out of the shower by now. He waited and then tapped a little harder on the door. Still no answer. She must have the TV on and can't hear me, he thought, and put a little more umph in his knock. Again he waited. Babe still didn't come to the door. Good grief! Had she fallen asleep? These burgers and fries were getting cold!

He knocked even harder this time and called, "Babe, let me in!" Still no answer. Raising his voice he made a fist, hit the door with gusto, and yelled, "Hey, Babe, it's me! Open the door!"

Suddenly the door was jerked open. Backlit from the light in a room overdone in yellow, stood a red-faced woman, gray hair dripping wet and wrapped in a towel.

With a tight grip on the towel she was holding around her, she blasted, "I am not your babe, buddy. If you have any sense at all you will hightail it out of here before I get dressed. I might not be as young as I once was, but I'm fast, and I'm mean when I get riled!"

"I . . . I'm . . . uh . . . trying—" Spike felt like a little boy caught in the cookie jar. He knew this poor woman was ticked and appeared to be ready, willing, and able to do what was needed to put him in his place, no holds barred!

"Lady, I'm really, really sorry. I must have the wrong room!"

"Really!" she replied sarcastically, raising her eyebrows.

"I was calling to my wife to open up because I have our supper and couldn't open the door, and I don't have my key," he stammered, tripping over his words. "It won't happen again!" Too late, he had remembered the number stamped on the door Babe had gone through before he left to get supper. He almost ran, looking for room number 6. He heard the door to what must be the yellow room slam behind him as he fled.

Spike got to room 6 and knocked lightly, just in case he might have the wrong room again. Babe opened the door and he sighed in relief. He came in and flopped down on the bed and informed her, "You'll never believe what just happened!

216

I can't be sure, but I think I just ran into Mrs. Crockett, my fourth-grade teacher. If it wasn't her, it was someone a whole lot like her."

The next morning Babe and a subdued Spike headed for home. He had been awake early and ready to make the drive. Babe figured he planned an early departure in an effort to avoid seeing the lady from the yellow room again. Babe looked at him as she was getting on the bike and, tongue in cheek, asked, "Are you going to tell Chuck about your meeting with your former school teacher?" Spike's answering glare told her the answer.

The rest of the ride home was peaceful and uneventful. They had had enough excitement during the last couple of days to last a lifetime.

Chapter 24

Spike came into the kitchen from the patio. "I think they'll get the mowing done without my advice. The condo lawn maintenance committee really chose a good outfit to do the mowing. I noticed that the guy on the blower following the mower blew all the junk out of the corners of the patio. He looks to be a kid, but he was tending to business. I appreciate that!"

"Spike," Babe said, "Martha called with an invitation. She and Jerry are planning a Halloween costume party at their house. Doesn't that sound like lots of fun?" She paused from wiping off the microwave and stood pondering. "What shall we dress up as?"

Spike tilted his chair back on its hind legs as he often did and thought for a few minutes. Then he offered, "Why don't we go as bikers? It's time everyone knows we have *Hog Wild* and that we intend to enjoy it!"

Babe added, "Martha and Jerry have known about our motorcycle since we got it and they can help us break the ice. I've always dreaded someone new finding out for the first time, but I think we can make this fun. Besides, we won't have to go to all the trouble of thinking up another costume. We'll put on our leathers and off we'll go."

Their group of close friends, eight couples, had been together for many years, starting when they had kids in the same grades in school. They usually met on Friday nights after basketball or football games. With tongue in cheek, they had called their group the "Friday Night Cultural Club." There wasn't much culture involved, but the group was a fun-loving bunch. Babe expected a crazy night.

Spike held up a hand and said, "Remember what Chuck said about bikers—how they are mostly a really good group and most of them ride as a hobby? Why don't we dress like the one percent of the bikers that are below the line, the ones you might call fast, mean, and dirty?"

Babe squealed, "Yes! Let's do it! We'll even arrive a little late, and Jerry can act really nervous about opening the door. Let's be so tough-looking we're scary!"

Spike grinned and added, "Right after we got *Hog Wild*, I thought about growing a handlebar mustache. Now I wish I had. It would have looked great about now with some gray speckled through it like my hair. Perfect for a party like this!" He straightened his back, put his hand under his chin, and struck a pose to help Babe imagine him with facial hair.

"Tomorrow I'll go down to the party store and see if I can find you a fake one. If they don't have a gray one, we'll use some Wite-Out to give it a few streaks of gray. This close to Halloween the party store should have lots of things, maybe things we haven't thought of!" She bowed her head forward a little, rubbing her hands together as though they had already pulled off a coup. They had two weeks to plan their transition from an ordinary couple to a couple of mean and downright dirty renegades, so there was no time to lose.

Spike was doing bookwork at the kitchen table the next

afternoon when Babe got home. She had gone shopping for groceries and said she would stop at the party store too. He smiled, remembering how excited she had been about the upcoming party. And her excitement was catching. He rubbed the ends of two fingers under his nose. He hadn't shaved that spot this morning, wondering how long it would take to really grow a handlebar mustache.

Babe came into the kitchen lugging several bags with the local grocery logo. She put them on the counter and turned to go back out.

"What's for supper, Babe?"

Not pausing, Babe ignored his question and said, "Wait until you see what I got! Just you wait and see! We are going to look so good at that party!" And with that she was out of sight, back in the garage. She reentered the kitchen with the biggest grin on her face, holding three bags from the party store straight out in front of her.

Intrigued by Babe's enthusiasm, Spike pushed his bookwork aside, rested his elbows on the table, and put his chin in his hands. "OK, surprise me."

Opening the first bag she pulled out a long fake mustache. "We can put a few streaks of gray in, but don't you like the way it will curl around your mouth? And look what is in the same package—little sideburns and two bushy eyebrows! And to add to your overall look, here's a fake ponytail for your helmet."

"That's great, Babe! I'm going to go try it on right now!"

Babe held up her hand to stop him from getting out of his chair. "First you have to see what else I got! Oh, Spike, you're going to love it!" she added enthusiastically.

Reaching in the second sack she pulled out what looked to

Spike to be two dog collars. Babe was grinning as though she had won a marathon.

"Babe, we don't even have a dog. What are we going to do with those things?"

Babe was busy taking tags off two black leather bands. Taking the smaller one, she worked open a buckle. Then she stretched it out and put the thing around her neck. It was like a small black belt with big silver spikes sticking out all around it. Handing him the other strip, which was a bigger replica of the first, she said, "Here, put it on!"

By this time Spike had the band around his neck and was struggling to buckle it. Babe came over to help, smiling all the while. Then she stood back and they looked at each other, admiring her purchase. The collars were like black chokers, with silver spikes a half inch long and spaced less than an inch apart. Spike noted that the sun coming in the west window of the kitchen made the spikes on the collars shine. He laughed as he said, "Be careful! Don't try to hug me or we'll kill each other!"

Spike started to sit down, but she again held up a hand and said, "There's more!" She reached into the last bag and pulled out a smaller sack. She opened it and held what appeared to be a stack of cardboard sheets covered with drawings, all in different colors.

"What are those?" Spike asked. Looking closer he saw the sheets were covered with pictures of skulls and crossbones, streaks of lightning, fire-eating dragons, lines of barbed wire, hearts with daggers through them, and one scantily dressed lady who appeared to be winking. There was also a good sized one of a heart with "Mother" written across it. All were different sizes. He gave Babe a puzzled look.

"Those, my wannabe bad biker, are fake tattoos to put up and down our arms and on our necks and even on your chest! You stick them on your skin, press down and then remove the clear tape backing." Babe took a sticker of a heart with a dagger sticking out of it and pressed it to the back of Spike's hand. Slowly she pulled away the backing; and, as easy as that, Spike had his first tattoo. "Don't worry," she said, "they will come off in the shower and will wash off by next Sunday. These things will morph us into two eye-catching bikers of the wildest kind! A biker and his babe going to a party!"

By this time Spike was picturing the whole getup in his mind, and he didn't think anything could improve the look they were after.

Babe spoke again, breaking his train of thought. "One more thing to tie it all together," she said, reaching into the last bag. She pulled out two fake leather vests. The larger one had a skull with crossbones on the back. The skull and crossbones' slight green tint looked like they would glow in the dark. She turned the smaller one to show the back where letters proclaimed, "Mama, I won't be home tonight!" also in glow paint. "Sleeveless vests are the thing to wear to show off all these tattoos! Let's hope it's warm that night, because we need to go bare armed to flaunt them as any bad biker would!"

Spike laughed so hard he had to sit down. He looked up at Babe, trying to speak through his laughter, and remarked, "When you set out to become a biker, you really work at it, don't you? I think you were born to be a biker!"

The next day Babe stopped at Second Chances to see if they had anything that would enhance their Halloween costumes. You never knew what you might find in that place. When she entered the store, she greeted May, who was standing behind the counter restocking her plastic bag supply. She spent nothing on packaging, since people brought their resale items in old grocery sacks, and May reused them to bag purchases going out of the store.

"Good to see you, Gwen . . . or is it Babe now? I can't keep track of all the changes you young people are making!"

Babe responded, "Call me anything but late for dinner! Isn't that what they used to say? I'm just looking to pass time today, May. Has anything good come in lately?"

May chuckled and answered, "Everything that comes in is good, Babe. It depends on what you're looking for or what you might need. Some of our best customers come in not knowing what they are looking for. Go have a look."

Babe walked through the kitchenware hoping to find another ten-inch pie plate. She had enough rhubarb in the freezer for two pies; one for Spike, and she would take the other to the Longs. They needed to keep track of that couple and keep encouraging them to come to church.

She found two ten-inch pie plates, and she decided to take both. You never knew when you would break one, and fifty cents apiece was a good price. With the pie plates under one arm, she walked to the women's clothing section. She had put the two navy blue dresses back the day she had to leave in a hurry with her leather pants. Maybe she would see if they were still there.

She thought she spotted one hanging on a rack in the other aisle and crossed over to check. Yes, it was one of the dresses she had planned to try on. She reached for it but drew back in a flash as she spotted a brown dress on a hanger tucked between the other dresses. Could it be? She grabbed the hanger and brought the dress out to get a better look. Yes! It was her brown dress. She looked at the price tag hanging from one sleeve. It said $6.98! She didn't know whether she felt miffed it was marked so low or to consider it a rebuy bargain. After all, she was buying the same dress twice! Take the dress and be thankful it's still here, she thought, as she headed for May at the checkout counter. In comparison to the price she paid originally, it was the best bargain she had ever come across anywhere.

* * *

Moving was always a hassle but a good hassle, Babe thought. It was challenging to find a place for all the things she and Spike decided to bring with them when they downsized into their condo. There was still a garage full of boxes to unpack. She wanted to unpack them slowly enough that everything could find a permanent place. Slow and easy wins the race, she thought. Spike had offered to help her, but men always unpacked quickly and worried about placing later.

Babe opened three boxes and set them up on the workbench in the garage. These were their good dishes and would go in the china cabinet in the dining room. She took each piece out of its newspaper wrapping and set it at the back of the bench. She loved these dishes. Some had been gifts at their wedding.

The doorbell rang, and Babe opened the door to see Kenny looking up at her with expectation. "Hi, Kenny! How are you today?"

Kenny had no time for conversational niceties. He headed straight to Spike's chair. If Spike had work to do, they had best be getting at it. "Can you come out and work, Spike?"

"Well, Kenny, there isn't any more work to do outside."

Kenny turned on the porch to look over the yard to be sure Spike knew what he was talking about. "Do you have any work in the house?"

"Well, Kenny, I have lots of work to do out in the garage, but I have been waiting to find a good worker to help me."

"Spike, don't you 'member how good I worked in the dirt?"

"Yes, I remember, Kenny. Do you have time to help me in the garage?"

"I have time to work, Spike!" And with that Kenny bypassed Spike and headed for the kitchen and the door into the garage.

"Wait, Kenny. You need to go tell your mom you're going to help me because we might not hear her call when we're inside the garage."

The little guy was off like a shot but stopped short when he got to the front door. He turned and instructed, "Spike, don't work until I come back, OK?"

"OK, Kenny, I won't." What a dear little fellow he was. Kenny was just the impetus Spike needed to empty those boxes. "I should have had a Kenny around back when I had all the yard work to do at the old house," thought Spike. I wouldn't have put anything off.

Chapter 25

"Babe, it's really nice outside, and there is going to be a beautiful sunset. Want to go for a little spin on *Hog Wild* while it's still light? We could go out to the park and sit on one of the picnic tables to watch the sun go down."

"Sounds good. Just let me get my sweater and put the rest of this cobbler in the fridge first."

Spike and Babe climbed on the bike and headed for the edge of town towards the park. It was a quiet night, and Spike kept the speed down so they could see what they were passing. They waved to Mrs. Kline, who was enjoying her porch as she did on many nice nights. They got to the outskirts of town and turned into the park. In the distance they saw lights, and every so often could hear the whack of a metal bat hitting a fastball. No one was playing horseshoes tonight and that area was dark. They found a picnic table where they could view the sunset, then parked the bike and sat on the table. They watched the view for a while and decided to head home before people at the ballgame started to leave. That way they would avoid lots of traffic.

Traffic picked up, though, as they headed towards the park entrance. The game must be over after all. They blended in with the cars headed into town going at a fairly slow pace.

Suddenly, Babe grabbed Spike's shoulders and yelled, "Spike, stop. Please stop."

Spike, hearing crisis mode in Babe's voice, pulled to the shoulder out of traffic. He turned to Babe and asked, "What's the matter? Are you sick?"

"No, I'm fine, but we have to go back right away."

"Did you drop something?"

"No, but there is a turtle crossing the road back there in all this traffic, and he's going to get run over if we don't go get him."

"Turtles don't get run over on the road, Babe. I've never seen a dead turtle on the road, have you? Besides, they have that hard shell to protect them."

He could tell by the *humph* she muttered that she wasn't buying that suggestion. That woman was just too softhearted. He waited for a chance and then turned the bike to head back. Sure enough, there was the turtle, about the size of a dessert plate, halfway across the highway. Babe hopped off the bike, waited for oncoming cars to pass, and ran to pick up the turtle. Holding the little guy, she again let a car pass; then she ran to the bike.

"Just put him down in that ditch and he'll be fine," reasoned Spike.

"No, I'm taking him home and away from this busy road." It was said in a way Spike knew was final and that no suggestions, no matter how reasonable, would change her mind. Spike took off slowly as they headed for home. He knew Babe was hanging on with only one arm while holding on to that blamed turtle with the other.

Spike drove into the driveway, dismounted, and helped his one-armed turtle protectress down from the bike. Babe was a

227

champion for anything living and breathing and always had been. When they had a mouse in their house, Spike had to trap it in the dead of night, plus get rid of the body before his wife got up.

"What do turtles eat, Spike?" asked Babe. When he didn't answer she said, "I think I'll try lettuce."

"You're not going to bring that thing in the house, are you? Just let him loose out there, and he'll find himself something to eat."

"I'm going to put him on the patio with some water and lettuce."

Spike rolled his eyes. It was dark so she couldn't see him; plus she was busy talking to the reptile, so there were no reprimands for the heartless ditching suggestions he had made. "With any luck at all," he thought, "that thing will run off during the night."

* * *

It was a Dirty Queens day, and they were meeting at Betty's house. Betty was a minor coconspirator because she knew something was going on, but not what. She liked to watch any intrigue in the group unfold. She was only told that Agnes and Mary Alice would arrive ten minutes after the specified arrival time of 2:00 that afternoon. No one was ever late, so ten minutes would work just fine and get everyone guessing. Betty just nodded and then asked, "Should I leave the windows and doors open?" Agnes just nodded in the affirmative and the stage was set.

Tess and Bess arrived first and parked in the driveway with Sissy close behind. Everyone was always sure to leave a space in the driveway for Sissy, no matter where they were playing on a particular day. She hated parking on the street.

Bert always tried to be the last one to let Lettie off to make sure everyone noticed his '57 Chevy. When he picked Lettie up he always asked her what the others had said about the car. None of the card players paid much attention to Bert and his car anymore, but Lettie always made up something nice that someone had supposedly said so he would feel good. She considered it as making her husband happy rather than telling a lie. Babe drove up just as Bert was turning around at the corner to make one more pass by Betty's house. She knew she was a minute or so behind schedule, so she hurried with Lettie to the door.

Betty welcomed the ladies as they entered. When Babe came in she looked around and noticed that Agnes and Mary Alice weren't there yet. Seeing Betty standing alone, she quietly asked where the missing two were. Betty just looked her in the eye, raised her eyebrows, and patted Babe on the shoulder. "Aha! Something is up," Babe thought, so she said no more. Those two were never late, and it was two minutes past the arrival deadline when she sat down. Babe patiently waited for the other shoe to drop.

The next minute there was loud honking coming from the driveway and what sounded like a motorcycle being revved up. Babe knew immediately what and who it was, but the other five were shocked off their chairs and were at the windows in a flash.

"Why, that's Agnes and Mary Alice," said Tess.

"What in the world are they riding on?" asked Bess.

"Heaven help us," Sissy said. "Agnes is going to fall off that thing if she isn't careful!" She looked a little closer and added,

"I think it's a big tricycle . . . no, that's a motorcycle. If they plan to get down, I hope the neighbors aren't watching! Look! They have skirts on!" and she turned away to avoid seeing what she was afraid the neighbors might see.

By that time Agnes and Mary Alice were at the door and Betty was welcoming them. They entered, and Babe gave each a hug as they came in the room, whispering, "You go, girl!" The room went quiet, but Sissy was in high fiddle. Her hands were covering her mouth, and her eyes were wide! She was staring at the two riders as if she was at a loss for words, which was very rare for Sissy.

Agnes, with her usual smile, announced, "We thought we'd ride over to the card game today and show you what we bought. We were in Sturgis, South Dakota two weeks ago at a motorcycle rally to see what kind we wanted. Life is too short to waste, and this is what we want to do!"

Sissy found her tongue and muttered, "Don't you think you're a little old to go riding around on one of those things? Plus, how did you talk Mary Alice into doing this with you?"

The normally quiet, soft-spoken Mary Alice, who had held her tongue so many times when she wanted to speak her mind, raised her chin a little and spoke out. "I am so glad Agnes asked me to drive the bike. I've wanted to take chances in my life ever since I was too shy to take the lead in the Community Days operetta. I decided after that I was going to do something out of the ordinary; and, lo and behold, she asked if I wanted to learn to drive her machine."

Sissy wasn't finished trying to talk sense into them. "Look at your skirts. Seeing you two climbing off and on that machine is probably more than this town can take. It just isn't decent to take the chance of letting your underwear show in public!"

Agnes gave Mary Alice a look and motioned, and the two went to the side of the room as the other six watched in fascination. "Let's show 'em, Mary Alice!" Agnes was a little stooped with age, but Mary Alice was standing straight with her nose a little high in defiance. They were standing side by side in their matching calf-length skirts. Then, in unison, they both stretched their outside leg sideways. As they stood there with hands on their hips, it was plain to see that the full skirts were stitched up the middle, making them pants. Then they put their legs back together and were wearing skirts again. They looked at each other, laughed, and spread their legs again. "They are called culottes and are as modest as anything!" explained Agnes.

"Oh," muttered Sissy, "I'm so relieved! I was so afraid people would start asking me about you riding around in skirts. It's bad enough to be seen on a machine like that, but it adds insult to injury if they think you are riding in skirts." Babe just pretended she hadn't heard.

Everyone settled down, and the card game began. There were lots of questions about the bike, and Tess and Bess quietly asked if they could have a ride sometime. Agnes told them of course, but they would have to go one at a time.

With a touch of sarcasm, Sissy asked, "And whose skirts are you two going to borrow?"

The twins both turned at once; and having seen Mary Alice stand up to Sissy, answered in unison, "We have jeans at home we wear when we're doing our housework!" That more or less satisfied Sissy, who was mentally thankful they just wore them inside their house.

To depart from what seemed to be a sensitive subject, Mary Alice asked Babe how her turtle was doing.

"He seems to like it in our yard because he stays around," answered Babe.

The afternoon progressed, and Babe thought the conversation seemed more uninhibited than usual. The group seemed to forget that age was considered by some to be limiting and had progressed to looking forward to new experiences.

Betty had been quiet up until now. When there was a lull in the conversation, she ventured, "My nephew has a motor scooter. If he will let me borrow it, can I ride with you sometime?" Agnes was quick to say yes, they would be happy to have her ride along.

Play continued, and suddenly, when everyone was quiet, Lettie commented, "Did you hear what Ann Lewis said she saw?" All eyes turned toward the speaker, and it was so quiet you could hear a pin drop. No one wanted to miss this! Ann was one of the biggest gossips in town, and even if you condemned gossiping, it was hard not to listen to what Ann said. She seemed to know everything going on in town.

Lettie, unaccustomed to being in the limelight, cleared her throat and began. "Ann said the other night her son brought her home from taking her out for supper. She says they were driving down South Street, and the sun was just going down. You're never going to believe this, but Ann says it's true. You will never guess what they saw!"

By this time she had her audience's full attention, and she continued in a softer voice as if she was going to tell something indelicate. "She said it was hard to tell what was coming down the sidewalk in the dark, but when it got closer she saw that it was a man in a wheelchair. But the strangest part was that there was a lady sitting on his lap, and she was wearing some kind of hat that covered her whole head and face."

At this point there were several loud intakes of breath and one face that blushed bright red. But everyone was so enthralled by what they were hearing that no one noticed the blushing face. Lettie continued, "It was one of those electric wheelchairs that runs by itself, and they just seemed to be riding along talking. Ann said it was too dark to see who it was. Don't you wonder who in the world would ride around like that—out where every Tom, Dick, and Harry in town could see them? Ann said she must be a floozy!" They all professed to be anti-gossip, so no one commented further about the wheelchair or the proposed floozy, but it was on everyone's mind. They just hoped Lettie would keep them up to date without them having to ask.

The card game ended, and after everyone had their dessert and coffee, Agnes brought up giving motorcycle rides to any and all who would like to try it. It was arranged that Mary Alice would give rides to Tess and Bess the next afternoon. Lettie had to talk it over with Bert first, and Betty decided she wouldn't go for a ride but was going to call her nephew about the motor scooter when she got home.

Babe was encouraging all of them to try it. She suggested that Tess and Bess come over to her house the next day. Mary Alice lived fairly close, and while she gave one twin a ride, Babe would visit with the other on her porch.

Everyone turned to Sissy and wondered if she was going for a ride. Sissy hesitated and then said, "I've been thinking I need to exercise more and I might get a bicycle. I know I would be more comfortable that way. I'm not into this motorized business. But I might follow you on my bicycle when you ride."

"Oh, yes, you can follow right behind Betty on her motor

scooter," suggested Agnes. "We aren't going to go fast because we want to see the scenery. You know, maybe we should start a riding club!"

This is going to be quite a parade, thought Babe to herself as they all departed for home.

Chapter 26

When Babe got home, Kenny was in the backyard sitting on the ground by the turtle. Spike was sitting on the patio thinking, "If I play my cards right, I may find a home for this turtle."

Babe came out on the patio and took a chair next to Spike. "You really have a nice turtle, Babe," said Kenny. "My Mom says I can't have a pet because she's 'lergic to 'em." I really like your turtle, Babe. What's his name?"

"I haven't given him a name, Kenny. What do you think his name should be?"

Spike entered into the conversation. "How about *Tortuga*? That is Spanish for turtle."

Kenny looked at Spike in dismay and replied, "I don't think Torgoos is a good name for a turtle, Spike. Why don't you just call him Gus?"

Spike thought for a moment and then asked, "Kenny, do you think your Mom would let you have a turtle in your backyard?" Then he glanced at Babe sitting beside him. She nodded in agreement.

"Do you mean this turtle?" he asked incredulously, pointing at the turtle. "This Gus, in my own backyard? Really, Spike?" His eyes lit up, and he turned to Babe and asked, "Would you let me take Gus to live at my house, Babe?"

Babe just nodded, adding, "But you would have to ask your mom first. Why don't you and Spike go over and talk to your mom?"

Kenny grabbed Spike's hand and pulled him out of his chair. They headed down the street as fast as Kenny could pull Spike. On the way, Spike said, "You know, Kenny, if you have the turtle in your backyard, he may want to run away."

"But I would be good to him, Spike, and not hurt him or anything. I would feed him and take care of him. Why would he want to run away?"

"Well, he's wild you know, and sometimes wild things don't like to be in one place all the time. It doesn't mean he doesn't like you or that he's afraid. He's wild and wants to explore. I just want you to know what could happen so you won't feel bad if it does."

Kenny and Spike reached the Welch house, and Kenny entered, yelling at the top of his voice for his mom. Spike waited on the doorstep. Mrs. Welch came running out of the kitchen wondering what could have happened. When she saw Spike she put her hand over her mouth and grabbed Kenny's shoulder, fearing that Kenny was somehow in trouble.

Spike spoke up right away, but she couldn't hear him because Kenny was talking as loud and as fast as he could, telling her about this new pet. Mrs. Welch motioned for Spike to come in and then tried to quiet Kenny. "Slow down, Kenny, so we can understand you," she said.

Kenny obediently stopped, took a breath, and said, "Mom, are you 'lergic to turtles?"

Mrs. Welch looked from Kenny to Spike in puzzlement. "I don't understand," she said.

Spike opened his mouth to explain, but Kenny was way

ahead of him. "Babe has a pet turtle, and she said I could have it, but you have to say it's alright before I can bring Gus home. Please, Mom! Please?"

When Spike could get a word in edgeways, he explained how Babe had rescued the turtle. Then he said he had told Kenny he could have it if she said it was OK.

"I don't know anything about caring for turtles, Mr. Miller, but I suppose I could learn. Kenny has wanted a pet for so long, and I'm terribly allergic to pet dander. This would be the answer if you're sure it would be alright with Mrs. Miller. Kenny said it is her pet."

That was all Kenny needed. He took off toward the Miller's condo, not even waiting for Spike. He reached the front porch and pounded on the front door until Babe opened. "Mom said I could bring the turtle home if it's still OK with you, Babe," he pleaded hopefully. "Can I take Gus home with me, please, Babe?"

Babe barely started a nod of approval when Kenny ran through the kitchen and out the back door. He skidded to a stop when he located the turtle. He knelt down on the grass and cradled the turtle in his little hands. "Mom said you could come live in our yard, Gus. You get to come home with me, and I'm going to take care of you real good. Please don't get wild and run away, Gus." With that he gave the unlikely pet a little hug and carefully walked back to the house. "I would stay and talk to you, Babe, but I have to take Gus home to show him where he's going to live. Do you want to kiss him goodbye?"

Babe struggled to keep a straight face and then said, "No, I think Gus is anxious to get to his new home. So I'll just wave goodbye to him." As she waved, Kenny, carrying his precious cargo, walked carefully past her and out to the sidewalk where he walked slowly toward home. He was busy explaining to Gus just how good he was going to take care of him as he passed Spike coming in the door. What looked so strange to Babe was that the turtle, nestled in Kenny's hands, was looking up at the boy as if he was listening to every word.

* * *

The next day dawned bright and sunny, and Babe was looking forward to watching Tess and Bess try something new. They showed up at her door at the designated time dressed in their jeans topped with long blouses. Babe figured they might do their housework in jeans, but she would wager good money they had never worn them outside of the house before today. The two opened their car doors and looked both ways; and, seeing no one coming, walked as fast as two ladies in their eighties could manage, straight toward the porch.

Mary Alice, driving the *Tri Glide*, arrived with Agnes in the passenger seat. Agnes climbed off and went to join the watching crew. Tess, first of the twins as always, ran to the machine, and Mary Alice showed her how to get on the passenger seat. They both waved at those on the porch and then slowly started down the street.

Agnes shook her head and confided, "Mary Alice is going to have to drive a little faster or I'll have to have a talk with her. She just goes too slow!"

Less than two minutes later the motorcycle came back down the street. Mary Alice parked in the driveway and got off to help a pale Tess climb off and walk to the porch. Mary Alice looked at the surprised group and said, "She got car sick . . .

or, I mean motorcycle sick, and wanted to come right back."

Babe pulled a chair over to Tess, who sat down, leaned forward, and put her head in her hands. "Would you like something to drink?" asked Babe.

"Oh, no," answered Tess. "I just want to sit here quietly."

Mary Alice looked at Bess and said, "Well, are you ready to try it now?"

Bess was quick with her answer saying, "No, if she got sick I'm sure I would get sick too! I'd better not try it." They all sat on the porch, and Babe served them lemonade, except for Tess who couldn't face lemonade yet.

* * *

Martha and Jerry's Halloween party was the next day, and Spike and Babe had lots to do. Excitement had built up ever since they began planning. In Babe's mind it was about equal to her surprise fifth birthday party, which had always been her benchmark for party excitement. No party had measured up to it until now. Martha and Jerry were in on the surprise, so phone calls had gone back and forth all week. Martha had wanted to see the paraphernalia they were going to wear, but that's where Babe drew the line. No, they wanted to walk in and surprise the entire group. Was it normal for adults to have this much fun with a costume party?

Both Spike and Babe woke early, anticipating the fun day ahead. Babe called it their pre-party day. They each had new boots with buckled straps over the arches—just what real motorcyclists wore, according to Chuck. But they looked too new. Spike was sure the renegades they wanted to portray would never be seen in new boots. He looked down at his new boots, contemplating how he could age them effectively. He'd worn them since he got them; he had even rubbed them on the front step and kicked at a tree or two, but they still looked new.

Ah, he thought of something to try. He went to the garage; and, taking off one of his boots, walked over to his workbench. He opened the vise attached to the bench and placed the heel of the boot between the jaws with the toe pointing towards the ceiling. As he was tightening the vise, Babe walked into the garage to see what he was doing.

Spike reached for the hammer and began beating the toe of the boot without loosening the grip of the vise. He slammed the hammer this way and that, giving it all he had! He paused and stood back to gaze at the shoe. The boot looked like he had hit it with a hammer, but it did not look worn. Babe approached to take a look. After all, she also had a pair of new boots that would need the same treatment.

Spike spoke a little dejectedly. "They don't look like they have been worn for years . . . like I want them to."

Babe stood looking at the poor, hammered boot and offered, "Why don't you try the sander?"

Spike reached under the bench, took out his sander, and plugged it in. Holding it above the boot he lowered it suddenly, touching the toe. He drew it back and surveyed it as Babe stepped forward to get a look.

"That looks better, Spike. Try going all over the front of the boot, and do the same to the other one." She suddenly thought of all the times she had polished and buffed shoes for the family to get them to look newer or at least neater. Their world had surely turned upside down!

Spike took the battered boot out of the vise and put his

other boot in its place. Babe handed him the hammer for the preliminary treatment. Spike raised it high and brought it down again with force. Finishing that stage of the process, he got his sander ready and gave the boot the same buffing. Then Babe's new pair got the same treatment.

Finally, all four boots had received equal distressing. They stood side by side on the workbench. Looking askance at Babe, Spike said, "I guess they are OK, but they still really don't look exactly how I want them to look."

Babe patted him on the back and said, "Let's go in and have a sandwich for supper. We've been at this all day. The boots will look better to you tomorrow."

When supper was finished, Spike pushed his chair back from the table and clasped his hands behind his head.

Babe looked out the window and noted the sun had set. "Spike, let's go for a bike ride after I get this cleared away." She had come up with an idea but didn't know if it would work. "Go get the bike ready and I'll come out shortly."

Spike was straddling the bike when Babe came out through the front door. She was carrying two long strands of yellow nylon rope and both pairs of boots. She centered each strand of rope around her waist, letting four long strips dangle. Then, to Spike's surprise, she tightly fastened the end of each rope under the tied laces of a boot until she had anchored all four.

"What in the world are you up to?" barked Spike.

She looked up at her husband, grinned, and said, "You had your go at making these boots look used, and now it's my turn. Your job is to drive us around several streets, hopefully where all the residents are gone or busy in their backyards! We are going to drag these boots around town until they look well worn!"

Spike was laughing so hard he could hardly start *Hog Wild*. He thought they had not had this much fun for a long, long time. Babe placed the boots on the ground carefully, each at a slightly different distance behind where she would sit on the motorcycle with the ropes around her waist. She climbed onto her seat, glancing over her shoulder to see that the boots still lay, each with plenty of bouncing room, behind her.

"OK, Spike, let's go! And don't spare the horses!" she quipped.

Shaking his head, Spike started the engine and took off slowly down the street as Babe glanced behind her. The boots bumped and bounced around, but the knots held as the motorcycle gained speed. What would they say if someone asked them what they were doing!

"I think it's working!" Babe shouted in Spike's ear. They went down the quiet streets at a leisurely pace; fast enough to keep the boots bouncing but not so fast that the cycle made lots of noise. Up and down they went until Babe yelled in Spike's ear, "Let's stop and see if it's working the way I hoped it would."

Spike pulled over into a park and Babe got off. She picked up one of the boots, carefully inspecting the results.

"Spike, it worked! Look at this! They look like we've been wearing them for years!" She picked up the now dirty, distressed boots in her arms and climbed back on the motorcycle, as they headed for home.

Chapter 27

The next morning Spike and Babe got out of bed early. It was the day of the party, and they had no idea how long it would take them to tattoo each other. They were concerned that someone would come for a visit while they were practicing their new art form. They decided if someone came to the door they would hide and not answer. They would answer the phone only if the caller ID said it was someone they didn't think would subsequently show up at their house. They were going underground for the day, and they burst into laughter whenever their eyes met.

With breakfast finished, Babe went to get her purchases. She had high hopes for their transformation from an ordinary couple to a big, bad motorcycle gang of two. Spike went to find the Wite-Out left over from typewriter days to age his fake mustache, sideburns, and eyebrows so they would match his hair. He carefully selected random strands of the artificial hair and applied the correction fluid. "It's looking good, Babe," he assured her as he put the lid back on the little bottle.

Babe was busy putting their new vests in the dryer to get out the fold lines. She watched them closely, because she didn't know how much heat the cheap, fake leather vests could take. A week earlier she had hung two new red bandana handkerchiefs outside in the sun on the patio trellis, hoping they would fade and look worn. The last thing this couple wanted was to look like they were new bikers.

Applying the tattoos proved harder than it first seemed. How close should they put them? How should the colors mix? Should they apply them by subject or by color? Nevertheless, they began applying them wherever they seemed to fit. Babe would choose one she liked and Spike would apply it. Then they reversed the roles, laughing all the time.

"Think about how this would hurt if someone was putting real tattoos on with needles," Babe said to Spike. Then she picked up several strips of what represented barbed wire and held them up to Spike's upper arm. "What do you think?" she asked. Shall I put it on both arms or just the one?

"Both, of course," replied Spike, "It's the real me!"

They applied the stickers, discussing back and forth about what should go where. Spike thought the scantily clad, winking lady should go on his upper chest, where his vest wouldn't spoil the effect, and it would still be below the spiked choker around his neck.

"She looks like she has a funny look on her face," remarked Spike as he looked in the mirror.

"She should," countered Babe, "going out in public with those short shorts!"

Babe applied a fake diamond on each nostril to look as if they were pierced. A row of small skull and crossbones went below her spiked choker. Then she reached in her pocket and brought out two long, dangling skull and crossbone earrings.

Still not completely pleased with the effect, Babe brought out black mascara and applied it liberally. Going back to the table where the fake tattoo materials were, she looked through what was left of the stick-on tattoos and smiled as she found what she wanted.

"Here, Spike, put this right here." She pointed to the outside corner of one eye. Carefully, his big fingers stuck it where she pointed. He stepped back to admire the addition of a big, black tear falling from the corner of her eye.

Next they put on their leather pants and the fake leather vests. Underneath the vest, Spike was going shirtless, and Babe had chosen a sleeveless blouse. She had let her white hair go frizzy after her shower that morning so it stuck out every which way. The worn and dirty boots came last. They stood together before the bathroom mirror to critique the results, and they hardly recognized themselves. Staring back at them were two of the most hard-core bikers they had ever imagined. Even after working on the persona for weeks, they were surprised at the effect they achieved.

Laughing loudly, Spike said, "Babe, it's perfect! It's exactly the way I thought it should be!"

Babe said, "Oh, I forgot," as she left the room. Spike heard the patio door open and then close. Soon Babe was back at the bathroom mirror, handing him a faded red bandana.

"What should I do with this?" he asked.

"Fold it in a triangle, and fold in the pointed end to make a band," Babe said as she demonstrated with the one she was holding. Having finished, she laid the folded cloth over her forehead and reached around to tie the ends in place behind her head of frizzy white hair. "I think they wear them under their helmets to keep the sweat from running into their eyes," she offered, and then added, "Don't forget to attach the ponytail to your helmet."

Spike slapped his forehead and headed for the utility room.

When he returned he was carrying his helmet and the fake ponytail. He handed them to Babe and asked, "How does this attach?" She took the thick, black hank of hair and showed him the little tab at the top. Taking a small piece of duct tape she attached the hair to the inside of the back of the helmet. Spike donned the helmet and turned to show Babe the effect. The blue helmet seemed to accent the black hair as it hung there in all its glory.

"Perfect!" she pronounced. "Just perfect!"

The supper party started at six o'clock that evening. They had arranged with Martha and Jerry to make their loud entrance a little before seven when everyone had arrived and the steaks were ready to go on the grill. Their friends seemed almost as excited about the new Harold and Gwen as Spike and Babe were. Martha had confided to Babe she thought Jerry was getting motorcycle fever.

The weather was nice for a patio party. Spike and Babe waited restlessly at home for their seven o'clock appearance time. They had turned off all the lights so no one would stop by. They kept grinning at each other as they waited, dressed in their bad biker gear. Babe suddenly noticed that Spike had somehow taped a small chicken bone to each of his ears. From a distance it looked like he had pierced ears! It just kept getting better!

Babe wondered whether their friends had heard rumors of their motorcycle purchase. This group socialized with each other mostly in the fall and winter months. They saw little of each other in the summer, since everyone usually spent those months going on vacation, visiting their children, or attending extended family reunions. Nothing was ever mentioned about the bike when they happened to meet at church or somewhere else. It was hard to tell who had heard of the purchase and who hadn't. It was surprising sometimes how gossip either missed some people or was misconstrued by the time word got around that the what or the who was no longer identifiable. Either way, Spike and Babe felt that the fewer of the group members to have already gotten wind of *Hog Wild*, the better. They would know for sure tonight.

Babe noted, "Lorraine will be there for sure, and I don't think she knows yet." Lorraine was the group's alarm system. She screamed at good news and bad, at spiders, when she met someone new or someone she hadn't seen for some time, and especially when she got scared. Lorraine would definitely alert the others.

Then there was Marge, who followed every style trend that came along. Marge was a free spirit with a sense of daring. Spike said they should start a pool, wagering on whether Marge would get biker boots or a helmet first.

Al had jokingly threatened his wife for years that he would get a tattoo, more to hear her repeat her anti-tattoo litany than anything else. They looked forward to hearing what he had to say when he spotted Spike's tattoos.

Then there was Lee; who, upon hearing or seeing something new, always remarked, "Why didn't I think of that!" All of them were nice folks and great friends. Babe hoped the group would have as much fun with this as they were having.

Spike pointed to the clock on the stove and said, "Blast off time, Babe. It will take us ten minutes to get to the alley." Babe went to the fridge and retrieved the large bowl of fresh fruit she had offered to furnish for the party. She put the bowl in a grocery sack and headed for the garage. They got on the bike and took off down the block at a quiet pace, as Babe balanced the fruit salad with one hand and hung on to Spike with the other. The plan was to noise things up as they got closer to Jerry's backyard where their friends were gathered.

Spike and Babe came to a corner, and Spike slowed to a crawl. "OK, here we go, Babe!" He roared the motor. "Let's scare the Billy gee whiz out of that bunch!"

Spike took off like a shot with the bike making all kinds of noise. Babe wondered how Spike knew how to make that much racket. She knew they were going too fast, but it was only a block. Spike had told her he planned to turn down the alley so the backyard party would hear them coming.

As they were about to make a speedy turn into that alley, lights flashed and sirens went off. It was a police car.

Spike knew the night patrol officer, Jake Kelly, and figured Martha or Jerry had probably told Jake to get in on the hilarity by activating the patrol car lights and siren at the right moment. So Spike kept going, not even slowing down.

The action was getting a bigger response than anyone might have planned. The cycle was whooping and vrooming along, followed by the siren and flashing lights of the patrol car. All along the alley lights were going on in houses, and yard lights were being turned on. Several dogs started barking, which added to the cacophony.

The patrol car sped up and passed the cycle in the narrow alley. "Whoa, Jake!" thought Spike. Jake was taking some dangerous chances here! The patrol car went ahead of the cycle and pulled in front at an angle, causing Spike to hit the brakes in a hurry! Babe was using only one arm for a death grip on Spike's waist and one arm to clutch the sack with the fruit salad. They were going at high speed; and if she hadn't had such a grip on Spike, his sudden braking would

248

have catapulted her over his head onto the patrol car. In her efforts to save herself, Babe let go of the fruit salad. When the bike stopped suddenly, the salad went flying. It flew out of the sack, up and over Spike, and made a three-point landing on the hood of the squad car. It was surprising how much car three quarts of strawberries, kiwi, pineapple, and blueberries could cover.

Spike was a little perplexed. Jake must be mixed up. They weren't behind Martha and Jerry's house yet. It was too early for the big climax!

The patrol car door flew open, and Jake jumped out with his gun drawn. Spike thought a drawn gun was a nice addition he wouldn't have thought of. He hoped those at the party were close enough to see all this action. If he figured right, Jerry's backyard must still be about two houses down.

Spike had his foot out to hold up the bike and had left the motor on. Babe was still hanging on for dear life, wondering what was coming next. She had no idea Spike had gone to such lengths to make their entrance to the party this spectacular. Even a gun, for goodness sake! He should have told her so she could have had a better grip on the fruit salad.

Jake got within ten feet of the bike and stopped, still pointing the gun at them. "Turn that thing off and face me, and I mean right now!" he shouted.

Spike turned off the machine, taking off his helmet and tucking it under his arm, and said jovially, "Hi, Jake. Your appearance really gave our entrance to the party a big impact. Thanks, buddy!"

"I don't know what you think you're up to, son, but you are trying to fool the wrong guy!"

Chapter 28

Norman Winter came through his back gate, walked up to Jake, and asked, "What's happening, Jake?"

"We have some funny folks here trying to pull something, Norm. Will you help me with this, please?" With that, Jake pulled a pair of handcuffs off his belt and handed them to Norm. "Put them on the guy. Have him put his hands behind his back." Small towns didn't bother with deputizing.

Spike was getting a little alarmed. Surely this wasn't part of their entrance to the party. There must be some mix-up.

Norm walked over to Spike and told him to put his hands behind his back. Spike, his face nearly masked by the handlebar mustache, bushy eyebrows, and long sideburns, looked at him and said, "Norm, it's me, Harold Miller!"

Norm frowned and said, "Sure, and I'm the Pope!"

Spike turned towards Jake and said, "Jake, it's me, Harold. We're on our way to a costume party at Jerry's."

Jake responded, "Son, never try to pull one like that in a small town where everyone knows everyone else. Now get in the squad car!" He roughly pushed Spike into the back seat, got something out of the front seat, and returned to where Babe was standing.

Looking at her in the dim light, he spoke, "I don't know

what you two are trying to pull, but you failed and you're both going to jail!" He had her put her arms behind her. Jake's reprimand continued. "It was a quiet night around this town before you two started your mischief!" With that he slapped handcuffs on her; and, none too gently, put her in the backseat with Spike. The two bad bikers just stared at each other, both of them two astonished to utter a word.

None of this was done quietly, so the partygoers two houses down had heard it after all. Jerry must have realized what was happening and enlightened the rest of the party. The entire group of partiers gathered along the back fence, everyone leaning over so they wouldn't miss a thing. As the squad car passed with the handcuffed culprits in the back seat, the assembled party goers raised their arms in a salute, yelling, "Lock 'em up, lock 'em up" in unison as they waved at the prisoners.

The entire party loaded into cars and followed the renegades to the city jail. After Spike removed his mustache and showed his identification, they were released into the custody of their friends. Even Jake had to laugh at the irony of it all. He returned to his nightly rounds of the town, and the party relocated to Jerry's backyard. By that time both Spike and Babe could see the humor in the entire scenario. What they thought their friends had added to their intrigue was actually coincidence. Who would have thought!

The steaks and baked potatoes were good, and no one seemed to miss the fruit salad lost on the hood of the town's only squad car. Jake had simply wiped off the windshield but left the fruit residue on the hood as he left to make his customary rounds. People in town should realize that his job wasn't always as easy as they might have thought.

The party ended about midnight, and Spike and Babe got on their motorcycle and headed home, thinking how much of a good time, albeit somewhat hair-raising, was had by all.

The speed going home was much slower than the ride to the party. Babe leaned her head against Spike's back and thought of all the things that had happened in the last few hours. She was sure it would be fuel for much reminiscing in the future, both for them and the group who experienced it all with them tonight. All of their friends seemed to have had a great time, especially when things went awry.

Spike slowed the bike as they turned onto their block. Babe noted their driveway light was on, and she didn't remember leaving it on when they left. She also saw cars in the driveway. Who would be there this time of night? As Spike turned in the driveway, Babe saw that the cars belonged to their sons. What in the world were they doing here at this time of night? Maybe the night's excitement wasn't over after all.

Spike parked the motorcycle on the grass in front of the front door, since there was no way to get past the cars to get the bike in the garage. He and Babe entered the front door, still in full bad biker regalia, and came face-to-face with all four of their sons.

Luke was the first to speak. "I can't believe what you two have done to yourselves!"

Spike said, "What are you guys doing here? We didn't know you were coming."

John broke in. "Maybe it's a good thing you didn't know we planned to come or we would never have realized what is really going on! What in the world do you two think you're doing running around looking like that! You don't look like you're going to a Halloween party! You look like you're going to rob a bank! What happened to you?"

Mark, always the mediator, came forward after putting up his hand to quiet his brothers, and said, "We came down this evening to celebrate Dad's birthday. I know it's early, but it was the only time we could all come together. We wanted to surprise you!"

Then Matt chimed in. "Yeah, and look who got surprised! I'm glad we put the kids to bed so they wouldn't see this. I don't know how we'd be able to field their questions! And look at those tattoos! How are we going to explain those? When my son gets to the age he thinks he should have a tattoo, what am I going to tell him?"

Spike raised his arms in the air and spoke in a stern voice, "I don't know what you guys think we were doing, but we went to a Halloween party."

Babe saw all this was getting them nowhere, so she jumped in and lighten things up. "We got all gussied up like this to go to a costume party at Martha and Jerry's. We waited until we were sure everyone else was there so we could make a noisy entrance. It was an entrance all right. We ended up getting arrested! Everything was done innocently, but we ended up briefly going to jail."

At that John threw back his head and covered his eyes with his hand. Luke hung his head and went to the couch to sit down, his arms dangling between his knees.

Matt, looking baffled, said quietly, "Mom, you told me you and Dad were just going to ride that thing around once in a while because Dad had always wanted a motorcycle. Now look what it has snowballed into! Jail! You have to have made that up! You are not the kind of people who get arrested! Why, this means you'll have a record!"

The spouses in the room stood still in a small group and watched and listened, their eyes going from speaker to speaker. But Babe thought she noticed two of them hide grins behind their hands.

Babe stepped forward, raised her hands, and looking at each one, said, "Let's all sit down, and we'll explain this to you." She was pulling a chair out from the dining room table when she noticed little Emma had come to the living room door. Her blond curls were mussed, and her eyes looked sleepy as she stared from one to the other wondering what all this loud talk was about.

Slowly the three-year-old looked everyone over and then went toward Spike, dragging her feet a little. She stood in front of him, tightly gripping the little blanket that went everywhere with her. She put her head to one side while looking, as if she wasn't quite sure who this was. Spike had taken off the helmet but was still wearing the false mustache, eyebrows, and sideburns. He still had the red bandana wrapped around his forehead and neck, and his arms and chest were covered with the fake tattoos.

Then Emma spoke softly. "Are you my Papa in there?"

Spike answered, "Yes, Emma, it's me," as he reached out to her.

Emma backed up, still studying this strange Papa, not ready to fully trust he was who he said he was.

"It's really me, Emma. Don't I sound like your Papa?"

"You looks really funny," she countered. Then she stepped closer and pulled the bandana off his head. Spike reached up and pulled off the fake mustache. Emma giggled.

"Eberbuddy, look! It's my same Papa under there, but Gramma drew pictures all over him!" She threw her arms around Spike's neck and climbed onto his lap.

Babe looked around at her sons and noted there was a somewhat sheepish look on all four faces as they watched little Emma love Spike for what he was to her. Leave it to a child to get to the crux of things.

"Now," said Babe, "Let's all get some sleep, and we'll talk over breakfast tomorrow morning. Let the kids sleep where they are, and the rest of you can head for the motel. Breakfast will be at nine sharp. We're having waffles, so first come, first served!"

It seemed that morning came earlier than usual after all the excitement of the night before. To Spike, their kids' arrival seemed to have enhanced the action of the last few hours. However, things had settled down. Also, their sons seemed to be mellowing and appeared less concerned about this motorcycle business as they headed back to their respective homes.

The day after the family had gone, Spike caught up on household chores that had been on hold for the past week. He couldn't help but laugh at everything that had happened. Life continued to be interesting, but slowing down for a spell would be good too. With all the chores finished for the day, he went out to the patio where Babe was watching the sunset, her favorite way to end a busy day. "A little early for the pretty part of sundown, isn't it Babe?" asked Spike.

"Sunsets have been beautiful the last couple of nights, and I don't want to miss tonight's if it happens to be a good one." They sat in companionable silence as the colors appeared on the western horizon. "See," said Babe, "I told you it would be lovely!" They sat watching until it was almost dark.

A few days passed quietly. Chores were completed, coffee

was sipped, and newspapers were read. Then one afternoon Babe said, "We need milk, Spike. Would you go down to Casey's and get a half gallon so we will have some for breakfast?"

"Sure, I need gas for the bike, so I can kill two birds with one stone. Why don't you come with me?"

Babe grabbed her sweater, and they headed for the garage. Spike always took off from the driveway at a fairly slow pace. They had heard no complaints from neighbors about bike noise, but they wanted it to stay that way. Since they were fairly new to this part of town, they hadn't gotten well acquainted with their neighbors yet other than Mrs. Kline. So, to be safe, they always waited until they reached the end of the block before gaining speed.

Very few people were out this evening despite the nice the weather. Spike took several turns down side streets so they could enjoy the ride a little longer than if they went straight home. Twilight had come by the time Spike and Babe turned the corner to their street. As Spike was turning they heard a squeal. They had hit something. Babe was first off the bike and saw, to her horror, a dead squirrel under their cycle's wheels. Babe let out an anguished yell that brought Mrs. Kline off her front porch and over to the curb to see what catastrophe had occurred on their quiet street.

Spike was off the bike, too, and the three of them stood looking at the poor squirrel they hit. "Spike, do something!" begged Babe.

"There isn't anything I can do, Babe. That critter has gone to the great walnut farm in the sky."

Mrs. Kline moved closer and offered, "I just hope that isn't Beulah's pet squirrel! She's going to be in a terrible snit if it is!"

"Who is Beulah?" asked Spike.

Mrs. Kline pointed to the house directly across from her house. "She lives there and told me she has no one left in her family so she 'adopted' a squirrel. That's what she told me; a squirrel is her only family now."

"Ohh," cried Babe, "Ohh."

At that moment the door Mrs. Kline had pointed out opened, and an elderly woman stepped out on the porch. "What's going on, Mrs. Kline?" she called.

Chapter 29

Mrs. Kline groaned under her breath and then replied, "The Millers hit something on their motorcycle, and I'm afraid it's dead."

Babe knelt by the little body, sobbing, and tried to give him chest compressions. Spike stopped her saying, "It's too late, Babe. He's gone."

Beulah came running to the curb, or running as fast as an elderly overweight person could run. "Oh, Mrs. Kline, it isn't Amos is it?" She stepped hesitantly into the street and slowly approached the three witnesses, afraid of what she would see. Babe got to her feet, and they moved aside so Beulah could identify the body. She looked down and immediately raised her arms heavenward. "Why you ruffians, you! Look what you've done to my poor innocent Amos! He never hurt anyone; and you two, riding around on one of those death machines, drove over him and killed him dead!"

"Oh, we are so sorry! We just didn't see him when he was running so fast!" wailed Babe. "I tried to save him, but he was already gone."

Spike, hoping to make a bad situation somewhat better, said, "I don't think he suffered, ma'am."

Babe sent her elbow into his ribs and put her arm around the

258

woman's shoulder. That was a wrong move, because Beulah turned quickly toward her house moaning loudly. Halfway to her porch, she turned and addressed the three. "You," pointing at Spike, "find a box for that little body. Put him in it carefully, and we'll have a service tomorrow at ten in the morning when I hope I will be able to face this!" With that parting shot she turned and went into her house.

Still standing over the little body, all three looked at each other, wondering what could serve as a casket for their victim. And then there was the aforementioned service. What kind of a service do you plan for a dead squirrel? And then . . . burial?

Mrs. Kline was the first to speak, "I have a shoebox at home that might fit."

Spike, doing an eye measurement, suggested, "I think a boot box might be a better fit, and we have one of those. This guy is pretty big. She must have fed him well. I'm going home to get a shovel to remove the body from the street, so stay here and see that no one else runs over it." And off he went to his garage.

The squirrel's body had been moved to the makeshift morgue in the Miller's garage. Babe took the boot box into the kitchen and went hunting for something to fancy it into a proper squirrel casket, whatever that might amount to. The best she could find was wrapping paper with little angels on it that she had used to for Emma's birthday present. Wrapping the box so it looked as if angels were fluttering all over it was the closest she could come to effectively turning a boot box into a squirrel casket. When she was done, she held it up for Spike's approval. "That looks really nice, Babe." With tongue in cheek he added, "It should take the little guy straight to squirrel heaven in style."

To finish the project Babe put cotton balls in the bottom of the box and lined the inside with an old silk slip she cut up. After it was in place she could see some of the lace hem ended up on the part that would pillow the little fellow's head. She hoped it would meet Beulah's approval of a proper send-off.

At that moment the phone rang. Babe was happy she had finished her casket project. Doing something like that could play havoc with a person's nerves! She picked up the phone and answered. "Oh, hi Jenny. No, I'm not busy. If I told you what I've been doing you'd never believe it anyway!" She was persuaded to confess and proceeded to tell Jenny how Amos the squirrel had met his end and who was on the bike when that end was met.

Jenny commiserated with Babe but was having trouble keeping the humor out of her voice. She asked if the funeral would be private or if the public was invited. Babe told her the burial site was still undecided and she was in charge of casket design only, so the burial site was Spike's wheelhouse.

Babe went in search of Spike to show him her finished work. Holding up the little casket she announced, "I think I may have missed my calling. Look at this work of art. Maybe I should put out my shingle: Miller Small Animal Caskets."

Spike reached for the box and said, "I think we should see if he fits." They headed for the garage and walked over to where the little body lay in repose on an old gunny sack. "I think this should do fine, Babe, but let's put him in it and see. Should he be on his stomach or his back?"

Babe studied the problem at hand and said, "If we put him on his stomach, what will we do with his tail? I think you should put him on his back and then lay his tail on his stomach. His little legs are already standing straight up. That way Beulah will be able to see his little face. Plus, it will hide the bump on the back of his head."

If only all problems were so easy to deal with, thought Spike!

"Oh," muttered Babe. "I forgot to make the lid for the casket! We'll need a lid, won't we?"

"How should I know," answered Spike. "This is the first time I've been involved in a squirrel burial, and I don't know what the protocol is in the case of squirrel accidental death." He stood looking at the squirrel in the box and shook his head.

"What now?" asked Babe

"I kind of hate to bring this up; but is he going to stink by morning? Maybe we should put him in the refrigerator tonight."

"Whoa there!" replied a startled Babe. "I think we've gone all out for this little fellow, seeing as it was because of us he met his demise. But I draw the line at putting the body in my fridge overnight! Think of another solution, because my fridge is off limits!"

Spike and Babe decided that since it was early November it might be fine to leave the little fellow in the garage. Babe went into the house to cover the lid for the casket with more of the little angels wrapping paper.

The next morning dawned bright and sunny. Babe was thankful, because having a funeral in the rain was probably more than poor Beulah could handle. Spike came out for breakfast in his red flannel shirt. Babe made him go back and change into his navy blue one, telling him he should always wear dark colors to a funeral. Spike turned back to the bedroom door and shook his head. Under his breath he muttered, "I didn't even really know the guy!"

The time came to head to Beulah's house for the service.

Babe was carrying the shovel and a bouquet of rather wilted mums from their backyard. She had stuck them in a quart jar as a last resort. Spike was carrying the dear departed in what he hoped was a respectful stance. He thought Babe should be carrying Amos, but Babe told him that pallbearers were usually men. Spike just shook his head and did what he was told. Somehow, he thought, this was getting a little out of hand. He wished this morning was over because he knew there could still be more guilt laid before all this was over unless Beulah had mellowed overnight.

They walked past Mrs. Kline's house, and she joined the funeral procession dressed in a black dress and black hat. She leaned over and whispered in Babe's ear, "I haven't had a chance to wear this outfit since my sister's funeral eleven years ago." Babe felt a little underdressed in her black slacks and print blouse. At least the print was black and white.

As the threesome turned to cross the street to Beulah's house, they saw her coming out of her front door. She was dressed in a black dress and was wearing black gloves. As Mrs. Kline walked up to put her arm around Beulah's shoulder, Beulah leaned over and said, "I couldn't find where I put my black hat. I hope I look alright."

Beulah turned to Spike and said, "I mulled over this thing all night and finally decided Amos should be buried under the lilac bush in the backyard where he liked to hide nuts." With that said she headed around the house toward the lilac bush. The procession, led by Beulah, included Spike as pallbearer carrying Amos, followed by Babe toting the shovel and the flowers, and Mrs. Kline bringing up the rear respectfully. Arriving at the lilac bush, Beulah said no more but pointed to the exact location she wanted Spike to dig.

Spike passed the casket to Babe, took the shovel from her, and began digging, hoping he got the right size and a do-over would not be called for. He couldn't wait to get home. When the digging was complete, Spike turned to Babe and took the little casket from her.

Beulah suddenly held up a hand for them to wait, and she headed for the house. She returned with a cardboard box and a small tablecloth. She placed the box beside the open grave, covered it with the tablecloth and reached for Amos. She put the casket on the box and took off the lid, laying it to one side. Then, looking at Spike, she announced, "Oh, doesn't he look nice! I will give the eulogy, and you can give the words of committal." She then turned to Babe and said, "Thank you for making such a suitable casket for him."

Beulah then turned to look at the casket and began her eulogy. "Amos came to my patio over a year ago as a little squirrel. I kept putting walnuts on the patio, and before long he would come get them out of my hand. Whenever I came to the door, he would make chirps that sounded like he was saying, "Andy, Andy." I thought he had named me Andy, so I thought it only fitting that I call him Amos. You've been a good friend to me, Amos, and I'm going to miss you. You were my family when I had no one. When I was down in the dumps you cheered me up. When you didn't see me for a day or so, you would climb up on my bedroom screen and look in to see if I was alright. I will miss you." She stopped and looked at Spike, tears running down her cheeks, to let him know it was his turn to speak.

Spike cleared his throat and began. "Thanks for being a good friend to Beulah. We send you on your way to where squirrels go when they die." He paused and took one mum out of the bouquet Babe was holding and laid it on the squirrel's chest, directly over his fluffy tail. "Goodbye, little fella." Then he placed the lid on the box. Carefully lifting the box he knelt down and gently laid it in the grave. Then he turned to the ladies and suggested they leave while he filled in the grave. He sank the quart jar holding the mums in the ground at the head of the grave. Finally he took a small stick out of his pocket and laid it below the flowers. He had carved Amos on the stick this morning. Amos now had the proper send-off and was in his final resting place. Afterwards, he joined the women in Beulah's condo to celebrate Amos's life with coffee and cake.

* * *

At the next Dirty Queens game day at Tess and Bess's house, the riding club idea was thrown back and forth, but Babe thought it was only in jest. However, she knew this bunch of plucky ladies could also be full of surprises.

That day Agnes arranged for Mary Alice to go with her to Freedom Park on a little excursion the following day. She asked Betty if the motor scooter idea had panned out. Betty was all set, since her nephew was going with a school group on a trip to Sweden.

Agnes next turned to Sissy and asked if she had found a bicycle yet. Raising her chin a smidgen, Sissy assured them, "I have indeed found one; it is pink and specifically built for women." It was said in a manner that suggested they might be questioning her ability to get a job done. Then she added, "Plus, it has a basket for any necessities I might need to take along on a ride."

Agnes hesitated, questioning Tess and Bess about the venture after the fiasco of Tess getting sick. She was afraid they would feel bad about not joining the group, so she rerouted the conversation, hoping they wouldn't notice.

Lettie said Bert had told her in no uncertain terms that no wife of his would ride around on either a motorcycle or a bicycle. Lettie added, "And I knew it was no use arguing with him!" The ladies sensed the regret in Lettie's tone, but they could think of no alternatives to offer. Babe wondered if Lettie had ever put her foot down on anything in her sixty-three years of marriage to Bert. But that wasn't something anyone needed to bring up or meddle in.

During a lull in the conversation Lettie said she had a request to make if it was alright with everyone. Sissy barked the OK in her low voice. "It's a free country! Just say it, girl!"

Lettie looked around and then said, "I can't join you, but I would like to knit you matching sweaters. If you like the idea you could be a real club, and people would know you belonged to the same club if you all had matching gray culottes." Then she added, "I knit really fast!"

They were all flabbergasted and looked from one to the other. Then Agnes answered for the rest, saying, "That is so sweet of you, Lettie," and quickly added, "it would be more fun if you were riding with us too!" She regretted saying it as she saw tears in Lettie's eyes.

Tess and Bess's faces lit up. Tess offered, "We have done knitting projects with you for the church bazaar, Lettie. We can help you knit the sweaters."

Mary Alice, sitting in the background quietly, offered, "If any of you would like a pair of culottes, give me your size and I will order them for you." A lengthy discussion was held on what color the sweaters should be. Agnes thought red—a dark red—would look good on all of them and the rest agreed. Babe didn't know what or who started it, but that afternoon as they were leaving to go home, the card players started hugging each other goodbye.

Chapter 30

The doorbell rang. It was after eight in the evening, and Spike and Babe wondered who could be at their door at this hour. No one would come visiting this late. Babe, who was sitting closest to the front hall, went to the door and looked out the peephole. She saw no one standing on their porch. She opened the door slowly and looked down.

Standing there was little Kenny. His dishrag hankie was hanging out of his pocket, and he was carrying a Spiderman lunch box. His untied shoes were on the wrong feet, and his T-shirt was on inside out. "Kenny, what are you doing outside at this time of night?" Babe asked.

"I'm running away from home, and I need to talk to Spike." Spike heard the running away part as he came into the hall.

"Hi there, Kenny. Why don't you come in and sit down and we'll talk about this." Spike sat down on the couch and motioned for Kenny to sit beside him. Kenny put his lunch box on the couch and climbed up beside Spike. Babe left the room quietly and went to their bedroom to call Kenny's mother to tell her the runaway was at their house.

Then Babe crept up to the doorway to hear about Kenny's rebellion.

With a frown and his head lowered somewhat, Kenny spoke.

"Mom says I have to pick up my toys. I'm just going to play with them tomorrow, so I shouldn't have to put them away. Mom says it's a house rule that I have to put my toys away before I go to bed. It's not fair!" Then he looked at both Spike and Babe, eyes wide, and added, "And I have to make my bed every morning too." His little chest puffed out in indignation as he added, "I have to do it before I even eat breakfast." He hesitated, and his little blue eyes clouded when he said, "I want to come and live at your house, Spike." He opened his Spiderman lunch box and pulled out a pair of Batman pajamas. "See, I brought my stuff so I can live here."

Spike ruffled Kenny's hair as he rose from the couch. "Well, I'm getting ready for bed pretty soon; but before I do, I have things I need to do. Will you help me, Kenny?" Kenny hopped off the couch and nodded in agreement. He followed Spike across the room. Spike picked up his coffee cup. "I need to take this to the kitchen. Will you pick up those newspapers for me? It's my job to put them in the recycling bin every night." Kenny ran and gathered the papers in his arms and followed Spike to the kitchen.

Babe, not to be left out of this teaching seminar, called from the living room, "Spike, don't forget to put the hammer and nails away that you used to hang that picture for me."

"Oh, I almost forgot. I used them last, so it is my job to put them away." He picked up the hammer and headed for the garage, the little runaway close behind. "It's one of the rules we have at our house."

"Are you done with your jobs now, Spike?"

Spike sat down at the table, pulled the little boy close, and put his arm around Kenny's shoulders. "No, I have one more chore I need to do every night. Since I'm the man of the house

I need to check that all of the doors are locked before we go to bed. That's the man's job every night. I need to be sure our house is safe."

"We don't have a man at our house, Spike," the little boy said sadly.

"Yes, you do, Kenny. You are the only boy at your house, so that makes you the man of the house. You need to help your Mom as much as you can because that's your job since you are the only boy who lives there."

The little guy sat still in concentration for a minute. Then he straightened his shoulders and stuck out his chest. He paused, still deep in thought. Then he looked up and said, "I can't stay at your house, Spike. Mom needs me to be the man of the house where we live, cuz I'm the only boy." He popped off the couch and started stuffing his Batman pajamas back in the Spiderman lunch box. When he was finished he said, "Spike, it's dark out. Will you walk with me to my house?"

Spike kept clearing his throat, and Babe could hardly hold back the tears as the two went out into the night. What a sweet little guy Kenny was.

When Spike returned Babe told him about her conversation with Kenny's mom. The mother told Babe she didn't even know Kenny had left the house. She thought he was in bed, but there had been problems about picking up toys. Spike told Babe the mother had come to the door when he brought Kenny home. Spike had to clear his throat again as he told how the little boy walked in the house and told his mother she didn't need to worry. He was going to keep her safe because he was the man of the house now. The relieved mother was brushing away tears as she told Spike thank you when he left to return home.

* * *

Babe thought The Seven was a more cohesive group now than ever before. There were many calls back and forth about sizes, when the first outing for the group would be, and what direction they would ride. It was a stated fact that they would only be gone one hour per ride. Babe smiled to herself because it was also known, but not talked about, that they were all practicing on their various vehicles. No one wanted to be left behind or have it appear she wasn't in perfect control of her own conveyance. They were all in a dither but seemed happier than Babe had ever known them to be.

Lettie asked The Seven to come to her house one afternoon. She said it was not a card game—just a social occasion—and they should all come. Babe was the last to arrive and noticed everyone looked as perplexed as she felt about this mysterious meeting. When Babe took her seat, Lettie announced, "We have something to show you."

Tess and Bess went to some boxes; and when they turned around, the others all oohed and aahed. They were each holding a handmade red, sleeveless V-necked sweater. They smiled at each other and then both looked at Lettie. Evidently more of the surprise was coming. Everyone was sitting on the edge of her seat. Even Babe, who was used to this crowd, was holding her breath.

Lettie smiled and explained, "They are sleeveless because we were short on time; and also you really don't need sleeves. We reasoned that you will be riding in the warmer months, so a blouse under the sweater will work fine. They are mostly to identify you as a club. I can't thank Tess and Bess enough for helping me get this done within the timetable. Now, I want you all to watch as they turn the sweaters around."

In unison, Tess and Bess turned the sweaters over so the backs were in full view. Everyone gasped. Knitted into the back of each sweater was an enlarged, black queen of spades playing cards. The words *Dirty Queens* was embroidered the top of the card with *Riding Club* under the card.

"Beautiful!" they all exclaimed as they each received their sweaters and began putting them on.

Then Tess, who was the spokesperson for the twins, added, "Bess and I want to tell you something too. We will be going on the rides with you because we have bought a tandem bicycle." Bess went back to the box and pulled out two more sweaters. The group clapped at the prospect of having this many active members riding together.

Lettie stood up and began serving lemonade and cookies to the group. This reminded them that all but Lettie now had a sweater. No one mentioned that fact. As Mary Alice was leaving, she looked heavenward, thankful that nothing was said about a man in a wheelchair or about the floozy riding on his lap.

First Ride Day, as it had been named, dawned bright and beautiful.

"Do you know what route you all plan to take?" questioned Spike.

"All I know is Agnes wants to prove that older women can still do what is thought of as young people pursuits. In short, she's saying, 'You didn't think we could do it, did you,' to as big an audience as possible. Mary Alice told me we are all to meet in front of Lucky's Market. I would think that means we plan to go down Main Street."

"That's right next to Murry's." Spike got on the phone and

told Chuck he thought a ladies' riding club would be passing his store.

Chuck laughed and said, "I figured there was something special happening today. Mary Alice has had an appointment for me to check out her *Tri Glide* on the calendar for weeks. I just looked it over this morning, and she seemed pretty excited about something. I'll call Jenny. If she missed something like this she'd never forgive me."

As soon as Babe was decked out in her red sweater and riding culottes, she turned to Spike and said, "I'm off to join the bunch. I've been in on this from the start, and I don't want to be late now."

"Good idea," answered Spike. "Here, how about I drive you, and that way you can ride along and wave at people!"

Babe turned and gave him an incredulous look. "I don't think so," she countered. "This is my group, and we are proclaiming that women can do just about anything we set our minds to! You are welcome to come along; but you will, I repeat, you will ride behind me. It is my day to be boss, and there will be no further discussion on this matter!"

In more than forty years with this woman, this was about the closest Spike had ever come to having his ears pinned back. There was nothing left for him to do but climb on the back of the bike and grab hold of Babe's waist. Just then Chuck drove up on his cycle with Jenny on behind. As soon as they pulled up next to them, Spike said, "Whoa, what's going on here, you two? You can't drive, Chuck. Didn't you know that this ride is some kind of women's statement to the world? If you're riding in this parade, Jenny will have to drive, and you can ride along for once."

As if to stop any argument on the subject, Jenny immediately hopped off the bike. She gave Chuck a playfully solemn look and said, "Move over, buddy. It's my turn!"

Chuck climbed off the bike, smiling as he muttered, "If you can't beat 'em, join 'em." Then he took his seat behind Jenny.

At ten o'clock on the dot, Mary Alice drove the *Tri Glide* up to the corner in front of Lucky's and pulled over to the curb. Agnes was sitting on the passenger seat as if she owned the world. Both were outfitted in their culottes and red sweaters. Right behind Mary Alice in the driver's seat was a metal box that had been welded to the motorcycle. It had slat sides painted green to match the machine. Those watching had to look twice to recognize what was in the box. Scrutinizing closely, it looked like an animal. The little head was covered with a little red cap that had a see-through visor over the eyes. It was tied under the chin.

Spike sputtered, "That's the hitchhiking cat! That rascal has joined the Magnificent Seven! Can't I ever be free of him?"

Babe volunteered, "They named him Prince and had a special box made for him on the bike so he could ride with the Dirty Queens Riding Club." As Mary Alice drove up to the meeting place, the cat hopped off the box and bounded over to a man in a wheelchair, hopping up in his lap.

"Well, I'll be. That's Edward Walters, the guy who gave Mary Alice a ride when she sprained her ankle a while back." Spike turned to him and asked, "Planning to ride with these gals?"

"No, I just heard about the parade and decided I should come down and watch."

"Ah, you should ride along! Chuck and I are going along, and you've already got your wheels!"

At this point, Mary Alice walked over and joined the conversation. It didn't take much convincing from her for him to decide to come along. The others left Mary Alice and Edward talking silently. Every so often Mary Alice would blush or look around to see if anyone was watching them.

Just then Betty pulled up on her nephew's motor scooter, proudly wearing her red and gray club colors. She and Agnes were talking back and forth when a pink bicycle came from the other direction.

"That's Sissy," Babe said, clarifying the rider's identity for Chuck and Jenny. "Frances Fullerton has changed her name to Sissy."

Jenny was about to question the renaming move, but there was more action on the corner. They saw a tandem bike pull up behind Sissy with Tess sitting in the front pilot seat and Bess riding shotgun on the second seat. Both were smiling as if all was right with the world. All the riders were decked out in their red sleeveless sweaters over white blouses, with the gray culottes completing the outfits. When they turned their backs, the Dirty Queens Riding Club logo identified them to onlookers. Smiles were worn by all.

Agnes, taking charge, yelled in a commanding military voice, "Is everybody here? Then let's be off!" Mary Alice put her machine in gear and was about to move out when they all heard someone call out, "Hey, wait for me!"

Coming down the sidewalk was Lettie, and she was wearing old-fashioned, high-top shoe roller skates. The skates looked scuffed and worn, and Babe thought they were probably from when Lettie was in high school, a time long before anyone had heard of in-line skates. By the time Lettie reached the rest, they had climbed off their various vehicles and were crowding around her. Lettie, all out of breath, explained, "We used to roller skate, so Bert finally said I could come along if I was on

274

my roller skates and stayed on the sidewalk near you!"

The Dirty Queens were all standing close together when Tess backed away from Lettie, looking closely at her sweater. Lettie's sweater was just like the others, but it stopped four inches above her belt and she had a small roll of yarn tucked in at her waistline. Lettie noticed the questioning look and explained, "I tried hard to finish my sweater, but there wasn't enough time last night. I figure I can finish it tomorrow if I can find the knot where I stopped."

"Well, are we going to get going this morning?" hollered Agnes. Her voice was definitely louder and more demanding as she assumed command. The parade took off at a leisurely pace with Lettie struggling to keep up as she skated on the sidewalk.

As the group watched they saw that Lettie was lagging more behind each minute. Just when they thought the club would leave her behind, they saw a turquoise and white Chevy pull up to the curb and Lettie climb into the passenger seat. After a few minutes, when the Chevy slowly caught up with the other riders, it stopped; and a rested Lettie got out and skated on the adjacent sidewalk alongside the others.

Babe was sorry she had misjudged Bert, thinking he just wanted Lettie to know that he was in control. She realized now, overprotective or not, he was genuinely interested in her welfare.

Bert joined the parade as Lettie grabbed the back of Edward's electric wheelchair whenever she got winded. The Millers and the Murrys, as the parade's rear guards, were shouting encouragement to the riders ahead of them. Agnes must have heard because she looked over her shoulder. She raised her right fist in the air and made a circle like a cowboy on a cattle drive, yelling "Head 'em up!"

Slowly but surely the parade was headed across town. They were approaching the Cromwell Heating and Air Conditioning offices, and the employees were gathered out front trying to see what all the commotion was about. As the end the parade came in front of the building, one of the employees yelled at Spike, "We see you're playing second fiddle, Spike. Riding shotgun?"

Spike kept one arm around Babe's waist, waved at them with the other, and yelled back, "It's a smart man who knows when to hold and when to fold! Besides, look what I get to hold on to this way!"

Babe slowed the machine and yelled, "Why don't you get in the company truck and join us! But you are going to have to let Ann, the bookkeeper, drive! No men drivers in this parade!" Spike kept his eye on the Cromwell door and soon saw Ann come out and climb in the driver's seat. The men climbed in the bed of the truck, yelling encouragement to those ahead of them in the parade.

Cars driving by pulled to the side of the street and stopped. People came to the curb from stores and everyone clapped. Lou, the owner of the music store, came out of his store with his trumpet and started to play, "When the Saints Go Marching In." Bert stopped his car, rolled down his back windows, and motioned for Lou to climb in the back seat. Lou climbed in the car, stuck his trumpet out the window, and kept playing. Slowly, from all over the little town, youngsters on bikes joined in the parade. The parade was slow moving, but its length was impressive considering the size of the little town.

The parade ended up at the small park at the edge of town, and everyone was wondering how it had come about when no one seemed to know about it beforehand. Sissy, true to form, climbed up and stood on the nearby bandstand and raised her arms to quiet the crowd. She looked at all the people and said in her low voice, "Fun, wasn't it?" People yelled and clapped their approval, and she continued, "Every year on March 1, let's have a parade just to show we can. Let's call it the Shelby County Parade!"

Everyone had a wonderful time milling around the park until one by one, people began drifting away. A reporter was still talking to folks and taking photographs of the surprise parade for the town's paper, but Spike and Babe just watched the scene.

Babe gripped Spike's hand tightly and smiled. She closed her eyes and simply enjoyed the moment: the chattering of old friends; the chirping of birds; the smells of motorcycles; and the outdoors mingling as one. They were not only watching this world in their retirement, they were living in it.

Babe opened her eyes and looked off into the distance. The breeze was soft and sweet on her face. She tugged on Spike's sleeve and pointed down a road leading out of town.

"Let's go somewhere," she said.

"Well, where do you want to go?"

"I don't care. Anywhere."

He smiled and revved the engine. They peeled away from the crowd and headed west out of town contemplating new adventures. They loved being with everyone, but what they truly loved was being with each other.

Acknowledgements

We would first like to thank our spouses for encouraging us every step of the way and for listening to us talk on and on about Spike and Babe. Thank you for encouraging us even in our most hair-brained ideas!

Also, thank you for our entire family for your support and your inspiration to us and our characters.

A special thank you to Maleah Bell, who edited the book and helped us sound smarter and more cultured than we really are.

Above and beyond all these, we want to thank Jesus. You saved us from the spiritual death from which we were dying, and have placed us in the world You created. You set us apart and have given us a calling and an abundant life full of friends and adventure. Thank you!

About Spike and Babe

(Written separately by each author, and merged to form a singular story.)

(Jane) Phil and I were blessed with four sons plus another 'son' we acquired through the years. They are a witty bunch and their horsing around taught me to never let facts get in the way of a good story as they verbally piled on whichever brother had goofed. After they have all been together I've been known to take flowers to a neighbor trying to compensate for their rollicking good time.

Traveling back and forth between Iowa and Arizona after retirement, I jotted down random thoughts in a notebook. I ran across it a few years later and it gave me fodder for some Spike and Babe antics. Some of what is now attributed to Spike and Babe actually started with incidents that happened to Phil and me. However I have not let facts stymie my storytelling. Other tales just grew in a mind that must be bent that way.

As our sons spread out and had families of their own, we enjoyed traveling to their homes hoping they had a 'to do' list that needed work. It was also a way to get acquainted with our ten grandchildren. Somewhere along the line, I told our Grandson Philip about a story idea I had about a retired couple. In my mind they were just Spike and Babe and they had a motorcycle. Why a motorcycle I'll never know, as I know nothing about those machines.

(Philip) A couple months into Bianca and my first year of marriage, we went up to Iowa for Labor Day to visit my grandparents, Jane and Phil Jorgensen. During that trip, we got a lot of time with them watching the birds, talking, and laughing. One morning out on the porch, Grandma began telling us about a fictional couple she had created who in their retirement years bought a motorcycle and renamed themselves Spike and Babe. She told us that years before she had begun thinking about this couple as they would travel. I encouraged her to start writing down her ideas and maybe one day send out a short story to the family.

After that visit, each time we talked on the phone, at some point in the conversation I would ask, "So, how are Spike and Babe doing?" Her answers grew from, "Pretty good, I haven't gotten around to writing it down yet," to "Not good. I don't think I will do it."

Then, three years later, at the start of 2016, I had a burning desire to write a book. I didn't know what to write about, even though I had several ideas. So I asked God to help me decide what to write about. During that week over and over again, I felt God impress on me that I needed to help Grandma write her story about Spike and Babe. But how would she feel about that? She hadn't seemed too interested in writing it down recently. But I figured I would give it a go.

(Jane) Then came the call when Philip announced, "I'm going to write this with you!" It must be somewhat unusual for a 28-year-old grandson and his 85-year-old grandmother to author a book. We might have lived many states apart but we consulted over the phone many nights.

(Philip) We had a blast writing this together. Every so often we would get on the phone to laugh and plan and laugh and plot and laugh some more. We would always say that even if no one liked it, it was just fun to write!

(Jane) Plots were hatched and elaborated on as we talked and laughed. Spike and Babe would never have materialized if Philip hadn't insisted, and I would have missed out on one of the greatest experiences in my life.

(Philip) As the book developed, I liked to think of it as a fictional autobiography of Jane and Phil. Some of the stories are based on their experiences, but several are not. However, Spike and Babe capture their spirit and their marriage. The way that Spike and Babe love each other is the way that Jane and Phil love each other. The strength, the togetherness, the wit, the 'who's the boss' playfulness . . . it is all captured in these pages.

CPSIA information can be obtained
at www.ICGtesting.com
Printed in the USA
LVHW040440140223
739360LV00001B/126